# Mirror Image

# Mirror Image

Beth Murray

COSMIC EGG BOOKS

Winchester, UK
Washington, USA

First published by Cosmic Egg Books, 2014
Cosmic Egg Books is an imprint of John Hunt Publishing Ltd., Laurel House, Station Approach, Alresford, Hants, SO24 9JH, UK
office1@jhpbooks.net
www.johnhuntpublishing.com

For distributor details and how to order please visit the 'Ordering' section on our website.



ISBN: 978 1 78279 482 0



A CIP catalogue record for this book is available from the British Library.

Design: Stuart Davies

Printed in the USA by Edwards Brothers Malloy

To my mum, for making this possible,
and to my dad, my unofficial proofreader.
Thank you.

# Prologue

*The door burst open, allowing the foul stench to reach the officers in the doorway. At first, they all backed away, trying to get out of reach of the smell of decomposing flesh. Then, hand covering mouth and nose, Jack Daniels took the first tentative step into the flat.*

*The curtains were drawn, and his vision was blurry from the sickly aroma, so it took the detective constable a few moments to take in his surroundings.*

*The dreary light that filtered through the dark curtains did little to brighten the flat, and the sparse furniture added only a sense of foreboding. Jack noticed, as he walked further in, that a small delicate layer of dust coated the floor. If the smell hadn't been enough, the dust would have been a good indication that nothing had moved in the flat for some time.*

*He walked into the bedroom, gagging as the smell intensified, and saw the single bed in the centre. It was this that Jack's gaze fixed upon.*

*Lying on the bed in a white dress, in a position of peaceful sleep, was the body of Sarah Fletcher. Her skin had bloated from death, her mouth partially open, allowing the almost-black tongue to be seen. As Jack looked on in disgust, a maggot emerged from her mouth and he realised that her whole body was heaving with them, burrowing into her rancid flesh. He tore his eyes away, and spotted a pillbox near her still body.*

*"Jack."*

*Jack looked behind him and saw John, a little green in the face, standing by a desk that had been tucked into one of the corners of the room. He was pointing at a book that sat on the solid wood, next to a white envelope, which had Jack's own name printed upon it.*

*Jack walked over and glanced at the envelope before turning his attention to the book. The words* My Journal *were printed in black on the front of the white leather-bound book. Taking a pair of latex gloves from his colleague's case, he ignored the noise from the other officers as they began to move around the flat.*

*The gloves soon covering his strong hands, he picked up the book and turned to the first page.*

# Chapter One

Sarah Caroline Fletcher was thirteen when her life changed forever.

The day started normally enough, just another Wednesday, just another school day. She woke, as she usually did, a couple of minutes before her alarm clock sent its shrill cry through her bedroom. She switched it off and slowly got out of bed. It was still dark, yet bright enough for her to be able to see her way through the jungle of her room, easily skirting past the clutter.

In the bathroom she washed, cleaned her teeth and brushed her hair, gazing at her reflection in the mirror. Unlike a lot of her school friends, Sarah was luckily un-plagued by acne, her skin smooth and unblemished, yet she still did not consider herself pretty. Not ugly, but definitely not pretty. Once she had done all she felt she could do, Sarah returned to her bedroom, switching on her small bedside lamp so she could see what she was doing a little better.

The light shone through the purple lampshade, illuminating the already-purple room. It was her favourite colour, as her bedroom proved; purple lampshades, purple walls, purple carpet, all slightly different shades. Even her white furniture – bed, desk for homework, and wardrobe – displayed her colour with small, delicate purple flowers stencilled on the surfaces.

Dressed in her school uniform, Sarah went downstairs. Like her own room, the house was comfortably cluttered: not enough to be called messy, but enough to add a lived-in look.

"Morning, Sarah." Her mum stood in the kitchen, already fixing herself her second cup of coffee of the day.

"Morning, Mum. Dad left already?" Sarah asked as she poured some cereal into a bowl, adding a large amount of milk on top.

"Yeah, there's some problem with the plumbing or something

at the office, and he's got to let them in to fix it."

Sarah nodded as she ate her breakfast, accustomed to her mother pottering and scurrying around first thing in the morning. She didn't know how her mum did it though, she never had any energy until about midday, but she had an idea that it had something to do with her mum's caffeine intake.

"Do you want a lift to school today?" Her mum popped her head out of the laundry room to look at her daughter.

Sarah stared out of the window, looking at the sun beginning to rise in the cloudless sky. "No, it's okay, Mum. Doesn't look like it'll rain. I'll chance walking."

"You sure?"

Sarah smiled. "Yeah, I'm sure, Mum."

"Okay." She went back to her washing before nipping back out again. "Don't forget, your Dad and I will be out when you get back from school, so you'll have to fix yourself something to eat."

"I know, Mum."

Still smiling, Sarah watched her mum go back to her housework, and was glad. She loved her parents dearly, but first thing in the morning all she wanted was some space.

With a glance at the clock, Sarah cleared her breakfast things away before rushing upstairs to pick her homework off her cluttered desk. She put it into her school bag and ran back downstairs.

As she was opening the front door, she shouted back into the house. "I'm going now, Mum. See you later."

Over the sound of the washing machine, she heard her mum's faint reply, probably wishing her a good day. Sarah set off to school feeling good.

"You daydreaming again, Sarah?"

The voice brought Sarah back from her own personal world, and she looked at Katy.

"You know me," Sarah said as the two of them walked to their lockers, which sat side by side.

"That means 'yes'."

As Sarah emptied everything out of her bag except the books that she'd need for the first two lessons, Katy leant against the lockers, applying a faint shade of lipstick and admiring her efforts in her small compact mirror.

Sarah laughed. "You know if Thorney catches you with lipstick on, he'll put you in detention. *Again*."

Katy caught the emphasis that her friend had put on the last word and laughed. "You make that sound like a bad thing, Sarah."

"Well," Sarah said, closing her locker. "It's not a *good* thing."

Katy shrugged. "Yeah, well, not everyone's a suck-up like some." Playfully, she pushed Sarah against the lockers, both of them giggling.

The bell for registration rang through the corridors, making Sarah jump. Together, along with the other hundred-odd students, they began to walk to their form-room.

"What lessons have we got this morning?" Sarah checked, ignoring the bustling bodies that tried to push her out of their way.

"Er, Maths then English, I think."

"Good." English was Sarah's favourite subject, the only one she actually had a knack for.

Katy regarded her with a look of disbelief, and shook her head, smiling. "See? Told ya. Suck-up."

Still laughing, they walked into the classroom for registration, saying hello to the rest of their classmates.

Their form teacher, Mr Arnolds, went through the register, noting the few absentees with disdain clear on his face, then sat at his desk silently, while his students talked about football, soaps, love lives, and everything else that they needed to catch up with.

Friends from pre-school, Sarah and Katy talked together, and only stopped when the door swung open.

A girl walked slowly over to Mr Arnolds and exclaimed in a loud voice, which carried to the entire room, "I'm Rachael Simmons. I've just moved here, and was told this is my class."

Sarah smiled and watched as the girl confidently strode straight into the midst of the 'popular' group.

In Sarah's experience, girls like this Rachael had in-built radar when it came to finding more of their own kind, which usually meant bullying and bitchiness, and treating others like rubbish. In Sarah's limited experience, girls like that were the sort to stay away from.

The main topic of conversation for most of the morning was the new girl – where she used to live, how she was dressed, what she was like. A half hour into the school day, Sarah was already sick of hearing about Rachael. As long as the girl stayed out her way, Sarah wasn't in the least bit bothered. Before lunch, Sarah knew that it wasn't going to happen.

In English, while Sarah had been asking their teacher about story writing, she had heard some sniggering from the back of the class.

When Mr Simmons had turned to write something on the whiteboard, Sarah had looked around to see Rachael surrounded by her newly acquired friends staring straight at her, still laughing. Ignoring them the best she could, Sarah turned her back to them and resumed her work, trying to concentrate. It was difficult with the laughter and snide remarks that were going on behind her, but she managed it somehow.

She wasn't upset by it, or even annoyed. She was used to being treated as a bit of an oddball. After all, she didn't go out of her way to make friends, she didn't slag people off to gain respect. But, after all that, she did feel confused; even if she wasn't especially liked, she had always felt accepted by her class mates.

At lunch, wanting to get away temporarily from the incessant taunts, Sarah rushed to the toilets and stood in front of the mirrors, taking deep breaths.

Looking at her red face, her brown hair doing nothing to disguise her embarrassment, tears standing out in her eyes, Sarah realised that she was more upset by it all than she'd wanted to believe.

The door swung open, and Sarah turned to see Rachael walk in, a menacing smile on her face.

"Hey, it's the teacher's pet. How you doing, Loser?"

Without responding, Sarah faced the mirror again, and watched the reflections as Rachael stood next to her. Sarah's eyes locked on to Rachael's, and a pain like a thousand needles attacked her eyeballs. The pain became unimportant though as something strange began to happen to the images within the glass.

The air began to shimmer before her, and as she looked into Rachael's eyes she realised that the air wasn't the only thing that was shimmering. Rachael's face seemed to be bubbling, her skin melting, changing shaped, dripping, like wax from a candle. The air suddenly stopped shimmering and Sarah was able to see the new reflection clearly.

Instead of the pretty, if arrogant, features, Rachael's face was now completely different. Her smooth skin was rippled, lumps having sprouted around her eyes, lips and nose, and was now a sickly greenish-yellow. In place of ears were loose flaps of skin that hung almost to her chin.

"What's up with you, Freak?"

Sarah heard Rachael's voice, normal and sarcastic, and saw the creature that had replaced Rachael in the mirror moving its ill-coloured lips.

Watching those lips move into a smile that exposed rows of tiny blackened teeth was the last straw for Sarah. She broke eye contact with the thing in the mirror and rushed into one of the stalls.

As she was sick, she heard Rachael laugh and the door to the toilets opening and closing as her tormenter left.

Sarah, on her knees in front of the toilet, closed her eyes and tried not to faint.

On the way home, she was lost in a world where she repeatedly saw the monster that had taken Rachael's place in the mirror, and she stayed locked in that world.

In the house it was cool and quiet, but Sarah noticed none of it – her head was trapped in a whirlwind and there would be no way out until the storm dropped. In an insight that she forgot about only seconds later, one that she never allowed herself to truly hear, Sarah knew that it would be years before this particular storm ebbed.

It was impossible for her to relax, alone in the house. She tried watching the television, but the programmes seemed too complex for her to follow. The radio was of no use either, and it too was soon switched off.

Making sure that the front door was locked, Sarah went upstairs and began to run a bath. Steam soon started to fill the aqua-coloured room, and she felt relieved when the cabinet mirror fogged up. While the bath filled, Sarah collected some nightclothes and her dressing gown from her bedroom despite the early hour.

Being occupied, even with a simple task like getting herself ready for a bath, made her feel better. But once she was laying in the bath, both her mind and her body relaxed, Sarah was unable to stop replaying what had happened. Over and over, she could feel the pain of thousands of red-hot needles being stuck into the backs of her eyes. Then the air rippling and watching Rachael's face melt.

She'd had enough! Quickly, almost slipping in her eagerness, Sarah got out of the bath after only ten minutes. She dried herself and dressed in her purple nightshirt, wrapping the dressing gown around her before the chill could seep in.

Knowing it was stupid, knowing that she should *know better*, Sarah began to hunt through the bathroom cabinet, looking for her mother's tablets.

Her mum had suffered from major insomnia on-and-off since her teenage years, so she always had some sleeping tablets around, in case of another bout. Sarah's hand tightly grasped the white box of pills and slowly popped one out of the blister pack into the palm of her hand. Careful not to drop it, she put the box back into the cabinet, hoping that it didn't look as if it had been moved: she didn't want her parents to worry.

She put the tablet in her mouth and took the small glass from next to the set of three toothbrushes. A mouthful of water washed the tablet down and she left the bathroom, and lay down in her bed. Almost the second that her head touched the pillow, the small cream-coloured tablet worked its magic and Sarah fell asleep.

The school was bursting with people, and Sarah knew that she was dreaming because there was no way that there were that many people at her school.

As Sarah looked at them all moving around her, she saw that all of them were Rachael. All had Rachael's black hair and her arrogant sneer.

Without warning, pain struck behind her eyes, making them water. The light in the school corridors began to flicker, like hundreds of strobe lights, and in the flashes of light, she could see all the Rachaels turn to face her.

They surrounded her, and Sarah screamed as their faces changed simultaneously. All lumpy and identically grotesque, they closed their circles tighter, closing in on her.

"See," one of them whispered, reaching out to Sarah. "You'll always be the Freak."

As Sarah screamed again, the lights stopped flashing and

began to grow dim. Sarah slipped easily from her nightmare into nothingness.

# Chapter Two

Sarah walked to the hotel that Tony was staying in, enjoying the fresh breeze that blew her hair away from her face. She felt guilty about lying to Serena, but until her friend accepted that Tony hadn't committed the crimes that he had been accused of, it was just easier to pretend that she and Tony had finished.

At seventeen, the things that had happened to her in her early teens were buried in the base of her mind, not forgotten but hidden. After the incident with Rachael Simmons, Sarah had seen no more of those images caught in mirrors. This was mainly because she had spent the last four years avoiding other people's reflections for more than a split second.

She walked into the hotel lobby and over to the elevators. As she waited for the doors to open, Sarah thought about how lucky she was. And how she'd never been so happy.

"Do you want a drink, Sarah?"

"Please." Sarah stood in the bathroom, brushing her long brown hair. The girl trapped inside the mirror copied her every move. She tied her hair back and looked into her mirror image's eyes, leaning forward so that her nose was almost touching the glass.

A hand crept onto her neck and, in the mirror, she saw Tony behind her. They had just made love and he wore only his boxer shorts. He bent towards her and began to kiss her neck. She closed her eyes and enjoyed the tingling feeling throughout her body.

She opened her eyes and watched their reflections as he began to caress her breasts, her neck, and her stomach. His other hand moved up the inside of her thighs and touched the cotton of her knickers. She uttered a small gasp as his fingers brushed gently against the most sensitive part of her. Their eyes met in the glass and she held his gaze. The mirror began to shimmer, and the images began to distort. Sarah was unable to tear her eyes away, her breath caught in her throat as memories of Rachael filled her mind. *This can't be happening. Not Tony, please, not Tony.*

The mirror cleared and the images were suddenly distinctive once again. She could see herself reflected there, her eyes wide, tears beginning to track their way down her cheeks.

Tony, though, was no longer there. In his place, still kissing Sarah's neck and unaware of her unresponsiveness, still touching and teasing, was a monster. It's bright-red skin, scaled and pitted, was touching her, broken only by Tony's blue boxers. Its black eyes were still locked with her own, and Sarah could see a combination of madness and lust in their otherwise dead depths. Yellow and ancient tusks protruded from its cracked black gums. Although she couldn't feel them, knowing that they weren't physically there, she could *almost* feel them, could imagine them piercing her flesh.

She looked away, seeing the images dissolve once more, and turned to face the monster. It was not there: only Tony stood there in front of her, still cupping her breasts, rubbing her erect nipples with callused fingers. Sarah looked into his eyes and saw the lust that she had seen in the monster's.

When Tony leant forward to kiss her, she viciously pushed him away, her eyes sparkling dangerously. Without realising she was doing it until it was done, she reached out and grabbed one of Tony's aftershave bottles. When Tony reached for her again, Sarah raised the bottle and quickly brought it down upon his head, watching as the alcohol began to mix with his blood.

His face screwed up in surprise and pain as it smashed, and Sarah was shocked to realise that she felt no guilt. Still holding the jagged neck of the bottle, she started to advance on him. He tried to overpower her, but she somehow managed to hold him off. She stabbed him over and over, letting her anger out, letting it take control.

Eventually she stopped. The room was splashed with blood, and so was she, and she felt sick. Yet she regretted nothing. Quickly, she showered, not wanting to risk being seen leaving the room covered in blood, letting the hot water wash it away from her body. She dried herself and dressed, then stood looking at the body that was motionless on the bathroom floor.

Repulsed by what she was doing but unable – and unwilling – to stop, she covered one finger in her late-boyfriend's blood and turned back to the mirror. She printed one word on the glass and then washed her hands, before collecting all of her things and leaving the hotel room.

Alone in the room, Tony's body laid still and quiet, guarded only by that one word on the mirror, the letters beginning to drip, so that it looked like an advert for a cheap and predictable horror flick.

EVIL.

Sarah hadn't even been questioned by the police. In fact, she hadn't been linked to him in any way, not even in the newspapers that she read.

SUSPECTED CHILD KILLER FOUND DEAD

Report by Tania Lloyd

Last night the body of thirty-two year old nightclub owner Tony James Aldridge was found in his hotel-room bathroom.

Seventeen months ago Aldridge was questioned by police after four children were found dead and severely mutilated near his home, in the outskirts of Millsbury. Despite forensic evidence linking him to the crimes he was never charged. After his arrest and subsequent release, parents of the deceased children plus dozens of supporters raged their own war on the nightclub owner, targeting his club and his home. For his own safety, Aldridge moved to the Maiden Hotel in the centre of Millsbury, where he took up permanent residence.

His body was found by one of the hotel's cleaning staff approximately forty-eight hours after his death. A police spokesperson said today that Aldridge had been attacked repeatedly with a broken aftershave bottle. When asked what they thought of the attack, the spokesperson refused to comment.

Tony Aldridge, originally from London, in a previous interview stated that he moved to this "quiet area to escape the chaos of city life", but investigations into his past have revealed that he was also suspected... (continued on page five)

After allowing the report to get through to her, Sarah angrily balled up the newspaper and threw it away from her. She sat quietly for a few moments before she found herself beginning to giggle, and then to laugh. A few seconds later her hysterical laughter turned into uncontrollable crying, and she spent half an hour sitting on the floor, hugging her knees and rocking back and forth.

Why hadn't she believed Serena? Why hadn't she trusted her friend's judgement, and finished it with Tony ages ago? How could she have ignored all those rumours, how could she just disregard it all?!

There was a photograph on the floor beside her and she picked it up, hands shaking with anger. It was a picture of her and Tony, both of them bundled up in jackets to protect them from the winter winds. He had his arm around her shoulders, and a gentle smile covered his face. Looking at the photo, his eyes sparkling with laughter, Sarah wondered again if he really could have killed those children. She dropped the picture onto the floor as the image of that red-skinned monster filled her mind once more. She knew that he had.

The anger resumed, burning up inside her, bubbling over like a volcano erupting after years of sleep, and she stood swiftly, nearly knocking over the nearby coffee table. She paced around the room for a few moments, before sitting abruptly back down.

As her breathing and her heartbeat slowed down to their normal pace, she realised that her anger was ebbing, or more accurately was mutating, into a sense of wonder.

*If he had stayed alive, he would have killed more. I've stopped him, haven't I?* she asked herself silently. *I've stopped him from killing again.*

Her eyes focussed on nothing as those thoughts rebounded through her mind, forming themselves in different ways, but always returning to that one point: that, by killing Tony, she had almost certainly prevented countless lives from being destroyed.

Before she could change her mind, Sarah posted the letter. Wondering if she was doing the right thing – and knowing that it was too late now either way – she walked away from the post box and back towards the bus stop.

# Chapter Three

*In his office, Jack put the journal to one side, and picked up the first letter that they had received. Her handwriting was already familiar to him, and he would recognise it anywhere, every curl and swirl of her penmanship.*

To whoever needs to know.

He killed those children, he deserved to die. He's the only one to be blamed.

Let it go!

*Jack had to smile. It was so simple, straight to the point. Still smiling, he turned back to Sarah's journal.*

# Chapter Four

By the time that Sarah's twenty-first birthday rolled around she had killed four people. And she only hesitated once, the second time.

Jackie Austin, nine years old, had never been what people would call a perfect child, although as far as everyone was concerned, including her parents, Jackie was sweet, well mannered, smart and (mostly) well behaved. When Jackie was six and a half, Melanie Austin found out that she was pregnant, almost four months gone. The news pleased everyone, including Jackie, who thought that it would be great to have a little baby to play with, even if she was a little hazy on the whole hows-and-whys of the subject.

Almost exactly a year later, when Nicholas Austin was just over six months old, Jackie decided that she had had enough. Enough of the crying, enough of the lack of sleep, of her parents always being tired, of never having any attention paid to her, of it always being Nicholas this and Nicholas that. She had just had *enough*!

Her parents went out for the evening, leaving Jackie and Nicholas in the capable hands of Louise Williams. Louise, twenty-three, had been babysitting for six years and had always looked after Jackie.

Louise got Nick to sleep at eight, and into his cot at quarter past the hour, and Jackie went to bed twenty minutes later of her own accord. Louise settled down to her college assignments, and was still working on her Shakespeare essay when Melanie and Josh Austin returned, not long after midnight. Louise went home, well studied and well paid.

Josh had had slightly less to drink than his wife so he was the one to check on the two kids. Jackie was emitting her usual lady-like snore, and he looked in on his son, noticing nothing wrong.

Jackie woke up with the sun shining through her curtains and a smile on her face. No crying had woken her and she felt well rested and happy. She crept past her parents' bedroom, smiling as she heard them both snoring, and went downstairs. In the kitchen, she got her mother's cereal out of the cupboard and put it onto the table. She did the same with her father's, and then set the table.

Josh walked downstairs at eight nineteen; a whole hour after Jackie had woken up. He saw his cereal on the table and smiled, despite his hangover. He appreciated the gesture, even though he would be unable to eat anything. He got himself a glass of water and sat down at the table opposite his daughter. "Morning, Jackie. Have a good night last night?"

Jackie smiled sweetly. "Brilliant." Still smiling, she continued to eat her breakfast, watching the small television that sat on the counter next to the fridge.

When Melanie screamed, Josh almost knocked his glass onto the floor. Blood pumping in his temples, he rushed up the stairs to find his wife, wide-eyed and trembling, holding their son.

Through all the commotion, through the screaming and the crying, Jackie sat patiently, eating her cereal, the morning's cartoons capturing her full attention.

A year and a half later the memory of what she'd done was still clear in her mind. But it had taken on an unreality – she could have seen it on the television.

As she washed her hands in the sink of the supermarket toilets, she let those memories play over again. The feeling she'd had when she'd held the pillow on her baby brother's face was the only thing that now seemed real. His struggles slowing down and eventually stopping altogether was distant, but the rush she had felt had made everything worthwhile. She'd done the right thing. After things had settled down, her parents, especially her mother, had doted on her. Anything she wanted, she got. And

Louise being blamed for Nicholas's death meant nothing to her.

In the mirror she saw a lady walk in. She knew her, but couldn't remember her name. She watched, still washing her hands, as the woman went into one of the empty cubicles.

Sarah – that was her name. She was quite friendly with her mum.

Behind her, the toilet flushed, and Jackie saw Sarah walk towards the sinks.

The woman with the brown hair and soft brown eyes noticed the nine-year-old. "Oh, hi, Jackie. How are you?" When Jackie didn't answer, Sarah looked around at the empty cubicles. "Where's your mum?"

"Outside."

"You been enjoying school?"

Their eyes locked in the mirror, and Jackie saw Sarah's open wide. She tried to look away, but found that she couldn't. Sarah's eyes, usually soft and understanding (and perhaps a little bit vacant) suddenly seemed intense. It was just her imagination – she thought so until later that week – but it looked as though Sarah's pupils were spiralling.

"Everything all right, Jackie?"

As the voice broke through to them, Sarah's eyes lost their intense look, and once again became soft as she turned to look at Jackie's mother.

"Hi, Melanie."

"Hi, Sarah. How's things going?"

"Not too bad. I rang up about that correspondence course you were talking about. I should hear back about it soon."

"Hey, that's great."

"Yeah. I'm feeling really excited about it." Sarah glanced at her watch. "Shoot, I'm going to be late if I don't get a move on. I'll see you later."

The words had passed by, but Jackie hadn't taken any of it in. Yet when Sarah's gaze locked with her's again, it felt as though she was thrown back into herself.

"Bye, Jackie."

She watched Sarah leave, keeping her eyes on the door.

"Come on, Jackie. Stop your daydreaming."

They left the supermarket, with one thought echoing through Jackie's mind. *It's impossible, but she knows. Somehow she knows.*

Jackie lay in bed, her nerves tingling. The streetlamps shone their lights through her curtains and she could see that everything was in its place. A draught from the window shifted the curtains, and she sighed. There was no way she'd be able to get back to sleep with the window open. She threw back the covers and got out of her bed, her bare feet making no noise as she walked across the bedroom. Once the window was closed Jackie felt a wave of relief wash over her.

She turned back to her bed, ready to go back to sleep. She was just about to climb back under the duvet when something touched her foot. Goose bumps broke out over her body instantly and she fought to hold back a scream. Looking down, she uttered a nervous giggle. Her rug had curled up and she had walked into it.

Feeling silly, she shook her head lightly. Before she could have another go at getting back into bed, a hand clamped down on her mouth and another on her throat.

She heard a small laugh, feeling the breath on her ear. "I know what you did."

Jackie woke, gasping for breath, the memory of Sarah's spiralling eyes burnt into her mind. She pulled her covers up to her chin and lay awake in the dark.

By Friday, Jackie had relaxed a little. She decided that it had all been her imagination after all, that Sarah couldn't possibly know what had happened – except at night, alone in her room, when she believed unconditionally. During the day, though, she wasn't at all bothered. So, she didn't mind when her parents told her that they were going out for the evening.

Melanie and Josh Austin told her that they were going to the movies, and then to dinner. Jackie looked at the possibility of spending the evening alone with excitement (she'd never spent an evening by herself before) and nervousness (the thought of Sarah still picked at the back of her mind). But, she told herself, she was old enough to look after herself.

At six o'clock, Jackie watched as her parents got into their car and drove away. When she was sure that they were gone and not coming back, she ran quickly up the stairs. Instead of going into her own room, a sly smile crept onto her face. She walked into her parents' bedroom.

After going through her parents' drawers and finding nothing of interest she walked into her own room. After turning on the CD player, she slumped onto her bed and picked up a magazine.

Startled, she looked up. Had someone knocked on the front door? Jackie shook her head. With the stereo on she wouldn't have heard it, plus they had a doorbell and she hadn't heard that chime. Thoughts of Sarah flickered through her mind, but she dismissed them; she was too old now for being scared of her own imagination! As always, she turned straight to the problem pages. She was so absorbed in what she was reading – How do I tell him I like him? Should I finish it? – that she didn't hear the footsteps on the stairs.

The bedroom door was open, and Jackie should have seen Sarah walking up to it, stopping and just standing there, watching. But she didn't. Nor did she see the knife that Sarah held by her side, held in a hand that, like the other, was covered in a leather glove.

Jackie should have recognised the sound of the back door closing, but she hadn't. And she should have sensed that she wasn't alone, but she didn't.

If things had stayed that way, Jackie would have been fine.

Sarah looked at Jackie lying on her stomach reading the magazine in front of her, her feet tapping out beats from the music.

Instead of rushing upon her and stabbing her, Sarah could only stand there, feeling impotently unsure. She didn't see the horror she had seen in the ladies' room, a horribly disfigured witch-like creature, but only a pretty young girl relaxing, just as she should be.

Had she really planned to kill this girl – this *child*! – because of something she had *thought* that she had seen? Sarah shook her head and prepared to go, until she heard Jackie gasp.

The magazine was really boring, and Jackie closed it, wondering what to do next. Her gaze wandered to the window and she looked outside. Her eyes focussed on the reflections in the window, and she saw Sarah behind her. Without wanting to, but powerless to prevent it, she felt herself roughly breathing air into her lungs. She could not take her eyes from the window, could not move at all.

At first, Sarah thought that Jackie had seen something outside. Instantly, she looked at the window to see what was so shocking. Instead of looking at the view, she found Jackie's eyes in the reflection and felt herself caught. A split-second later, the images began to change and Sarah saw the blonde-haired girl morph into something else. Only a second had passed but now Sarah found that her eyes were locked by a different creature.

Its features were the same – long blonde hair, blue eyes – but nothing else was. Its skin had become the colour of diseased mushrooms, and looked as though the texture might be roughly the same, with deep scars covering it. As Sarah watched, a new line formed on her cheek. It suddenly split open and bugs, tiny and black, spilled out.

Not wanting to see any more, Sarah wrenched her eyes away.

It took a few moments for Sarah to stop looking at the window, and Jackie should have done something before Sarah returned her eyes to her. But she still half-believed that it was a dream. And the moment of safety passed.

They looked at each other, and although she was only nine, Jackie recognised the look that fell into Sarah's eyes for what it was: hate. She didn't know why, but she was smart enough to know that the woman in front of her, holding a *knife,* hated her.

She didn't move when Sarah began to walk forward. It was only when she saw Sarah holding the knife pointed slightly towards her that her paralysis broke, and she rolled away, pushing herself away from the bed.

Sarah started around the bed, and Jackie realised that two things were between her and the door: Sarah, and the bed. If she tried to get over the bed, it would slow her down and Sarah would catch her. If she tried to get by Sarah, she'd be stabbed.

Without knowing why at first, she felt a smile on her face, and it grew as Sarah faltered for a second.

As Sarah once again began to walk forwards, Jackie backed away towards her bedside cabinet, hands held out behind her. When she bumped into her furniture, her hands happened on the very thing she wanted. When Sarah came closer, Jackie brought the object out.

As soon as the aerosol deodorant was in front of her, she pushed down on the top, not noticing the direction of the nozzle. For a second, she was annoyed when the spray hit nothing but the empty air to her left.

Pain flared, first in her chest, then all over her body. As she was trying to understand what was happening, her mind was already replaying the last few seconds: Sarah ducking to one side and simultaneously forcing the knife up and into Jackie's chest.

The pain centred itself in her chest and she looked down to see the handle of the knife juddering up and down as she breathed. The front of her clothes were sticky and warm, and she hoped by some miracle, even when she saw the rich crimson, that it was only sweat. She looked into Sarah's eyes, and the last thing she thought was that the eyes in front of her seemed to be spiralling again, growing and growing. And finally, she was lost in the whirlpool.

# Chapter Five

*He jumped as the hand touched his shoulder.*

*"Sorry, Jack."*

*Jack placed a hand over his heart and willed it to slow down. In his other hand he held the girl's diary.*

*"It's all right, Maggie." He looked at his wife, and started to grin. It didn't feel totally right on his face, but it was better than nothing. "I guess I'm just a little jumpy." He noticed that Maggie was in her negligee, and glanced at the clock mounted on his wall. It read one forty. Stunned, he looked at the digital clock on his desk. Its red digits confirmed the time. "Christ, is it really that late?"*

*Maggie nodded, and Jack ran a hand over his mouth and chin, wincing as his fingers scraped over stubble.*

*"Are you coming to bed?"*

*He shook his head. "Not just yet. I just want to finish this bit."*

*She nodded expectantly and walked to the door. She paused, and then turned back to her husband. "Can't you get someone else to read that dammed thing?"*

*Jack looked back at her, half-amazed and half-angry. "I know this case better than anyone, Maggie. No one else would do."*

*She nodded. She'd been expecting that, too. Without pausing again, Maggie left him alone in his study.*

*His eyes stayed on the door until he heard their bedroom door close, and then sighed. He looked at the journal in his hand and placed it on his desk. Rubbing his eyes, feeling tired, he walked out of his study and into the kitchen. He made himself a large, strong, cup of instant coffee and returned to his study.*

*"More comfortable than work," he said to the empty room, and laughed. It sounded strange, more than a little eerie, and he promised himself that he wasn't going to do that again. With what he was reading, Jack didn't think that he had to worry about breaking* that *promise.*

*He sat back down on his leather chair and turned to his desk. He put the cup down after taking a small sip and brought forward the file that he had brought home. It held the photos and reports of all the murders that had been linked first, and then to Sarah Fletcher.*

*Jack opened it and looked through, searching for the photographs of the Austin murder, and forensic and pathology reports. The one photo that most disturbed him was the one he now held. It showed the bedroom window, and written in the girl's blood was the word* EVIL, *just as it had been with Tony.*

*He let the photo drop from his hand and picked up his drink. His eyes focussed on nothing as he sipped from his cup.*

*The most frightening thing for Jack was that when he was reading Sarah's diary he felt as if he was being sucked into her world, the same way he felt when reading a really good novel. When he was reading it, he believed in everything she wrote – he* believed *that she could see people's souls, he* believed *that she'd had to do it. But when he arrived back into his own world, he realised, all over again, that the acts she wrote of were* real, *and he felt ashamed of himself.*

*He could remember walking into that little girl's room, smelling the blood before he had seen a single drop. He had seen what was written on the window before he'd seen the body and knew –* knew *– that the killer was the same person that had killed Tony Aldridge, two-and-a-half years earlier.*

*It had taken all of his resolve to look at what had been done to that little girl. One reason – and he believed, as he always had, that it was the* only *reason – was the girl's age. At the time of Jackie Austin's murder, his and Maggie's niece had only been a few months older than she was.*

*But he had done his duty, he had looked at the dead girl and he had noted all of the injuries. The injury to the girl's chest was the one that he always saw in his mind, the others only minor and on their own not life threatening.*

*Jack finished his coffee and set the cup aside. He picked up the leather-bound book and began to read again.*

*By the time that he had read Sarah Fletcher's own account of leaving quickly through the back door, completely unnoticed in the dark night, it was after four. Exhausted, he climbed the stairs and lay next to his wife, holding on to her in his sleep.*

# Chapter Six

Sarah closed the door behind her and leant against it, eyes closed and breathing deeply. She held her hands out in front of her, looking at the skin. Although they had been protected by the leather gloves, blood had still managed to find a way in. It traced her lifeline, embedded in the lines of her palms, like a bad omen. As she watched, the blood, still wet, began to move, to run. Now, instead of tracing the lines on her hands, it spelt the word evil on each palm.

She screamed, the noise echoing through her empty house, and ran up the stairs, holding her hands in front of her. She rushed into the bathroom and turned the taps on in the sink, leaving red marks on the silver surface, and put the plug in its hole. When the water was hotter than she could stand it, she plunged both hands into its depth, using her nailbrush to scrub the blood from her flesh.

The water turned pale pink and, as her hands continued to wash each other, her mind made a despairing connection – for a second, she saw herself as Lady Macbeth, crying, 'Will these hands never be clean'. Needing a distraction, she raised her head. Her throat locked, refusing entry to the air that her lungs needed so desperately, as she saw what was reflected in the mirror.

Jackie Austin's mirror image, grey-skinned and scarred by unknown sources, grinning a sickening smile, re-opening wounds, allowing black insects to again tumble from her face.

Sarah bolted up in bed, barely holding the scream in check, covers clutched to her chest. Sweat stuck her nightshirt to her back, and more ran freely down her face. A drop ran into her left eye, and she rubbed it, trying to ease the stinging.

Shaking, she put her hand out to find the lamp switch. Her nerves were shot and they screamed at her, telling her that something was going to grab her wrist; something was going to drag her into its lair. She did her best to ignore what she felt, and was relieved when her fingers touched the switch. In anticipation, she closed her eyes and pressed it down.

Light tried to push its way through her eyelids, but Sarah simply waited until it no longer hurt her head before she allowed her eyes to open completely.

Her eyes wandered over her room, making sure that nothing had been moved, that nothing was out of place and, after she had had a quick look under the bed, just to be sure, she let her hands drop the cover and she relaxed a little.

Knowing that she would never be able to get back to sleep, she threw the covers from her body and swung her legs over the side of the bed. She reached down and picked up her dressing gown from the floor. It was soon on and wrapped tightly around her, and she felt the last bit of chill left over from her nightmare fade.

Sarah felt almost completely human after a cup of coffee, with an added splash of whiskey, and a cigarette. She made herself another drink and took it into the conservatory. It was dark, and her eyes kept trying to peer into the darkness outside. But she refused them permission; she didn't *want* to know what might be out there, didn't want to see something looking back at her, and didn't want to see it smile its witchy grin.

Something fell over outside, and the loud crash made Sarah jump. She swore loudly as some of her hot toddy spilt onto her partially exposed legs. Her eyes immediately sprang to the uncovered windows. She saw nothing outside, but her imagination showed her dozens of possibilities. Realising that her nerves would soon be completely out of control if she stayed in there, she went back into the kitchen, closing the blinds behind her so she wouldn't be tempted to look back outside.

She ran the cold-water tap and used a cloth to soak some of it up. Her left hand held the compress to the now raw patch of skin on her leg, while her right hand supported her weight. When her leg felt a mildly better, she threw the cloth back into the sink. With the remains of both her drink and cigarette held securely, she walked into the living room and sank onto the sofa, feeling the material mould itself to her shape. She reached out to the table and used the remote control to turn the television on.

As the hours passed, two ideas echoed through her mind.

At six o'clock, Sarah showered, relishing the hot water as it rolled over her body. With regret, she turned the water off and towelled herself dry as quickly as she could. As she had the night before, she wrapped her dressing gown around her and, with the towel in her hand, walked downstairs. She wrapped her hair in the towel, fixing it so it wouldn't slip off her head. Stifling a yawn, she made herself another cup of coffee, resisting the powerful compulsion to add a splash of whiskey, and sat down at the table. She retrieved her pack of cigarettes from the pocket in her gown and shook out the last one. One-handed, she crumpled up the now empty packet and dropped it onto the table.

Sitting still with no background noise to distract her, Sarah began to feel the effects of only having had a couple of hours sleep. Feeling her eyelids beginning to drop, she quickly drank the coffee, doing her best to ignore the way the liquid burnt the back of her throat and rushed through her cigarette, roughly stubbing it out in the ashtray.

She stood and took her cup to the sink. Before she had time to feel tired again (or before she began to *really think* about things), she began her housework.

Within two hours of starting, she had cleaned her entire home: she'd polished everything that needed polishing, she'd tidied the living room, cleaned the bathroom and kitchen, put her clothes in the washing machine and started the cycle, and vacuumed all through.

Only one job left, she filled her watering can up in the kitchen sink and walked, head held up defiantly, towards the conservatory. She didn't hesitate. She pulled the blinds back and felt a smile fill her face as the sunlight burst towards her.

Feeling better, she walked through the doorway and was shocked as the built-up heat hit her. Her eyes moved to the windows as she watered the plants, and she didn't try to stop them now. With the sun shining, she didn't feel the tiniest bit nervous or afraid.

An hour later, feeling totally refreshed, she left the office supplies shop with her purchase safely in its carrier bag. Instead of going straight home, Sarah walked around and enjoyed the tranquillity of the day until she began to feel a little tired, then walked back to her car.

She placed her shopping on the passenger seat, and drove home with the windows open and her radio on loud, feeling better, more alive, than she had for some time.

When she arrived home she picked up the mail that had been pushed through the letter box and took her shopping inside. In the kitchen she put the kettle on, and while waiting it for it to boil, she opened her letters

"Yes!" Quickly, her hands opened the letter she had been waiting for. She removed the contents from the envelope and began to shift through the pages. She sat down and began to read about the different sorts of correspondence courses she could do, ignoring the kettle as it boiled and switched itself off.

Her special purchase remained in its bag, pushed aside for the time being.

It was only when she was lying in her bed eleven hours later that her thoughts returned to her shopping expedition. With the lights off and darkness obscuring her vision, her heart began to thump dangerously loud in her chest. She began to think once more of Jackie, which soon became thoughts of Tony. In one final leap, she began to think about her parents.

In the dark, Sarah began to cry. Whether it was with sadness, regret, or loneliness, even Sarah didn't know. She sobbed quietly, but with such force that she felt that her heart would burst from the pressure. She cried the way she had cried after the fact that her parents were dead had finally sunk in.

When she had herself under control, she threw her covers from her and walked angrily downstairs. After lighting a cigarette, she sat down at the kitchen table and brought the bag towards her. She took the book from it and gently traced the words that were printed on the front. The smell of new leather rose towards her, and she opened the book to its crisp white first page.

Picking up a pen, she started to write.

Sarah was in the kitchen, preparing herself a big breakfast. After writing in the journal the previous night, she had felt a lot better and had slept soundly.

The television was on in the living room, and she could hear the news reporter speaking in her usual monotonous tones. She was just starting to check how her bacon was cooking when she heard something that fully caught her attention.

"Jackie Austin, the nine-year-old girl that was brutally murdered in her home in Millsbury two days ago, has been connected to a murder that happened almost three years ago."

In the kitchen, Sarah dropped the bacon onto the floor.

The woman on the TV continued. "Anthony Aldridge was murdered in his hotel room, and his killer was never brought to justice. Our reporter asked the detective constable, Jack Daniels, his take on both murders."

Still in the kitchen, totally unable to move, Sarah lost all colour from her face.

"DC Daniels. Can you tell me in what way are the murders of a young girl and a notoriously known nightclub owner connected?"

"Due to a number of details that have never been released to the press, we have been able to link the murders of Jackie Austin and of Anthony Aldridge. We are pursuing all leads at present. Thank you."

"That was Penny Grey, reporting with DC Daniels. Now, the weather from your region."

Slowly, Sarah turned the cooker off, breakfast now the least of her concerns, and grabbed a bottle of vodka from one of the cupboards. She took it to the kitchen table and left it there while she fetched a notepad and pen.

Back at the table, the bottle of clear-oblivion in front of her, Sarah began to draft a note.

DC Jack Daniels

Leave it alone. Let me do what I need to do. As little as I liked it, those people were what I said they were.

Let it go.

She had driven out of town to post the letter and the return trip took her close to her were her parents lay. She parked up and stood by the gates, watching the people begin to drift away from the open grave at the far end, waiting until the last of the mourners left the graveyard before she walked in, making her way to her parents' graves.

It was cool under the shade of the oak tree, and she sat against its huge trunk. Her brown eyes looked at the headstones and she realised that the scripture on the stones was wearing thin already, that time and weather were doing what they could to erase the words.

Tears began to fill her eyes as she thought of what time was doing to her parents in the ground, and immediately decided not to stay. She had cried enough over the years since their deaths and she'd be damned if she was going to start all over again. It was comfort and understanding that she had come here for, not more sadness and loneliness.

A cloud passed over the sun, and a chill made its way up her spine. She looked at her bare arms and saw that goose bumps had broken out on her flesh. She rubbed them briskly, and when the bumps began to go down she noticed that the cloud had gone and the warmth had returned to the air.

Sarah spent a few moments tidying the grass from around the gravestones, told her parents that she loved them, before going home, giving the pub a longing glance as she passed.

# Chapter Seven

He slowly walked down the street, black briefcase full of papers to be marked swinging by his side, cigarette held in his other hand. As it always did after a day of work, his mind ached. Not his head, but his mind. It was always the same on a Tuesday. The little shits he taught all day on a Tuesday, *all day*, didn't have a clue, and he spent most of the day going through things again, and again, and again, until the words lost all meaning even to himself.

*At least,* he thought as he walked home, *I already know that most of the papers are wrong. I don't actually need to mark them.*

He walked slowly, prolonging the time when he had to walk through his front door and deal with everything that waited for him there. The first thing he'd do, after putting his feet up for five minutes, was to ring the garage that was holding his car. It had been in for three weeks, and Anthony was getting fed up of having to walk to work.

He arrived home – too soon for his liking – and walked up the drive. For a few seconds he just stood before his house, thinking of nothing in particular, enjoying the emptiness. He took a deep breath and, feeling as though he was about to tackle Everest, he stepped up to the front door.

A sigh of relief escaped from between his lips as he found the door locked. Placing his briefcase by his feet, he reached into his trouser pocket and pulled out his keys. Hands shaking from exhaustion caused by the shortl walk, he unlocked the door and, after retrieving his briefcase, walked in and closed the door behind him.

He walked up to the bedroom he shared with his wife, Liz, and began to undress, enjoying the stillness of the house. Two minutes later, he was dressed in jeans and a T-shirt and feeling a lot more human for it, his work clothes in a pile on the floor.

Anthony walked back downstairs and headed straight to the kitchen. He put the kettle on and while he was busying himself on the simple task of making the coffee, his eyes fell upon the envelope propped up against the salt and pepper shakers on the kitchen table.

Curious and with his drink made, he picked it up. Liz's elegant writing of his name made him smile; it was just so different to the *physical* her that he couldn't help but see the funny side.

He opened the envelope and, occasionally sipping from his cup, he read the short letter aloud to himself. "'Anthony. Mother's not well. Have taken Carla and William to visit. Know how busy you are, hope you can cope all right. Will ring as soon as I can. Love Liz'."

A mean-looking smile had crept slyly onto his face. So the old bat wasn't well! Maybe they'd get lucky and the bitch would croak. Knowing the way she milked everything for as long as she could, no matter how insignificant, Anthony knew that he could have the house to himself for at least two days, probably longer.

He'd miss the twins, naturally, but the idea of a couple of days alone, *totally* alone, filled him with excitement. He wouldn't even have to make up any excuses.

The cold wind did nothing to make him reconsider. If anything, it only made him more excited. It was the idea of doing something to keep himself warm that kept him where he was.

He crouched low next to the row of hedges, his shadow blending in perfectly. His jogging trousers were warm and, up until a few moments ago, fitted perfectly. But since his thoughts had turned to his expectations, his erection began to push his trousers out. The material rubbed, not uncomfortably, against his otherwise uncovered penis. He heard footsteps and risked a peek from behind his hiding place. It seemed he was in luck. Walking his way, alone, was a trim-looking brunette. He smiled and sank back, once again concealing himself.

It was four days since Jackie's death, yet Sarah felt better than she had for quite a while. She'd written about herself to begin with, about what she saw when she stared at people's reflections. Her words had come slowly, inhibited, and she had felt quite stupid. And then she'd started to write about Tony, and her writing had begun to be little more than scrawls as she rushed to purge herself from the thoughts she'd held onto for years.

Slowly, Sarah walked down the well-lit street, not noticing when the tidy neighbourhood – well-kept gardens, tidy drives – began to change into a dirty, littered mess. The hedges overhung the path, pushing Sarah closer to the road. Cigarette packets, crisp packets, and even a used condom, were stuck in the overgrown hedges. She was too involved in her own thoughts, so she didn't notice the figure rise from behind the hedge and step onto the pavement behind her.

"Excuse me. Do you have the time?"

The voice made Sarah jump, and she turned to face the man who had spoken to her, her heart beating loudly.

"Sorry. I didn't mean to startle you."

Sarah laughed, a little self-consciously. "That's okay." While she got over her fright, she took in the details of the man in front of her.

His brown hair was shaved close to the skull, and his dark eyes were hidden under thin-framed glasses. From his few words, she realised that, although far from posh, he was well spoken, and she could picture him in a suit. He didn't really look right in the tracksuit that he wore.

Her discomfort was beginning to creep back as she realised that, as she was appraising him, he appeared to be appraising her. Discomfort soon made way to the start of total disquiet as she saw the smile on his face.

"No, I don't have the time. Sorry." She smiled once, hoping

that it was disarming, and turned and began to walk away. She resisted the temptation to peer behind her and see if the man was following her. Her heart sank and started pumping even harder in her chest when she heard his feet striking the pavement.

Reaching into her pocket she brought out her pack of cigarettes and with shaking hands lit one. She kept her lighter in hand, which comforted her slightly.

"Hey!"

The blood was pumping harshly everywhere in her body, especially in her temples. Her feet, seemingly under their own power, had stopped and she willed them to continue, without success. Again, she began to turn towards him.

He roughly pushed her into the bushes before she could completely turn to face him. Sarah hit the ground, simultaneously hitting the side of her head and her stomach, her lighter flying out of her hand. She felt her breath being pushed out of her, but that seemed unimportant. An unnatural blackness filled her sight, dozens of white lights dancing before her.

Only when she felt her jeans being unzipped and tugged from around her hips did she understand the danger she was in. Part of her, a scared and nervous part, told her to lay still, to just wait until it was over, to survive through it. But, even as that side of her was trying to reason that it was the best thing to do, another side began to wake up. *This* side of her screamed out, demanding to know how she could just let this happen, demanding that Sarah fight back.

The moment she felt those rough, cold hands pulling at her knickers the decision was made. Anger welled up and, still unable to see clearly, she managed to lift her legs, knees reaching her stomach, and kicked out. Her satisfaction as she heard his shocked, and pain-filled gasp as her feet made contact was short-lived.

Sarah reached down and began to fumble with her jeans. She had them back around her hips when his hands were once again trying to push her flat against the ground. She could hear his heavy breathing, could feel it on her face. Instead of freezing with fright, she suddenly found herself pushing his hands away from her. The white dots left her sight and she could now see her attacker perfectly, despite the poor light. His face was red, sweat running down his forehead. She could see the enjoyment in his eyes.

As quick as she could, ignoring the spell of dizziness that tried to force her back down, she stood and moved slightly away from him. By her feet was the rock that she had fallen onto. Without taking her eyes from the man in front, she slowly reached down and picked it up.

Understanding flashed into the man's eyes, and Sarah shuddered as that look gave way to one of cunning. He stepped forward and, without meaning to, Sarah stepped back.

He was quick but Sarah was quicker. As he rushed towards her, Sarah sidestepped to her left and raised the rock above her head. An instant later she brought it back down, using as much force as she could. She couldn't have timed it better. She felt nothing as she heard his skull crack, and even when her mind registered the vibrations in her own arm, she still felt nothing.

Anthony fell forward, landing in a sprawled heap upon the ground.

Sarah raised the rock again, just in case, and held it tight as she approached him. With a small jabbing motion, she poked him with her foot. No movement. Once again, just to be sure, she kicked, this time harder.

Muscles suddenly failing her, she dropped the rock and fell after it, landing harshly on her backside. She stared at the body in front of her, her own completely numb. Little by little, her senses began to return, and she could feel bruises waiting to be born on her skin. It was a couple of minutes later that she felt the stinging just above her right ear. Hands trembling (either through the cold or the shock, or both) she reached out and winced as she found the spot. She brought her hand back in front of her and stared at the red liquid that now rested on her fingers.

The shock faded into denial, but the blood in front of her eyes was no illusion. Slowly, she shifted her gaze to the body. Her old friend, Anger, was creeping up on her again and she soon found herself staring down at him.

She rolled him over, ignoring the blood that was pooling around him. She realised for the first time that his grey trousers were no longer on his body, his still-erect penis pointing towards the sky. It was that sight that made her realise it was no longer anger she felt – it was fury. As she looked at his body, the old saying surfaced in her mind: hell hath no fury.

Close by, her lighter lay on the ground and she retrieved it slowly, hoping her body wouldn't fail her again. Sarah got her cigarettes out from her pocket and looked at the packet as though she'd never seen it before. Through everything, the box was miraculously undamaged. Her hands no longer trembled as she lit it first try. Bending her knees, she crouched over him, holding the cigarette as though she was about to stub it out.

Grinning meanly, she lowered the burning object towards his penis, relishing the contact. The smell as his skin burnt didn't deter her in the least. She moved the cigarette to the man's chest and, with the precision of a tattooist, using cigarettes instead of a needle, she wrote EVIL on his skin.

She held the cigarette (the third she'd gone through) up to her face, deciding what to do with it. The grin having resurfaced again, she inserted it into his eye, her mind ignoring both the sound and smell as she walked away.

She was fine until she locked the door.

She'd walked the rest of the way home without faltering once. Her hands didn't shake as she unlocked the door, nor did they shake as she walked in. But as soon as the door was locked, the bolt at the top securely fastened, she began to shake, her legs feeling weak, and she felt as though she was leaving her body behind. Moving slowly, she made it through the hall and into the living room without fainting. She collapsed onto the sofa and just stared blankly at the fireplace before her, her mind refusing to digest the situation.

She gave herself a few moments then stood, being careful not to move too quickly, and walked into the kitchen. Her destination, the cupboard with the alcohol in, seemed to move closer to her rather than the other way around, and she reached out and opened it. She saw the bottle of vodka and took it out. The cap soon spun off, and she swallowed a mouthful straight from the bottle. Fire exploded, first in the back of her throat and then in her stomach. Although she hated the taste of straight vodka, her senses thanked her for it. She put the cap back on the bottle and felt a hell of a lot better for it.

No longer worried about fainting, she went to the bathroom to clean the cut on her head. A bump, very tender, was forming behind her ear, but the cut wasn't very deep.

She glanced at the mirror and, for the first time in all her years, Sarah didn't stare too long at her own reflection.

# Chapter Eight

*Jack read from the journal, not realising that he was reading aloud. Maggie stood by the door, unobserved by her husband, her face growing paler as she listened to the words he spoke, tears making their tracks down her cheeks.*

*"That man. I'm beginning to wonder what the point is. For each evil person I get rid of, there seems to be loads more to take their place. And yet, I know I could not stop: if I don't stop them, who will?*

*"My hands are shaking again as I think about what he tried to do. For once I didn't have to see his reflection, didn't have to see his true image to know he was evil – his actions told me that.*

*"I'm confused. I'm scared that I am losing my mind, but deep down I know I'm not. I almost wish I was insane, then this responsibility wouldn't be mine: I wouldn't have to do this anymore. Although, I must admit that I am getting some satisfaction from it.*

*"It's that that worries me. If I enjoy it (which I'm starting to), doesn't that make me as bad – if not worse – than the people I kill. But I saw my own reflection and it didn't change.*

*"'It's been four hours, I've had two showers, but I can still feel him on me, still smell him. Every time my eyes close, I can feel his hands touching me, and I want to scream."*

*Maggie watched Jack turn the page before continuing.*

*"I think I'll take a holiday, go abroad somewhere, just relax. I know I can't escape seeing people, but if I just don't look, then maybe I'll be okay."*

*Slowly, Jack closed the book, one hand holding it down on the desk as if to trap everything inside. His other hand rubbed at his eyes. Silently, Maggie walked into the office, white nightgown flowing over her feet. "Jack?"*

*He whirled around, and the first thing she saw was the look of pure fright on his face. Then she gently caressed his cheek, holding her finger out for him to see. "You've been crying."*

*Jack smiled sadly. "So have you."*

*Maggie wiped at her own face, surprised when her hand came away wet. The silence started to become uncomfortable, so she asked the question that she really needed answering right then. "Was she attacked?"*

*Jack shook his head. "I don't know. The way Freeman was found was just the way she described it. But, to be honest, it scares me."*

*Maggie nodded, her own sad smile forming. "You mean, if that's true then how much else is?"*

*"That's exactly what I mean."*

*She nodded, gently kissed his cheek, and walked back to the door. Before she left, she turned again to her husband, her eyes locked onto his. "Do you believe it?"*

*"I'm beginning to," he said, without hesitation.*

*The door closed, and he heard Maggie's footsteps as she went to bed. He looked at the journal on the desk. "Yeah," he said to no one. "I think I'm really beginning to."*

*Two hours later, the darkness outside beginning to lighten, Jack closed the book. He rubbed his eyes, weariness washing over him. He closed his eyes, just for a second, and felt himself beginning to drift away. Images instantly started to crowd into his mind, images of the people that Sarah had killed. Instead of seeing their physically mutilated forms as he had for years, the evidence photos having long been ingrained on his memory, he saw them how Sarah must have seen them, monsters in the guises of people.*

*Jack jerked awake, heart beating painfully loud in his chest. The colour outside his window was a lot brighter, and he knew that he'd slept for at least an hour in his chair.*

*The photographs from the file were scattered over the desk, and his eyes moved over them, as they had so many times before. He didn't really need them, he knew every part of them, but he kept them out regardless.*

*He knew every single person that Sarah had killed, all ten of them.*

*He'd seen their dead, mutilated bodies, had spoken to their families, and, as a mark of respect, had attended most of their funerals. Jack knew that he had been a bit obsessive and, if his desk was anything to go by and if he was honest with himself, he knew that he still was. But he just wanted to finish this case completely, and that included reading the journal to its end.*

*"Jack. Sarah's here."*

*Jack turned and could only stare at his wife, the name burning in his brain and his gut.*

*She saw the look of shock on his face, because she shook her head and sighed. When she spoke, she sounded annoyed and angry. "Sarah. Our* daughter."

*Jack had recovered from the name, but the venom in his wife's voice hit him hard, like a punch in the stomach. He watched as Maggie turned away from him and walked out. It was then that he realised just how drained she looked, how tired. He tidied the photos away and put them in the top drawer of his desk. Jack placed the journal inside and closed the drawer. His hands locked it automatically, removing the key and putting it in his jeans pocket.*

*Walking slowly, trying to get the case out of his mind, he left the office and walked into the sitting room. As his daughter turned to face him, Jack stopped cold. In front of him, instead of the light brown hair and light brown eyes that she had inherited from him, he saw Sarah Fletcher, eyes sad and remorseful.*

*He watched as Sarah and his wife exchanged a worried look, and that seemed to pull him together. When she looked back at him, it was his daughter that he saw.*

*"Dad? Are you okay?" She rose from her chair and walked over to him.*

*His smile felt a bit weak, but it was still a smile. "Yeah." The smile felt a bit stronger and a bit more natural as they hugged. "I just forget how big you are now."*

*Sarah smiled back, and led her father to the sofa. She sat and took the packet of cigarettes from the coffee table. She lit one and, trying to keep the smoke away from her parents, inhaled deeply.*

*Both Jack and Sarah watched, unbelieving, as Maggie also took one from the pack.*

*"Mum? When did you start smoking again?"*

*Maggie lit it and walked to the door, without answering. "I'll go and make us all something to drink."*

*"What's going on, Maggie?"*

*As soon as Sarah had left, Jack had gone upstairs to find his wife sitting on the bed, another cigarette in hand, staring out of the window.*

*"When did you start smoking again?"*

*Slowly, Maggie turned to face him. Set deep in her pale face, her eyes seemed to take a while to focus upon him. As Jack watched, a tear from each eye was set free.*

*"You've got to give someone else that diary." Her voice was as expressionless as her eyes.*

*Jack shook his head. "We've been through this before. I've got to finish it."*

*She nodded and turned away, not really noticing when her husband of twenty-nine years walked away.*

*Jack went straight to his office. He took the journal and photographs from the drawer, his hands shuffling them to find the photo he wanted.*

*He held the photograph of Sarah Fletcher, seventeen years old and without a care in the world, for a few moments before reopening the dead girl's journal.*

# Chapter Nine

She was on the beach, feeling totally relaxed. For the first time in four days Sarah had the beach to herself. In the distance, she could hear music, drunken voices and laughter. She never ached for the crowds, which was why she sat alone in the moonlight. Whenever she was among lots of people she felt strange. The crowds seemed to crush her; the voices were too loud, the smoke too suffocating. But on her own, the waves attacking the sand and the moon reflecting on the water, the voices were distant and the air was pure.

She lay on the sand in a swimsuit and sarong, torch illuminating her book so she could read it. The heat had given her a pleasant tan and, unlike England, the heat was a constant, so even in the middle of the night she could get away with lying on the beach.

Sarah had managed to stay out of people's way. Whenever she had seen a reflection she looked away hastily. She was on holiday, and she just did not want to know. She hadn't slept enough but, to compensate, she'd drunk too much, smoked too much, and kept her nose in too many books. So she was completely rested, completely relaxed, and ready to do whatever she had to when she returned to England.

At two o'clock in the morning, Sarah left the beach and walked past the clubs to reach her hotel. With only four hours before her flight was scheduled to leave, Sarah saw no point in trying to sleep. Instead, she put the shower on and, naked, stepped under its stream, her face tilted up, the water cascading down on her.

The mirror to her left soon steamed up and she turned her attention to it. A sudden compulsion made her step out of the shower, and she stood in front of the fogged-up glass. Suddenly, she wanted – *needed* – to see her own reflection, her *true* reflection. Slowly, her hand lifted itself and began to wipe the moisture from the mirror. Her hand stopped moving and Sarah forced herself to look away, no longer wanting to see.

By the time she stepped back under the water, the compulsion had entirely left her. And the mirror had steamed up once more.

Waiting for the plane to start moving, Sarah looked around her. The flight was half-empty, so there was plenty of room for people to spread out. A man across the aisle kept trying to catch Sarah's eyes and, not wanting to talk to him, she averted her eyes.

She had no intention of striking up a conversation, so she reached into her hold-all and took out one of her books. Carefully, she put the bag into the storage space above her seat and sat back down. Her fingers opened the book randomly and, without reading the words written there, turned the pages regularly.

Sarah could still feel his eyes on her, appraising her, and sudden memories of the man who had tried to rape her sprung into the front of her mind. She wanted to see if this man looked anything like the man she had killed, wanted to look casually over. But, if their eyes met, he could take that as a sign that she was interested, and she had no intention of letting *that* happen. And even if, by pure coincidence, he *did* look like the bastard that had attacked her, so what? It didn't mean anything, except that she obviously wasn't as relaxed as she'd like to think.

Sarah ran a hand through her hair, trying to dispel the thoughts that had come to mind. Why was she doing this to herself? She'd just had a brilliant holiday, had refused to let anything bad happen, and had relaxed. So, why now? She didn't have the answers and refused to think about it anymore. Determined not to torture herself any longer, she began to read the book, losing herself within its pages. She was so involved in the story, one that she'd already read, that she hardly noticed when the plane finally took off.

Sarah was greeted back in England by an unsettling article in a newspaper.

After stepping off the plane, she collected her luggage and went into a cafe outside the airport, her stomach rumbling. She put her bags in an empty booth, and walked to the almost non-existent line. Sarah got her food – a fried breakfast and a pot of tea – then noticed a small selection of papers on a stand near the till. She added a copy of one of the tabloid papers to her tray and, after experiencing a slight touch of contempt at the overall price, paid.

Trying her best to balance her tray full of goodies without spilling anything, she slowly walked back to her seat. She uttered a sigh of relief when she noticed that she was in a smoking area, and sat opposite her luggage. Her body told her what she needed first, and she lit a cigarette, gratefully filling her lungs with the grey-blue smoke. The first drag made her feel a bit dizzy and light-headed, but her body soon remembered, and relaxed.

Within a few minutes, she was slowly eating her breakfast, flicking idly through the newspaper. It wasn't until she saw the small headline on the fourth page that her stomach began to roll. As she read the first lines her hand stopped in mid-air, fork holding a piece of bacon that soon slipped off and landed back on the plate.

Her eyes moved over the words as she lowered her fork to her plate and pushed it all over to one side.

UPDATE ON THE SMALL TOWN SERIAL KILLER HUNT
Report by Charles Gordon

The small eastern town of Millsbury is still in the middle of a hunt for a serial killer. DC Jack Daniels told this reporter that for the past three and a half years he has been investigating.

"The first death was of a man named Tony Aldridge, who was 32 years old when he was killed. At the time it was thought to be an isolated case. But almost a year ago a young girl, nine-year-old Jackie Austin, was found dead in her home by her parents. Small details connected the two killings, and forensic details have concluded that the murders were committed by the same person.

"Five months ago, I investigated another death. Thirty-nine-year-old Anthony Freeman was found behind some bushes on an abandoned industrial estate in Millsbury. He too had injuries that have connected him with the two previous deaths."

When asked if there was any sort of connection between the victims, the DC shook his head. "None at all. Tony Aldridge had no relatives in the area and lived alone. Jackie Austin was only nine years old, lived with her parents, and was a normal little girl. Anthony Freeman, a teacher, was married with two children. There's no connection, and no obvious pattern."

At the end of the interview, the Detective Constable asked to go on record as saying, "I will not rest until this case is closed with the arrest of the killer."

Sarah closed the newspaper, hoping to block out of her mind what she'd just read. Although it was now only lukewarm, she drank her tea. Now that she was back in England, the memories were harder for her to ignore. It seemed no matter where she looked, those memories were there, fighting to be heard.

Her appetite no longer there, she gathered her things and walked outside to find a taxi to take her home.

Sarah had started writing in her journal almost as soon as she'd arrived home, and an hour later she was still writing.

The doorbell rang and she jumped, the unexpected noise startling her. For a split second, Sarah imagined police officers waiting at the door. She quickly banished the image from her mind, closed her book and shot to her feet. She hurried to the display cabinet that stood in the living room. Putting the journal inside the bottom drawer, she closed and locked it, removing the key. She put it in her jeans' pocket as she walked to the front door.

She opened it with a smile. "Serena!"

"Welcome back, Sarah."

Serena Dawes stepped into Sarah's arms and they hugged, laughing. They walked into the house and through to the kitchen.

"So? How was the holiday?" Serena sat at the table, facing Sarah, while Sarah made them both a cup of tea.

"Brilliant."

"Anything happen?"

Sarah looked at her neighbour and laughed at Serena's raised eyebrows, knowing exactly what she meant by that question. "No."

Serena lent back, looking at her friend. "How is that possible? Have you *seen* you?" Her long red hair, naturally curled, swung around as she shook her head, her green eyes sparkling as they always did when she smiled.

Sarah was used to Serena's one-tracked mind, so didn't blush. She brought the cups to the table and sat opposite. Serena shook out two cigarettes from her pack, and held one out towards Sarah. "Unless you made a life-style change while you were away."

It was Sarah's turn to shake her head. "No. I'm still slowly killing myself."

They both laughed at the old gag, knowing that it wasn't really a joke, and lit their cigarettes.

"So, how's things between you and Henry?"

Serena's eyes dulled, and Sarah instantly regretted asking. But, without resentment, she knew she'd listen and, if she could, help.

"Not too good." She sipped her drink, turning the cup around on the table. "I don't know what's wrong."

As it darkened outside, Sarah listened as Serena talked about the worsening state of her marriage.

Henry Dawes could have explained properly, but he didn't have the courage to.

In the dark he walked around, half of him hoping to find what he was looking for, the other half disgusted with himself. He knew that it was unlikely, but he prowled anyway, His motto in life was, you never know your luck.

Henry walked slowly, hands in his pockets, collar turned up against the cold. The sweets in his pocket rustled as he moved, and the sound seemed too loud in the silence around him. He kept his head down, just in case anyone was watching him, but his eyes moved slyly around, looking for what he wanted.

The streets were deserted, the lamps shining their orange glow onto the ground. It was the perfect place for him to roam, the shadows cast by the insufficient light extending further than they should, giving Henry more places to conceal himself if he had to. Not that he ever *did* have to, but it created a comfort zone for him. His feet moved him to his new haunt, the playground.

Up until a few weeks ago, Henry had never played so close to home, always using his work to find opportunities further away. But now the excuses for going were becoming thin and no longer plausible, and he couldn't just stop! So, he was having to fulfil his needs a little closer to home.

He passed through the gates and just stood for a few moments, looking. The swings were on his left, the two slides on his right. As he always did, he moved stealthily, despite his size, to his left. He sat on one of the swings, doing his best to ignore the squeaking as the chain moved, his feet gently moving him backwards and forwards. His eyes were on his feet, watching the slight movement.

Henry looked up towards the gate as he heard voices. *Young* voices. A boy and a girl, by the sounds. "Damn." His voice barely reached his own ears, so he knew that it hadn't reached theirs.

He looked back down at his feet as he saw shadows entering the park.

Carla and her brother stopped talking as they saw the figure on the swings. They were both eleven, and knew enough to be realistic. Before their father had been killed, he'd talked about all the sick things that happened in the world, so Carla knew the sort of people that hung around in kids' playgrounds at night.

"What'd you think he's doing there?" she asked softly.

"Don't know," William said with a shrug, moving protectively closer to her.

Together they watched as the man stood and walked away from them and out of the park.

After a few minutes, they went to the swings and sat next to each other, talking about their father. Every now and then, Carla stroked the plait that reached the middle of her back and William fiddled with his glasses.

The two children of the late Anthony Freeman never found out just how lucky they had been.

Henry walked home, annoyed at his bad luck. If it had been just the girl it would have been fine. Or even two girls; he could have coped with that. But he knew from experience that boys had an image to maintain, and would protect the girls they were with. He'd been attacked by a boy before, after he'd had fun with the boy's little friend. The boy had found a broken beer bottle nearby and had slashed at Henry, giving him a nice cut on his arm. Henry had spent the rest of that night avoiding Serena so that she wouldn't notice.

Luckily, the kids hadn't been able to give the police an accurate description, and Henry had learnt his lesson. Never make a move while boys were around.

"What are parents thinking of, anyway?" he muttered angrily under his breath. "Letting kids out in the middle of the bloody night!"

He walked down the narrow road, walking on the right so that he'd be seen by any oncoming traffic. He glanced at Sarah Fletcher's house as he passed. As far as he could see, all the downstairs lights were on, so he figured that Serena was still there. Relief flooded into him when he saw that his own home was dark. His night had been bad enough without having to put up with all of *her* bloody questions.

"Have a good day at work tomorrow." Sarah heard Serena laugh as she stood by the door, watching her friend and neighbour walking away. As soon as Serena was out of sight, Sarah went back inside and locked the door behind her.

She felt exhausted, but in a good way. Serena always left her feeling that way, and it was something she'd always be grateful for. She went upstairs, turning off the lights as she went. As soon as she got into bed she fell asleep.

It was dark when her eyes opened; the red light of her digital clock gave the room a bit of illumination. She was completely alert and knew that something must have woken her. Her ears picked up no sounds, and she couldn't see anything wrong in her room, so she closed her eyes again.

After ten minutes, she sighed heavily and sat up – there was no way she was getting back to sleep. She got out of bed and walked to the bathroom, trying to shake off the cold that had suddenly come on her. She was sure that she'd put the heating back on when she'd come home, but the goose bumps all over her body told her otherwise.

When she'd finished in the bathroom she went back into her bedroom. Instead of getting back into bed she moved over to the window and parted the curtains. Looking at the moon always relaxed her, and she searched the sky for it. It was hidden behind a cloud, but Sarah could still define its edge. The grey cloud shone silver, and a feeling of utter peace settled over her. Calm,

Sarah looked out over her back garden, past the fence, and over the fields behind.

Movement, caught out of the corner of her eye, made her look below her. A metre away from the side of the conservatory, almost completely hidden in the shadows, stood a figure. By the shape, size, and stance, Sarah could tell that it was a man. He was all in black, his face completely lost in the shadows. And, although she couldn't be positive, Sarah thought that this man was watching her.

In the moonlight, the figure turned his back to her and began to walk away from the house. Sarah felt frozen, unable to move, yet her eyes continued to trace him as he walked through the garden. He wasn't rushing, seemed to be strolling, taking in every detail of the garden. When he reached the bottom of the garden, he stopped.

Sarah could hear the blood pumping around her body as she watched his still form. Her breath stopped dead in her chest as the figure started to move once more. Instead of continuing to walk, he slowly turned back to face the house. Sarah still could not see his features, even though nothing overshadowed him, but she knew that he was looking directly at her.

She stumbled back, hitting the back of her thigh on the bedpost when a bony finger, completely out of proportion with the bulky figure, pointed straight at her, and then began to beckon her.

She awoke with grey light filtering into her bedroom. A breath of relief escaped her as she found herself in bed.

"Just a dream. Thank fuck for that." Her almost hysterical laughter was cut short when she saw the window. The thing was, she shouldn't be *able* to see the window. The window should have been concealed by the curtains, but the curtains had been drawn back. Just as she had done in her dream.

"No way. No fucking way. I just forgot to close them, that's all!"

She jumped out of bed, and uttered a shrill cry as pain bolted down her leg. Gingerly, she touched the back of her right thigh and winced. Unnerved, she went as quickly as she could to the bathroom.

Her hands grabbed the small mirror and she positioned it so she could see the back of her leg. She almost dropped it as she saw the bruise on her leg, the dark purple mushroom that had exploded overnight. This time she did drop the mirror (seven years bad luck avoided when the glass stayed in one piece) as the muscles in her hand began to spasm. Her knees buckled and she landed heavily on the rim of the bath.

Sarah stared at the wall opposite. She stayed like that for almost thirty minutes, with absolutely no idea of what to think.

Three hours later, still in her nightclothes, she was sitting on the sofa, a tumbler of neat whiskey in her hand. She still had no idea about what had happened that night, but with the amount of alcohol she had in her system she no longer cared. The ashtray on the seat next to her was almost overflowing with ash and butts, but Sarah had hardly smoked. Instead, she'd light a cigarette, have a few drags then just let it burn down until she could feel the heat near her fingers and then stub it out.

Her eyes remained fixed upon the electric fire in front of her as the phone rang, never shifting.

An hour later, and still in the same position, a rapid tattoo on the front door brought her out of her stupor. Yet still she did not move. Sarah looked towards the door, heart pounding in her chest as she remembered her mysterious visitor from last night.

"Sarah? Are you okay?"

She heard Serena's voice, but still could not find the courage to go to the door. She was scared, but she was also ashamed. Ashamed of how she had reacted to the dream, or whatever it had been.

"Look at me," she whispered to herself. "Just look."

Moving as quietly as she could manage, she walked into the kitchen, hoping that Serena hadn't seen or heard any movement. Without second thoughts, without any hesitation, she tipped the glass upside down, watching as the dark amber liquid flowed down the sink. She reeled away as the smell reached her, not ashamed of herself now but totally disgusted.

In a fit of insanity, Sarah rushed to the front door, meaning to show her friend the journal and to tell her everything. As quickly as she could, Sarah threw back the bolt, unlocked the door, and yanked it open. To glimpse Serena walk out of sight.

# Chapter Ten

*She looked over the crowd, searching for Rob. She saw his dirty-blonde coloured hair, and felt a small pang of lust as she imagined running her fingers through it. Maggie knew that as soon as she looked into his deep blue eyes that feeling of need would instantly double. One second's worth of guilt was all she would allow herself though. It wasn't fair on Jack, but he wasn't being fair on her; his obsession with that murdering bitch had driven her into the arms of his best friend.*

*She moved to the small table where her lover sat, and she resisted the urge to touch his shoulder. What they were doing felt right, but neither of them wanted to hurt Jack. No matter what it took, their affair would not become common knowledge: they refused to be too indiscreet.*

*"How's Jack?"*

*Rob always asked about Jack. Maggie supposed that it was his way of dealing with his own guilt. "The same. Still reading that bloody thing."*

*"What about you, Maggie?"*

*His sad eyes showed only compassion, and tears began to fill her eyes. She rubbed at them, trying to deter the tears from falling, but as she spoke, her voice cracking, they began to slide down her cheeks. "It's destroying me. I can't cope anymore." She stopped talking so she could get herself under control again. After a few moments, she looked up into Rob's eyes and forced a sad smile to her lips. "I just don't know how much more I can take."*

*Rob wanted to take her hand, and it was hard for him to stop himself. He hated to see what Jack was doing to his wife, yet he could understand why Jack was so obsessed.*

*Rob had worked with Jack through most of the murders that Sarah Fletcher had committed. He'd had the same feelings of annoyance, of incompetence, as Jack had. But, whilst the rest of the investigation team had taken it almost like a fact of life, Jack had taken it as a personal insult – as if, just because she'd written to him personally, it was all his fault. The fact that both he and Jack had spoken to Sarah must have almost destroyed him after the realisation had dawned. But no one else had reacted quite so badly.*

*While Maggie was being led into Rob's home, Jack sat at his desk, thinking. As he'd read the thoughts and actions of Sarah, he'd begun to recognise the first signs of her becoming unhinged. And that led him to another thought: Did that mean that she'd been all there to begin with?*

*Jack pushed himself away from his desk and walked to the window. The sun was shining. Looking at the warm garden, Jack felt a longing for normality, for his wife, and for a bit of relaxation.*

*Quickly, he strode from his office, calling out his wife's name.* Maybe a picnic, *he thought,* or maybe just a day in the garden. *In the kitchen, he noticed the stillness of the house, the emptiness that filled every room. Loneliness filled him, and he stood unsure of what to do next.*

*Jack saw a piece of paper propped up against the kettle.*

*'Gone to meet a friend. Won't be back late.' He screwed the paper up in one hand, contempt filling him for a second before the loneliness returned. "Great!"*

*Deciding to do something constructive, he walked back to his study. Sitting once again at his desk, he stared at the journal without touching it. He knew exactly what it was doing to him, had known it for some time, but like any addict he needed his fix. He'd gotten into Sarah's head and he couldn't get out, didn't* want *to get out. The whole thing was insane, utterly crazy, but it also made a weird kind of sense to him.*

*For the dozenth time since first opening the journal, he wondered if he would do the same thing. If he could see that someone was evil, would he kill them? Would he stop them from hurting others? And for the dozenth time he answered himself. Yes. Without a second thought, yes he would.*

*"Maggie? Are you okay?"*

*"Yeah. I'll be out in a minute."*

*She stood in the bathroom, looking at herself in the mirror. What was she doing? How could she be doing this to her husband? She shook her head, trying to summon up anger to displace the guilt. How could* he *be doing this to* her*? She'd always been there. Through the late nights, the holidays ruined by a single phone call telling him about another killing. The drinking. The arguments. The distance. The awkward silences. She'd stayed with him through all of that and more.*

*Thankfully, relieved from all her doubts, she ran the cold tap in the sink, ducking her head towards the water. Gently, she washed her face, washing away not just the puffiness from her eyes, but all the bad feelings.*

*"Better?"*

*Rob stood outside the door, a hot cup of coffee held out towards her. Gratefully, she took the offered drink, holding it to her chest to steal its warmth. She nodded, worried that if she tried to speak, her emotions would betray her once more.*

*Rob sat on his sofa. The small flat was all he needed for himself, and Maggie was grateful that it bore no resemblance to her own home. She sat down and leant against him. He wrapped his arm around her shoulders, and Maggie sighed with happiness. She couldn't remember the last time she felt so content. Or so safe.*

*"Have you thought any more about what we're going to do?" He felt her shake her head against his chest. "I can't think about it, Rob. Not yet." She almost broke down again, but her stubbornness overruled. "When Jack's finished with that sodding book of hers, then I'll be able to think. We just have to be patient."*

*It dawned on Maggie just how much rested on the conclusion of the journal.*

# Chapter Eleven

It was Henry and Serena's fifth wedding anniversary and to celebrate they were having a party. Close friends and family only, and Sarah felt out of her depths because she only knew the hostess and host.

She'd been trying to catch Serena alone all night, but her friend had purposefully been avoiding her. Ashamed about something, and Sarah could guess at what. As soon as she'd entered the house, she had seen the bruise that was mostly hidden by Serena's hair, perfectly situated on her right temple. But Serena had given Sarah no time to ask any questions. As soon as she had stepped over the threshold, Serena had catapulted Sarah into the room with the rest of the guests and had disappeared.

So Sarah had spent the last few hours trying to find her, and her tracking led her into the kitchen, to discover only Henry. He was standing looking out of the window, nursing a can of beer. While everyone else had made an effort, Henry wore his usual dirty jeans and T-shirt. He turned at Sarah's approach and his sombre expression was replaced by his normal fake grin. "Hi, Sarah."

Her distrust of her friend's husband had increased when she'd seen the bruise on Serena's head. It went up a few more notches when she saw his drunken smile. "Henry." She looked around, still hoping to catch a glimpse of Serena. "Where's Serena?"

He shrugged his shoulders, obviously not bothered. "Don't know." He turned his back to her to continue looking out of the window.

The hatred she felt when he turned away from her was intense. She *wanted* him to be evil. As she caught his eyes in the glass, the image instantly began to move, and Sarah felt sick. Her reaction had never been so strong, and she felt scared as her head started to throb, as needles stabbed her eyeballs, as sweat seeped from her skin and as bile began to rise in her throat.

She didn't know if the figure she now saw could be called a man; she wasn't even sure if it could be called *human*. The shape of the skull was right, but nothing else was. The skin was white – not pale, but *white*. Ivory skin, seemingly illuminated from within, was stretched taunt across the bones and seemed to be tearing in places. Sarah found herself no longer staring into eyes, but into smooth white hollows where eyes should have been. There were no nostrils, not even a bridge of bone to support a nose. There were no lips and no mouth, although as Sarah watched a slight slit appeared in the skin, disappearing seconds later, leaving no indication that it had been there.

Below the head, with no neck joining the two, were elongated shoulder blades, each stretching out half a metre as if trying to escape the horrific body they were attached to. The bones were visible as no skin hid them, and Sarah was glad that the window cut off the reflection just below the chest.

Feeling sick, Sarah looked away, making sure that she turned away from Henry, not caring if she appeared rude, just wanting to make sure that she didn't have to look at either image of Henry Dawes.

Sarah didn't make it to her house. A few steps down the road, she quickly moved onto the grass verge and, holding her hair back with one hand, vomited. When she thought she had finished, more erupted from her throat. Finally, she stood up, her spare hand cupping her mouth. She felt empty, entirely drained, and totally confused. Why had her reaction been so strong to Henry's image?

Slowly, she walked along the road, grateful when she reached her driveway. Hands shaking badly, her whole body shivering, it took a little while for her to unlock the door. With relief, she managed to get in, and locked the door behind her. She was utterly exhausted and made her way to the bathroom.

Without turning on any lights, Sarah lay down beside the toilet, just in case, still puzzled about the ferocity of her reaction.

Seconds before falling asleep, it came to her. It was because she loved her friend. And because she wasn't sure if she'd be able to kill him.

Henry left the party after hurting his wife for the second time in as many days.

"Stupid bitch, shouldn't have been snooping."

She'd found some DVDs the previous day labelled 'Private', and had known instantly that they were pornography. When she'd suggested to Henry that they watch one, he had lost it, shoving her away from them and she'd hit her head on the edge of the wardrobe.

Henry hadn't apologised, too shocked with himself to really comprehend what had happened. Feeling more ashamed than he ever had before, Henry had put his collection back into his cupboard where they belonged, and pretended that nothing had happened.

During the party, he'd gone to tell his wife that Sarah had made a hasty – and puzzling – exit and the anger had resurfaced as he saw Serena going through his shoe box of photographs. He ignored the tears rolling down her face, his shame hiding behind his anger. Snatching the photographs away from her, he felt his face beginning to burn in embarrassment.

The moment that Serena had started to ask what was going on, he'd lost it. Moving gracefully, he'd stepped closer to her and punched her squarely on the nose. The feeling of bone shattering under his knuckles made his stomach roll, and he was sure that he was going to complete his wife's indignity by throwing up over her. Luckily for them both, Henry managed to get himself under control and walked quickly out of the house.

"Stupid fucking bitch."

The vast amount of alcohol he had consumed – which hadn't helped his temperament – did little to keep him warm as he moved through the park. He spotted a young figure hidden under the slide and stopped. A sick smile, which would have sent the strongest person reeling away, appeared on his face.

The young girl, upset over an argument with her parents, hadn't even realised that she was no longer alone in the park, so when the hand clamped down over her nose and mouth she was more than a little surprised.

He could feel the twelve-year-old struggling under his hand and at last he began to feel better. One hand already unzipping his jeans, he leant closer to her. "Don't make a sound."

Serena asked their friends to leave, doing her best to ignore their pitying glances at her ruined nose. She'd taken some heavy painkillers before going downstairs, and the pain had become a distant throb, but her shock also helped. It wasn't just the fact that he'd started to beat her again – she'd honestly thought that part of their relationship was over – but the photographs she had found.

Tears rolled silently down her cheeks, and only when they touched her damaged nose did she notice them. Like her neighbour, she was now totally exhausted and, as Sarah did a hundred yards away, Serena slept.

When he saw her lying on the sofa, he felt a pang of lust. He hadn't felt that way about his wife for nearly two years, and had never thought that he was denying her anything. As far as Henry was concerned, sex was for a man's pleasure only, and that a woman was just a useful tool.

And that was why he walked over to his wife and dragged her to the floor.

Her eyes sprang open and, realising that something was desperately wrong, breathed in deeply and prepared to scream.

She felt sick as his fist hit her in the stomach, pushing the air from her lungs. The first breath she tried to take in stuck in her throat, her lungs demanding the air yet refusing to accept it.

*I'm going to suffocate,* she thought desperately. *I'm going to fucking suffocate in a room full of air!* Just as she became sure that she *was* going to suffocate, her lungs expanded a little.

With her mind no longer on the subject of suffocation, Serena actually became aware of what her husband was doing. Her black velvet dress had been shoved up to her waist and her knickers had been pushed aside.

He entered her roughly, and she bit down on her bottom lip to stop herself from crying out. She felt something inside herself tear, and bit down even deeper, almost choking on the taste of her own blood. Tears ran from her eyes. "Stop. Please, Henry. Please stop, please, please, please."

His breath, stinking of beer, was pushed into her face as he moved above and inside her. He didn't see his wife below him, his mind giving him images of the young girl he had used earlier, and his pleasure increased.

Serena started to pray for it to be over and within minutes her prayer was answered. She felt him climax and hoped that there would be no more torment. He pulled out of her, and she closed her eyes, not wanting to look at him.

Henry looked down at his wife and shock washed over him. The shape of her once-perfect nose, her dishevelled hair, the blood running from her lip, the tears rolling down the side of her face. Before he could register anything else about the state of his wife, Henry walked out of the living room and ran up the stairs to the bathroom. He closed the door behind him and shot the bolt.

Serena lay there for a few minutes, sure that it was a trick, that he would be back to hurt her more. Finally she opened her eyes and looked around her, starting to get up. The pain all over her body nearly stopped her, but she kept going, self-preservation now spurring her on. She passed a mirror and stopped in front of it. Horror disfigured her features even more as she saw what her husband had done to her. She was tempted to put a brush through her hair to try to make a little improvement, but she knew that it would just be the beginning. She'd brush her hair, then she'd wash the blood away, then take some more painkillers. Then it would be too late; she'd be too embarrassed to go anywhere.

Instead, Serena walked bare foot from her home, disregarding the gravel from the drive as it pressed against the soles of her feet, the cold biting at her bare arms. She walked down the road, finding comfort in the darkness, and headed towards Sarah's house.

The doorbell rang just once, but it woke her up. A sense of urgency gripped her and she fled from the bathroom, almost falling down the stairs, and reached the front door. Sarah only waited for one second, visions of her visitor from the previous night filling her mind, before unlocking the door and opening it.

She couldn't speak at first, too shocked to say anything. "Serena? What the hell…?" She ushered Serena indoors without waiting for an answer to her unfinished question, and closed the door. Still leading her, they went into the living room, and Sarah left her friend on the sofa while she fetched the whiskey from the kitchen. She returned with the bottle and two tumblers. Once they were half-full she handed one to Serena. "Drink that."

That was all it took. Serena's resolve broke and she started crying. Between sobs, the whole story was blurted out: the films, being pushed into the wall, the photos, the broken nose, being winded. Being raped.

Sarah felt rage growing inside, like a malformed foetus, as she listened to Serena speak, eyes wandering over her friend's body, noting all of the visible injuries that had been inflicted upon her.

A vein pulsed in her forehead and she could almost hear the blood as it pounded there.

The glass in Serena's hand had emptied, and Sarah was relieved to see that most of her friend's shakes had departed. One hand under Serena's chin, Sarah turned her to face her.

"I want you to trust me, Serena."

Silent, Serena nodded.

"I'm going out for a little while." She tried to ignore the blood draining from her friend's face. "And I don't want you to go anywhere, or call anyone." Slowly, she stood, trying not to notice the panic on Serena's face. "Don't have a bath or wash yourself. Don't even comb your hair. Okay?"

Without waiting for an answer, Sarah walked from the room, with Serena following her; she took keys from her pocket. "Lock the door and don't open it for anyone. I've got another set hidden."

She walked from her house, relieved when she heard Serena closing and locking the door straight away, and headed towards Serena and Henry's house, with the darkness covering her.

Henry opened the bathroom door and stood for a few moments on the threshold. He heard nothing, and the density of the silence told him that the house was empty. But still he waited, the shame he felt as a result of his actions keeping him where he was.

For his own sanity, Henry began making excuses about what had happened, laying the blame on his wife. It was *her* fault that he attacked young girls. It was *her* fault that he'd hit her. It was because of *her* and that damned dress she'd been wearing that had *made* him rape her – she'd *wanted* him to.

By the time he had reached the kitchen, he'd resolved most of his inner conflict, and was simply ignoring the rest. All that was left was for him to find his inner peace again. And there was only one way he knew how to do that. He needed the relaxation of the park.

So he walked outside and towards his destination, with no idea that Sarah was following.

Sarah had hidden in the living room, the knife she'd taken from the kitchen drawer clasped firmly in her hand, and waited for Henry to walk away.

She followed him down the road, hearing, even from the distance she had allowed between them, him muttering to himself. Her anger forced her on, while every other part of her herself told her to stop, that she was being stupid, that after what he'd done to Serena, his own *wife,* he was capable of anything. Then she remembered the way that Serena had looked, standing on her doorstep with nothing on her feet, and the anger killed any doubts that she had.

Henry had entered the park, and Sarah stopped, struggling with what she had planned. Then she wondered if there were any children in the park, and that thought got her moving again.

He was sitting on one of the swings, his back to her, as she moved closer. His feet pushed him gently backwards and forwards, totally lost in his own world.

"Hello, Henry."

He looked around sharply. He saw Sarah standing behind him, and then sprung away from the swing when he noticed the knife in her hand.

Without speaking they looked at each other, the swing still moving gently between them. Uncertainty shone from his eyes and he felt the need to plead his case, but found that no sound would come. He couldn't meet her eyes, instead he stared at the blade as it caught the moonlight. Henry saw the blade moving closer, and knew that the woman who was holding it also had to be moving closer, but he could still not look at her.

"You're not gonna do it again, Henry."

The voice came from a distance, through a haze, and Henry finally looked at Sarah's face. The first thing he saw was a vicious and dangerous smile that made him back up a couple of paces. And then he noticed her eyes. Her usually dull brown eyes now sparked with hatred, and he was scared. The eyes he now looked at were the eyes of a killer.

"Never again."

Sarah began to stride towards him, and he continued to back away, his eyes never leaving hers. Because of his distraction, he never saw what he was about to step in. He slipped over, and black stars filled his vision as his head hit something hard. Pain shot through his body, and a shadow fell over him.

Sarah laughed. "Poetic justice, really. Shit slipped up on shit." She stood over him, knife held by her thigh as she looked at him.

Henry moved his head so that he was no longer looking at her, and dizziness swallowed him. His head was pounding, and he could feel the blood leaving from wounds in his back caused by the chunks of glass that were stuck in him.

"Oh, dear." Her voice was full of mock-sincerity. "Looks like you've hit your head. There's quite a lot of blood."

He knew that she was still talking, but he could no longer distinguish the words. As he looked around the playground a magical quality came bursting in front of him. The silver moonlight made the swings and slides shine, it made each blade of grass different from the last. It made everything perfect and innocent.

Something caught his eyes, and he gasped when he saw the figures coming towards him. Relief flooded through him as he imagined those figures coming to his aid, to help him get away from the woman towering above him. But relief soon changed to distress when he saw that his 'rescuers' were too young to be of any real help. Distress turned to disbelief when he began to recognise the girls as they moved closer. All of them. Every single girl he had ever attacked. All of them standing there around him.

He could still hear Sarah in the distance, somewhere in the darkness away from the silver light, still talking, unaware that they all stood around him, watching and gloating as the blood poured from his body.

Henry died with no sudden movements, no half-uttered false sentiments of remorse. He slipped out of consciousness, then slipped out of life.

Sarah stood where she was, waiting to see if his chest would resume its rise and fall. After a while she knew that he was dead, and moved so that she could see his face properly. She knelt before him and raised the knife.

After washing the knife clean of his blood, scrubbing and scrubbing with antibacterial soap rather than washing up liquid, then drying and putting it back into the drawer, Sarah walked upstairs. In Serena's bedroom wardrobe she found an old suitcase and placed it on the bed. She was putting some of Serena's clothes inside when she noticed the shoebox that was also on the mattress.

As she packed, her eyes kept returning to it. Once she'd gotten as many of Serena's clothes in the case as she could, Sarah gave in and moved to the other side of the bed so that she could see the contents.

She only saw one photo, and that was enough. It showed a girl, no older than seven, standing completely naked with her arms behind her head in a super model's pose. Bile began to rise in her throat as sweat swept down her face, and Sarah quickly put a hand to her mouth and turned away.

Having seen more than she'd wanted to, Sarah grabbed the case and walked downstairs.

She left the house without locking the door, and half-carried half-dragged the case along the road. Instead of going to the front door, Sarah walked around to the conservatory. The step that led to the conservatory door was loose and Sarah lifted it easily. She plucked the key out from the dirt and replaced the step.

The noise of the key in the lock brought Serena into the conservatory. Despite her injuries, the relief on her face as she realised that it was Sarah made her look about a hundred times better.

Sarah walked in, still dragging the suitcase, and locked the door behind her. "Right, now we call the police."

The relief quickly drained from Serena's face.

Sarah waited for the kettle to boil, absently wiping away tears. In the living room she could hear Serena talking to the female officer between crying fits.

"That was a foolish thing you did, Miss Fletcher."

She looked behind her and saw the other officer standing in the kitchen doorway.

He was in his fifties, maybe late forties, and Sarah found her eyes repeatedly drawn to the scar above his top lip. His hair was dirty-blonde – Sarah was grateful that it was a shade lighter than Henry's – and his eyes were a light shade of blue and, unlike Serena's husband's, those eyes were full of compassion. Sarah thought of it as a fatherly look.

She smiled tiredly. "For one, it's Sarah, not 'Miss Fletcher'. And two, I don't know what you mean." She turned back to the kettle.

Rob Donnelly nodded, expecting a response like that. He looked around as he walked towards her, enjoying the homely feel of the kitchen. It was the complete opposite of his own shoebox one-bedroom flat. "Mind if I smoke?"

Sarah turned her head and smiled. "Go ahead. I'll pour these then join you."

He leant against the cupboards next to her and watched as she made the drinks. With two cups in her hands, she began to walk towards the living room. Rob placed a gentle hand on her arm. "I'd leave 'em to it for now."

For a second, Rob caught a glimpse of fury as it flashed in her eyes, and then she smiled and nodded. She returned the two cups to the side before handing the officer his and moving her own a little closer to herself.

They smoked and drank in silence for a few moments, Rob watching her closely. "So? Why did you go?"

He watched as she put the cup down, a sad smile playing on her lips. But as their eyes briefly met, Sarah's looked guarded. Then her smile became a bit more genuine, and that look in her eyes was lost.

"Her clothes." She turned fully so she could look him in the eyes properly. "I didn't want her to have to go back there to pick up her own things. And, if I'm honest, I was angry." She looked towards the living room. "I suppose I wanted to find him, to confront him, look into his eyes and ask him how he could've done that."

He smiled as she looked nervously at him, as if expecting him to arrest her. "I'd probably have done the same thing."

They continued to drink in a silence that was entirely comfortable.

# Chapter Twelve

It was a week after Serena's rape, a week since the death of Serena's husband, and Sarah lay awake in bed. For five nights, Serena had been unable to sleep through the night, waking up sobbing after a nightmare, calling out for Sarah. And Sarah had been there every time, to hold Serena, to tell her that it was all over, to stop the tears.

Last night, Serena had slept soundly, not waking up once, but Sarah hadn't been able to. She'd been sure that as soon as she closed her eyes, Serena would wake up and need her. So it as easier to just stay awake.

Hoping that Serena would continue to sleep, Sarah got out of bed. She picked up her jeans and fished out the key from the watch pocket. Being as quiet as she could, she walked downstairs and into the kitchen, where she poured herself a double shot of whiskey.

She put the glass on the table and walked steadily through to the living room. She crouched in front of the cabinet and unlocked the bottom drawer. She was sure it had never done so before, yet as Sarah pulled the drawer open a squeak screamed out at her, terribly loud in the silence.

Her heart hammered in her chest and she remained still, ears ready to pick up any sound from upstairs. After only a minute, although it seemed to last hours, Sarah removed her journal and closed the door. She left the key in the keyhole just in case it had to be locked again in a hurry. Almost tiptoeing, she returned to the kitchen and set the book down next to her drink. Sarah sat before them and stared out of the window. She knew that she had to write in her book, but she had to get her thoughts in order first.

When what Sarah thought of as the worst was over – Serena's physical examination and the statements – there had been another visit from the police.

DC Daniels had told Serena – in Sarah's company – that Henry had been found dead in the park. Sarah had done her best to act shocked (mainly by making no reaction at all), but she found the man unsettling. He seemed familiar to her, but more worryingly was that he seemed *aware*. His eyes seemed to be everywhere, taking in every little detail.

He'd then asked to speak to Serena alone, and Sarah had left, grateful just to be away from him.

Afterwards, with Serena crying once more, Sarah had learnt the details of the conversation.

He'd told her that a young girl, prompted by an angry mother, had reported being raped, and that the description had fitted Henry to a T. Tests performed on the semen they had taken from Serena during her exam had matched samples taken from the girl. Henry was also being linked to attacks on other young girls.

Despite the sickening things she was hearing, Sarah had taken it all in her stride. Until Serena continued. "He says Henry's death, although accidental, might have something to do with a serial killer." She looked at Sarah with wide eyes.

Unable to speak, she put an arm around Serena's shoulders and squeezed gently, but on the inside she was screaming. Why had she marked Henry?

Sarah couldn't relax, despite nothing being linked to her. And it was because of Jack Daniels. *He* was the problem. Knowing that he was looking for her, that he was the one trying to track her down, was unsettling. She'd seen him around Millsbury, and knew that he and his wife lived nearby. And the idea that he was close, *so bloody close,* sent a sliver of fear down her spine.

Sarah looked at the journal to see that she had written everything down, without being aware that she had done so. She reached for her glass of whiskey and was shocked to find it empty. Her hand hung in mid-air before she let it fall back to the table.

"This can't be good."

She sat up straight as footsteps moved above her. She waited, sweat escaping from her skin, waiting to hear the footsteps on the stairs. Instead of Serena coming downstairs, she heard the upstairs toilet flush and the steps as Serena traced her steps back to the spare bedroom.

Breath that she hadn't been aware of holding was forced viciously out of her lungs. Feeling exhausted, drained and empty, Sarah put her hands protectively over the journal and placed her head on top.

It had been a long week, all told, and she had been living on her nerves for most of it, but now her strength was failing, falling away from her. And, thinking that she must stay awake, must continue writing, her will was overridden by her body's need, and she fell asleep.

Her dreams were confused and jumbled to begin with.

One moment she was walking along the pavements in the middle of town, feeling content and happy. The next, she was sitting in front of her parents' graves, feeling ashamed and alone. A split second later, she was *inside* a coffin, completely terrified, unable to breathe, hammering on the silk-lined wooden ceiling inches above her, with not even enough air in her lungs to shout or scream. The next piece of her dream started out brilliantly, especially when compared to the confinement of the last. She was strolling down the road that led from her home towards town. The sky was blue, not a cloud in sight, birds talking aimlessly to each other, the air warm. A small gentle breeze brought the sweet smells of the different flowers that littered the path to her

As she walked, she became aware of people walking behind her. She turned her head and saw couples also strolling, also enjoying the scents of the flowers, and she smiled at their obvious peace and happiness. When she faced forward again, there were more couples in front, walking towards her. Suddenly, the narrow road, which was really nothing more than a glorified dirt track, was full of people, and Sarah felt goose bumps break out over her entire body. She felt as she had in the coffin, utterly claustrophobic. There was now too many people. They were bumping into her, shoving her aside, knocking her into the paths of others. She caught sight of a man in the distance, and recognised him in an instant.

Although the day was bright, everything illuminated, the man who had visited her in the night – a lifetime ago, it seemed – was wrapped in shadows, moving through the crowd, parting couples the way that Moses had parted the red sea. He was walking away from her, and Sarah struggled to follow. People wouldn't move for her, wouldn't move out of her way no matter how hard she pushed them. She had to confront him, had to see who he really was. As she managed to clear a few people out of her way, she was disappointed to find that the man had disappeared.

After a few minutes, the dark figure reappeared only a few feet in front of her, and she stopped, shocked. So close, yet she still could not see his face, could distinguish nothing about him. He pointed towards her, like the famous ghost had pointed towards the grave that Scrooge just *had* to see, and a chill worked its way down Sarah's spine. Then he spread his arms and pointed to the crowds around them, and was gone.

Sarah closed her eyes, still feeling people pushing against her, and counted slowly to ten. When she opened her eyes again she slowly looked around at the crowd.

Her heart missed a beat as she saw the things that now surrounded her. Instead of the friendly faces that she had seen there were now monsters. Every figure was deformed, each body grotesquely out of shape, out of proportion.

One man bumped into Sarah and, as she took in his features, she swallowed a scream.

There was no skin covering his muscles, nothing to protect the nerves from the breeze. As she watched, blood began to seep through his clothes, the white suit absorbing the red liquid. He walked away from her, seemingly still taking pleasure from his surroundings, and Sarah could hear his shoes squelching as they filled with blood.

A woman walked before her, stopping to pick a handful of flowers, and bile rose up into Sarah's throat. Growths sprouted from her limbs, black and scaly, pushing against her clothes.

Sarah once again looked all around her, seeing the things that walked beside her. She could feel eyes upon her. They had all stopped moving, stopped what they had been doing. They were all staring at her.

Sarah screamed silently as the world was plunged into darkness, and she stared upwards, trying to see what had happened to the sun. As soon as she turned her face to the sky, the world was hit with the silver light of the moon.

There were differences again in the people around her. Their bodies were still deformed and freakish, but their faces chilled Sarah more than ever.

In every face she looked at, Sarah saw herself.

This time when she screamed it wasn't silent.

The house was still quiet as she sat up, but she listened anyway, just in case, unsure as to whether she had actually screamed or not. When she was confident that Serena had not been disturbed she looked down at the table beneath her hands. Instead of seeing the journal as she'd expected, she saw the key used to lock thc cabinet.

She held it in front of her eyes, turning it around, as if seeing it for the first time. She clamped her hand around it as footsteps once again moved above her. Instead of walking to the bathroom, Serena descended the stairs.

Without any time for Sarah to wonder when she had put her journal away (or where her mind had been when she had), Serena stepped into the kitchen.

"What're you doing up?"

It was asked casually enough as Serena got herself a glass of water, but Sarah believed – just for a second – that Serena was trying to dig at her, that she *knew something*. And, for that same second, Sarah thought of telling her everything, just letting go.

"Not a thing." The madness had passed, and she looked down at her glass. Her throat burned for one more – just one more – shot of whiskey, but she didn't want Serena to know how much she was drinking.

"Come on, Sarah. Something's bugging you. What's up?"

Sarah stood and walked to the sink, glass in hand. She let the water run before filling her glass, and drank half of it (trying not to taste the slight hint of whiskey that tainted the water), her back still to Serena.

"Just everything that's happened, I guess." Although it hadn't really occurred to her before, not consciously anyway, Sarah realised that it was true. Everything that had happened had completely knackered her out. She turned and looked at Serena.

The metal of the key suddenly felt very hot in her closed hand, and she looked down at it. The fever had caught her again. "Sit down, Serena." Sarah walked into the living room and straight to the cabinet. The burning in her hand increased and she almost dropped the key trying to insert it in the lock.

Hands shaking, Sarah removed her journal from its drawer. Voices in her head started to shout out, ringing the warning bells, but Sarah refused to listen. The drawer closed, and the shouts were closed inside. "Fuck it." The words were spoken in a whisper, and Sarah was shocked at her own calmness.

She felt no restraint as she stood up and began to walk back towards the kitchen, even though she'd expected (and half hoped) to be frozen to the spot. Instead, she moved easily and looked at Serena sitting at the table.

"I've got something to tell you." She sat opposite her friend, her journal on the table and her hands placed on top. To herself, she added, "Where the fuck do I start?"

Serena waited as Sarah tried to get her thoughts in order. She could see lines appearing on her forehead as Sarah concentrated, could see her struggling.

"Have you ever had a feeling, an intuition, about someone? Known that someone was horrible just by looking at them?"

Serena said nothing. She simply looked at the book before her." I haven't, not really. I've never *sensed* that anyone was evil, never looked at a stranger and felt a chill. But I see what a person's like, what a person *is*." She sighed, knowing that, although she wasn't being very clear, Serena was catching the drift. She also knew that if she said what had to come next then things would change for good, no going back.

"When I look at a person's reflection, when I make eye contact, sometimes I see their soul."

Slowly, Sarah looked at Serena. All she saw in her friend's eyes was incomprehension.

"What do you mean you 'see their soul'?"

"I mean I see them, not the physical them, but the real them. The soul."

Images flashed inside Sarah's mind: Tony's bright-red skin, the black bugs from Jackie, Henry's alien-like appearance. For better or worse, she was committed now. And she decided to commit herself completely. "I think you'd better read this." She slid the journal over to her friend, picked up the whiskey bottle and Serena's cigarettes, then walked into the living room.

When Sarah was out of sight, Serena picked up the journal, and gently caressed the raised surface of the words before opening it.

# Chapter Thirteen

Serena walked slowly back to her home. Sarah was sound asleep, she'd made sure of that before leaving, she didn't want any interruptions. Her mind was a total blank as she moved through the dark, unable to think properly. Too much had happened to her recently. Her friend was ill, that was the only thing that was clear to her. Sarah needed help – help that Serena could not possibly offer.

She felt calm and her hand did not shake as she unlocked the front door and locked it behind her again, her feet guiding her forwards. Serena knew that it would be there, she had no doubt. Henry always had it lying around in case he needed it for towing a car. She opened the cupboard under the stairs and saw it immediately. The blue nylon rope was cold when she picked it up, and she wondered if it would still be cold when she slipped it around her neck.

As she climbed the stairs to the main bedroom, she knew that there were other ways, dozens of them, painless. Still, painkillers could be taken beforehand. But morbidly she wanted to feel everything. She thought that it would, in a way, balance out what Sarah had done to Henry.

After several tries, Serena managed to make a loop that, she hoped, would work and moved to the window to look down at the ground.

Being careful not to slip (although she had to wonder why, considering what she was about to do), Serena leant forwards and threw the rope over the overhang that jutted out above the window. Clumsily, she made a knot that secured the rope, and slipped the noose around her neck and readied herself.

Before she could discover a reason to back out, she stepped over the ledge.

She was falling for an eternity, and she was sure that she

wouldn't stop, that she'd fall into and through the earth without hitting anything. Then fire bit into her neck as she was pulled backwards, her body flung against the bricks of the house. The pain was phenomenal and, far too late, doubts formed in her mind. Pressure was building up in her head and Serena felt her eyeballs trying to escape their confines, her tongue trying to push its way between her lips. Black spots danced in front of her eyes, her lungs fought against what was happening, trying to get just a little bit of air. She clawed at the rope, trying to loosen it from around her neck.

The fire was spreading through her body, and finally it consumed her.

Sarah woke up, wincing as she felt the pain in her neck. *Well,* she thought, looking at the sun-filled room, *that's what you get when you sleep on the sofa, you silly cow.* She sat up slowly, expecting pain to filter through from every part of her. Relieved that the only discomfort was in her neck, she stood and walked into the kitchen, moving her head in circles to try to ease it off.

Her journal sat on the table, and Sarah felt a cold hand touch her neck. She suppressed a shudder, the fear leaving her as quickly as it had arrived. Nervously, she laughed at herself, trying to figure out why she was feeling so weird.

As she put the journal away, she shouted up the stairs. "Serena? Are you up yet?"

She made two cups of coffee, resisting the urge to stir in a shot of whiskey into her own.

"Serena, you lazy bugger." Leaving her on cup on the table, she carried Serena's upstairs. With her spare hand, she knocked on the door of what had become Serena's bedroom. "Serena? You awake?"

She opened the door slightly and poked her head through, looking into the sunlit room. Serena wasn't there. Sarah pushed the door open completely and stepped inside.

That cold hand was back on the base of her neck, and another had joined it, this one in her stomach, roughly kneading it, as she saw that the bed hadn't been slept in.

Sarah backed out of the room and closed the door. Slowly she made her way back downstairs, still carrying the coffee. Steadily, she went into the living room and put the cup on the table.

She picked up the phone and dialled Serena's number, wondering if her friend had just gone for a walk to process everything. She didn't notice the way that her hand shook.

It rang, and Sarah felt an urgency building up in her. "Come on, Serena, answer the fucking phone!"

After the sixth ring, Sarah threw the phone away from her. "Shit!"

She became aware of how unstable she felt: her legs were rubbery, her hands were shaking, and her head felt too light. There was only one thing she knew of that could help her come together again.

She lit a cigarette as she walked into the kitchen. From the drinks cupboard she grabbed the open bottle of whiskey, and with no time to use a glass or a cup, she raised the bottle to her lips.

When the alcohol exploded in her stomach, sending its warmth to the rest of her body, Sarah took the bottle from her mouth and recapped it. Her body ached for more – just a little more, just until oblivion arrived – but she needed to find her friend.

Now that she was sure that her legs would hold her, she walked to the front door. Although closed, it was unlocked and the keys still hung from the keyhole. Without thinking about it, she took them and put them in her trouser pocket, and left the house, closing the door. The cold bit into her flesh through the thin layer of clothes, but Sarah felt no need to go back in for her coat.

The road was deserted, and for that Sarah was grateful – she was in no need for pleasantries with anyone. She wanted to run, that sense of urgency increasing its volume, but her good sense held her in check. If she ran then she would panic. If she panicked, she wouldn't be able to do anything of any use.

Her feet crunched over the frost-coated weeds, and she abruptly moved to the centre of the road without bothering to check to see if anything was approaching. She thought that if she had to listen to that crunching sound much longer she was just going to snap.

Finally she reached the beginnings of Serena's driveway and walked down towards the house, searching the windows for any sign of her. Finding none, she went straight to the front door. It was locked, but that didn't worry Sarah. All she had to do was go around the back and get the spare key. She knew exactly where it was kept.

She started to pass the house, walking towards the far end of the garden, when she saw a flash of red from the corner of her eyes.

"Serena, there you are..."

Everything stopped. Sarah just could not believe what she was seeing. It was impossible. It was a trick of the light, or a trick of her over-stressed brain. It had to be something else, because there was just no way it could be real.

Serena's left shoe had fallen off, and Sarah could see that the white sock which was now uncovered was beginning to fray near the toes – not real. Serena's hands hanging limply by her sides – not real. Her face, the colour of a bruise that was starting to fade – not real. Her red hair, seeming duller than usual, stirred by the breeze – not real. Except it was. A few strands of Serena's hair had caught on the house-bricks as the breeze moved them, and that managed to break through where nothing else had. Sarah sank to the ground, staring at the still body of her friend, hoping with every part of her soul that she was still asleep on the sofa.

After a few moments, she stood and turned her back on the

house. A couple of deep breaths and she slowly walked away again to the small shed in the garden. She knelt in front of the door and picked up a good-sized rock that lay on the left. Underneath, as she'd known there would be, was a silver key.

Sarah stood with the key in hand and walked back to the house keeping her eyes on the ground in front of her, refusing to look up at Serena even though she felt compelled to. When she reached the side of the house she felt a weight lift from her. Sarah went into the cool house, leaving the door open. In the living room, she picked up the phone and dialled 999.

While she waited for the call to connect, she became aware of two things: the heat from her early morning whiskey was gone, and that she badly needed another.

When PC Bradshaw walked into the house after having first looked around the back, she found Sarah Fletcher at the kitchen table. In front of her was a bottle of brandy with the cap off and a packet of cigarettes. Her left hand was curled protectively around a glass while she smoked with her right.

Karen Bradshaw neared the table and saw half a dozen cigarette butts on the floor, surrounded by a small littering of ash. "Miss Fletcher?"

Sarah looked up, her eyes red from the amount of alcohol she had consumed, nearing oblivion but not quite there – she hadn't drowned the pain yet. She looked at the officer steadily and spoke clearly. "She's dead." With no warning, Sarah swept the bottle from the table, and buried her head in her left arm.

The tears she had refused so far now broke through the floodgate and rushed out, and her body was racked with sobs as the tears exploded from her. She dropped her cigarette and used her hand to hold her chest, but it did nothing to stop the pain. Her heart was breaking.

*Jack put the journal down, rubbing his eyes with his thumbs, creating dark patterns in his vision when he pressed too hard. He pushed himself away from his desk and checked his clock. Five thirty. Maggie wasn't back yet, and she would probably eat out wherever she was. He had time.*

*He grabbed a piece of paper from his desk, took a pen and scratched a small note to Maggie in case she returned while he was gone. He stood up, wincing at the pain in the small of his back, and left the office. A quick detour to the kitchen, leaving the note where Maggie had left hers, and then he was gone.*

*Using the button on his key ring, he unlocked his Jeep, relishing the sting of the cold breeze on his skin. It seemed to him that he hadn't been outside in years. Almost regrettably, he got into his car. He started the engine, revving it a little to make sure it caught. He pressed the clutch, put it into gear, and then released the handbrake.*

*"Maggie's being unfaithful, you know."*

*Jack's foot slipped off the clutch, and the car lurched forwards a little before stalling. He looked behind him, sure that there was someone in the car with him. With his left hand he massaged his chest over his heart, also sure that he was about to have a heart attack.*

*When he was certain that he was alone and, more importantly, not about to suffer a coronary, he pulled the handbrake up, switched the ignition off, put the car back into neutral, and just sat there with sweat trailing from his forehead.*

*When he was a little calmer, he found that he could think about what the voice had told him. Unfortunately, he found that it made perfect sense. The meetings with old friends, the way she seemed to be drawing further away from him, starting to smoke again, and her disinterest in sex. Not that they had ever been sex maniacs, but it had always been healthy enough. Jack tried to remember the last time, but found that he couldn't.*

*He sat quietly, recalling all the times that Maggie had returned from her outings with a contented smile on her face. He realised that she almost always took a shower straight away when she came in ("Got to get rid of the smell of town, dear."). In his head, Jack inventoried all the gifts – CDs, stupid soft toys, bottles of brandy and whiskey – that she'd bought him over the last year or so.*

*"Guilt presents," he muttered, completely unaware that he'd spoken. It was all straight in his head now, but he didn't feel angry, only sad.*

*Jack realised that he no longer felt like his little outing that he'd planned, but he knew that he couldn't stay in the house. He climbed from his car, first making sure that the handbrake was on securely, and locked it again. He walked down the drive and onto the road.*

*As he walked, he realised something else. Although he had taken a walk every day for the last God knew how long, it had been at least six months since he'd done this. He'd been so obsessed with Sarah Fletcher. But for the fist time in months, Jack Daniels' mind was on other matters.*

She knew she was dreaming, but it seemed to make no difference. Repeatedly, Sarah found herself walking towards the bottom of Serena's garden. Repeatedly, she saw a flash of red out of the corner of her eye. And, repeatedly, she found herself turning back to the house, to see Serena hanging by the blue rope. Each time she tried to stop herself from turning, but each time found herself unable to resist.

The last replay before she awoke didn't end with her turning to see Serena. Instead, she walked straight over to the house and stood looking up at her late friend. She saw Serena's shoe lying in the grass below her dangling feet, and bent down to retrieve it. Sarah straightened up with the shoe in her hands, and as she felt the coolness from it, tears formed in her eyes. Knowing that Serena would never wear her shoe again just seemed so final.

"What's wrong, Sarah?"

Sarah looked up quickly, searching Serena's lifeless body for signs of movement. Nothing. Only the same breeze, moving the same strands of her lifeless hair. Hastily she looked away, feeling the breeze moving her own hair around her face. She saw movement again and looked back up.

Serena's head, which had been hanging limply against her chest, was now upright; her eyes, which were still red from the burst blood vessels, now looked at Sarah with consciousness. "All right, Sarah?"

Sarah was frozen, unable to move.

Serena's hand caressed the noose around her neck, and a smile that looked more like a snarl crept onto her face. "Necklace is a bit tight." A low chuckling rose from her throat.

Rooted in place, Sarah couldn't think, couldn't tear her eyes from Serena's. Those eyes, dead yet still seeing, looked into the depths of Sarah's soul, and seemed amused by what she saw.

"Feeling guilty, Sarah?" It was said in a pleasant could-you-pass-the-sugar voice. As her lips parted to form the words, plump white maggots fell from her mouth. "Yes, Sarah, you should feel guilty. After all, it's your fault. *Everything* is your fault."

Sarah felt something wrap around her neck and, when her fingers investigated, she found that the noose was a perfect fit. Sarah now looked over Serena's back garden, the sunlight beginning to make an appearance over the horizon; she had taken Serena's place. Desperately, she looked to her right, the pressure on her throat increasing. Despite there being no air in her lungs, Sarah somehow managed to scream anyway when she saw Serena hanging next to her, a sick and vacant smile on her face.

Still screaming, she blacked out.

She was still screaming when she woke up.

Her bed was in disarray, quilt on the floor and the bed sheet pulled out, which had wrapped around her feet.

Sunlight shone through the light blue curtains, illuminating the room, but Sarah's heart still beat too quickly, and she still trembled. Her eyes jumped around the room, expecting to see her dead friend standing in a corner, arms crossed, watching her. Even though she didn't see Serena, her nerves told her that

Serena was there. As the minutes passed she was able to accept that it was all just a residue of her dream, Sarah managed to get out of bed.

She breathed deeply, and it hurt. Not physically, but deeper than that. It wasn't from crying, but from knowing that Serena would never take another breath. Sarah's heart had broken and it wouldn't mend easily.

Without dressing, throwing only her dressing gown on over her nakedness, Sarah walked downstairs. In reflex, not really interested, she picked the mail up from the floor in front of the door, directly below the letterbox. Her eyes passed over her own address as her hands shuffled through the envelopes.

She stopped in mid-stride, hands beginning to shake, dropping all of the letters except one. She walked into the kitchen and sat at the table, still holding the envelope, shivers working through her body. She tore the envelope open and took out a sheet of paper, glancing at the end of the letter and feeling no surprise at seeing Serena's name at the bottom, feeling only that constant ache at the thought of her friend.

Sarah

My thoughts are all messed up. I love you, Sarah, but you are ill. You've got to be able to see that. You can't honestly believe that you can see the evil in people. It's just not possible.

You've written that you've killed three people, one of them a little girl. A little girl Sarah! Whether you think they deserved it or not, it makes you a murderer! And you wrote that on my husband's forehead, after watching him die, when a phone call could have saved his life. Henry was no saint, but he didn't deserve that.

I'm begging you, Sarah. Please, please, get some help. Hand yourself into the police, and ask for the help that you need. Go and see DC Daniels – he said he was investigating the murders.

I can't cope with this on top of everything else, Sarah. It's just too much.

I will love you always.

Your friend, Serena –X–

Get help. Please

Sarah was not crying, nor was she saddened by the letter. She crumpled it up and threw it away from her, wiping her hands on her dressing gown to get rid of the dirty feeling, as if she'd been contaminated. She wasn't upset. She was angry! How the hell could Serena say that? How the hell could Serena say that it was all in her head? How dare she, when she had no idea? And how could Serena kill herself and then blame it on her!

Sarah could feel the anger eating away at her, and realised what was really making her mad. *Henry was no saint, but he didn't deserve that.* It was unimaginable! The sick bastard had been a paedophile, had raped young girls, had beaten and raped *his own wife*, but Serena had ignored all of that. Of course he deserved that. That and more!

She stood up and walked around the room, close to stomping her feet like a child throwing a tantrum. "Stupid, stupid bitch!" She kicked the table, relishing the sting in her toes. "Stupid bitch."

Anger forced tears from her eyes, and she used her fists to wipe them away. Her tears only angered her more, yet they flowed more freely. She stopped and slumped to the floor. "Stupid bitch." It was said without conviction, and she cried harder.

The next few days were almost a complete blur to Sarah; she remembered drinking and smoking constantly, letting the hours, the days, slide past her. She didn't bathe, didn't dress, didn't open the curtains. Thick stale smoke hung in the air, but Sarah didn't open a window. She felt content to slowly choke herself to death.

Sarah was neither happy nor worried about it – it simply wasn't an issue. Nothing mattered to her just as long as she had enough alcohol to find her way back to oblivion. For days she stayed there, not caring if she was falling further and further into it – the darkness seemed no different to the light.

It was two days before Serena's cremation when Sarah realised who the shadowy figure was that beckoned to her in her dreams. And she was dragged back into the light, kicking and screaming, and with one hell of a hangover.

# Chapter Fourteen

The knocking on her door got through to her eventually, and Sarah left the kitchen and walked to answer it. She didn't care who it was, she just wanted them to stop banging – her head was too fragile this morning.

The men who stood before her seemed vaguely familiar, but she couldn't place them, and she wasn't overly inclined to. Whatever they wanted she didn't care, just as long as they went, so she could get back to her bottle.

"Miss Fletcher. I'm DC Daniels, and this is DC Donnelly, we spoke before."

At the mention of his name, Sarah snapped out of her fog. She didn't want to – it hurt too much to think, and her head was killing her – but reality caught her. She became aware of their looks of pity, and knew why. Disgust filled her as she saw herself reflected in their eyes: unwashed, in her dressing gown, with a cloud of cigarette smoke and alcohol fumes surrounding her.

"Come on in." She stepped aside to let them in. "Sorry about the state of the place, but—"

"It's fine, Miss Fletcher."

Sarah looked cautiously at Daniels, and felt that tiny sliver of fear pass into her heart. This was, after all, the man who was trying to track her down. Another fear moved into her – what if Serena had sent a letter to *them*, telling them everything?

*Well,* she thought, *if she did, I'm not going anywhere like this. I do have* some *pride left.*

"Could you make yourselves drinks, while I have a quick wash?"

They both smiled, disarming Sarah. Donnelly nodded. "I can remember the way to the kitchen, Miss Fletcher."

Sarah left them and went quickly upstairs to the bathroom, no longer worried about their presence – if they had come to arrest her, they wouldn't have allowed her to go anywhere unsupervised. She turned the shower on then moved to the bedroom and grabbed some clean clothes.

As soon as she stepped under the spray of warm water, Sarah could feel the dirt and grime leaving her. She washed quickly, scrubbing at her body and hair, and then stepped out before she was tempted to just stay there. Once dressed, she roughly rubbed her hair with the towel, not caring that it wasn't completely dry. The only thing she *could* care about was that, for the first time since Serena's death, she felt whole, completely there.

Before going back downstairs, Sarah took some migraine-strength painkillers in the hope that they would head off her hangover before it took over.

When she got downstairs she found the curtains and windows open, a cool autumn breeze chasing out the stale cigarette smoke.

"Hope you don't mind, Miss Fletcher." Daniels said, carrying two full cups into the living room. "It was a little hard to breathe."

"No problem."

Donnelly was looking at the photographs on the mantelpiece, as Daniels gave him one of the cups. "Your parents?" He looked over his shoulder at her.

She nodded. "Yeah."

Daniels brought the second cup of over to her. "I didn't know if you took sugar or not, so I left it out."

"It's fine," she said, without tasting it.

He disappeared back into the kitchen for his own drink.

Sarah emptied the over flowing ashtray into the living room bin and took it over to the armchair. She sank into it, letting it mould around her body. She lit a cigarette and, unlike the one she'd had only an hour ago, it tasted as fresh as the air.

Donnelly left the mantelpiece and sat on the sofa. "They look like a fun couple."

Sarah smile sadly, remembering them. "Yeah, they were. They died when I was seventeen."

Donnelly sighed. "Shit, I'm sorry. It seems that the only reason I open my mouth any more is to change feet."

Sarah laughed genuinely, feeling at ease in Donnelly's company. "I visit their graves every now and then. It makes me feel that they're still around." She saw Jack Daniels re-enter the room, and her caution jumped up a gear.

He sat next to his partner. "The reason we're here, Miss Fletcher, is that we need a statement about how you found Mrs Dawes."

For a split second, Sarah found herself once again looking up at Serena, holding Serena's shoe, watching Serena's hair catch on the bricks. She shook herself out of the memory and nodded.

"Now, you don't have to go to the station. You can write your statement out here if you'd prefer – no problem." He smiled reassuringly at her, his eyes no longer looking at everything else.

"I would prefer to do it here."

"No problem," he repeated, almost offhand. He glanced through the conservatory, and then looked back at her, almost demurely. "I don't suppose I could have a quick look around your garden, could I? My wife's been bugging me to do something with ours, but I have no idea what. I'm always looking for inspiration."

She forced herself to smile, sure that the DC was up to something. *Oh, for fuck's sake, Sarah,* she lectured herself. *Don't you think you're being a bit paranoid. He just wants to look around the garden. What are you worried about? You think he's looking for grave markers and murder weapons? Grow up!* "Sure. Go ahead."

She escorted them to the conservatory and, before any doubts could resurface, Sarah unlocked the outside door and opened it.

Daniels walked outside, while Donnelly stayed with Sarah. She'd brought her cup with her and, as they both watched him walk around, she drank from it. She was pleased to see that

Daniels was looking around like a true gardener and not like a cop.

A feeling of déjà vu crept up on her, and her forehead creased in concentration as she tried to figure out why the officer looking around her garden seemed familiar to her.

He reached the bottom of the garden and stopped.

Sarah seemed to stop breathing. Although she still saw him in the sunlight, another part of her was watching him from an entirely different perspective.

She was watching from her bedroom window. It wasn't day, it was night, and the moon was hidden behind a cloud, obstructing most of its light. He wore black instead of his current brown suit, but his build still showed. Any minute now he'd turn around and his face would be a shadow. And he'd look at her in the dark and beckon to her.

She was flung back into the sunlight and saw that, as he had in her dream, he had begun to turn. Her cup slipped from her fingers and shattered on the tile floor.

Daniels was smiling. He'd just had an idea about his own garden, and was very pleased with himself.

Sarah didn't see his smile. She'd fainted.

"I'm fine now, honestly. I just need to have something to eat."

"If you're sure?"

She nodded at Donnelly, trying to keep her smile natural and not desperate.

"We'll send someone to take your statement," Daniels said, and lightly touched her arm, and then they both left the house.

Her smile was frozen on her face, and she could still feel the residue of his touch. She closed the door quickly, and rushed to get her journal. She had a lot to write down.

*Jack sat back on his chair, frowning. Had she really had a vision of him? Or was it just another part of her delusion?*

*He could remember her fainting, could remember the shock on Rob's face as he barely managed to catch her before she hit the floor. Jack had gone on the run to see what had happened.*

*It had only taken a few seconds for her to come round. Was it his memory playing tricks on him, or did he actually remember Sarah giving him a strange look when her eyes had focussed on him? No, he was sure that she had looked at him wearily, frightened.*

*At least now he knew why.*

*He stood up and walked to his office door. The silence in the house told him all he needed to know – Maggie still wasn't home.*

*As he thought back to that day with Sarah, he realised something important. The voice that had told him that his wife was cheating on him had been Sarah's. She had uttered those words, had told him something that he'd had to face up to.*

*He just had to figure out what to do next. Not about Sarah – he'd carry on reading the diary, there was no question about that – but about his wife. How the hell was he going to sort* that *mess out*

*"I'm going to have to go, Rob." Maggie slipped out from Rob's embrace and got out of bed. Despite her age, she didn't feel that she had to hide her nakedness from her lover and she walked towards the wardrobe where her clothes hung.*

*"Can't you stay a bit longer?" He propped himself up on his elbows to watch her as she got dressed.*

*She shook her head. "Can't. Jack'll be wondering where I am."*

*Rob continued to watch her. "Are you ever tempted to just tell him about us?"*

*Maggie looked around at him, trying to work out if he wanted an honest answer. She sighed, and went back to the bed and perched on its edge, buttoning her blouse. "Course I think about it. Especially when he's got his head stuck in that sodding book." She looked straight into his eyes. "Sometimes I feel like packing a few bags, walking up to him and saying 'Jack, I'm leaving you for Rob'. Christ, it's so tempting." She uttered a high-pitched laugh." A lot of the time I have to concen-*

trate *not* to."

"So why don't you?"

Maggie looked at him, shocked. "Because of *her!*" She heard the contempt in her voice and did what she could to push it aside. When she continued she was calmer. "He's so absorbed in his work, with Sarah Fletcher and everything about her, that it wouldn't be fair. He'd either ignore what I said, or his work would suffer. It's not the right way."

He looked at her, grateful that she could be so honest with him, yet a little unnerved at her hatred towards the serial killer. The *dead* serial killer. "It'll get easier, Maggie, I promise you."

Maggie had been home for over half an hour before Jack realised that he was no longer alone in the house, and walked into the kitchen to see her.

"Hi, honey. Had a good day?"

She allowed him to kiss her on the cheek. "Yeah, pretty good. I bumped into Rob today."

"Yeah?" Suspicion was the furthest thing from Jack's mind. "How is he?"

"Seems fine. He said that he might pop over in a couple of days, take you out for a few pints."

Jack smiled, the first truly natural smile in just about forever. "That'd be good." When was the last time he'd seen Rob? A month? Two? It was about time they caught up. "So how was your old friend?"

"Michelle? Yeah, good. A lot of changes since I last saw her, but definitely for the better."

The smile on Maggie's face was so genuine that Jack almost believed her, wanted to believe that he was just being paranoid. But as soon as he saw the glimpse of guilt in her eyes, that possibility was destroyed. "Good. I'm glad you had a good time."

"Do you want something to eat?"

"No. I'm not really hungry." He started to walk away. "I'm gonna go back to work for a bit."

"What a surprise!" she muttered sarcastically under her breath.

*Jack found himself in front of Sarah's house. He walked into the back garden, remembering how it had been when he'd walked around it last: beautifully maintained, elegant, attractive. Now it was the opposite, a total jungle. Weeds had taken control, destroying the flowerbeds by pushing out the other plants. Everything that had been previously cared for was ruined. Jack felt a sadness that had nothing to do with Maggie. The garden was the source of his sadness.*

*He moved deeper, stopping in the same place he had stopped on the day that Sarah had fainted.*

*He was being watched.*

*Jack had never laughed at the idea of intuition. He believed in it, had always trusted his hunches. And now, his hunches were telling him that someone was watching him. He turned sluggishly and looked at the top floor of the house.*

*Sarah stood in the window, looking at him. The moon, hidden behind a thin cloud, showed her face clearly – she was petrified. For a reason unknown even to himself, Jack stretched his arm out, raised his hand towards the window, first pointing at her then curling and uncurling his finger, beckoning the dead girl to him. The moon escaped the confines of the cloud, and the darkness lightened slightly. Sarah no longer stood at the window – if she'd been there at all – and Jack dropped his arm by his side.*

What the hell was that all about? *He shook his head, doing his best to clear it.*

*Although he could no longer see anything out of the ordinary, he still felt as though he was being watched. The jungle he stood in didn't feel sad anymore, it felt menacing, as if it was hiding one of a hundred monstrous things. Or maybe* all *one hundred.*

*Without running, he walked as quickly as he could, escaping the garden, and keeping away from the house. He reached the Jeep, and fear stole over him again. He hadn't bothered to lock it.*

*Jack approached it carefully. Like a child looking for the nocturnal monster that hides beneath the bed, he checked the back seats and then the front seats. Sure (well,* almost *sure) that nothing was hiding in his car, Jack got in.*

*The door closed and he pushed the lock down, satisfied when the central locking system secured all the doors. Again, he checked the back seat. However he didn't feel completely safe until he got home and locked the house door behind him. And even then, he continually checked over his shoulders.*

*He thought of going upstairs, but he couldn't imagine sleeping in the same bed as Maggie, sleeping* next *to her, knowing that she had also been lying in someone else's bed. In his mind he could see himself screaming at her, totally losing it. He wasn't going to let it happen. So, instead, he went back to the one place in the house that was truly his.*

*He sat down and looked over his desk. Instead of reaching for the journal, Jack found himself picking up the photo of Sarah. Her features were so clear, yet she looked totally different to the scared-looking girl he had seen earlier. He knew that he couldn't possibly have seen Sarah Fletcher – she was dead, so there was no way.*

*But his heart told him that it* had *been her. No matter what he wanted to believe, they were connected somehow.*

# Chapter Fifteen

It was four days after Serena's funeral, which Sarah did not attend. The knowledge that her head was aching terribly, met her halfway between sleeping and waking, so she wasn't surprised when she sat up.

"Shit." The word sent another dagger of pain through her skull. Her mouth felt dry, and her tongue felt as if it were coated in cement. Her first attempt to stand from the sofa failed, and she plopped back down. She groaned at the pain in her head and tried again. On legs that felt worryingly unstable, she walked to the kitchen, eyeing the almost empty bottle of vodka with suspicion, as if it were going to attack her.

One hand massaging her temples, Sarah made herself a cup of very strong coffee. While she waited for it to cool enough for her to drink, she grabbed a couple of paracetamol. She took them with water, grimacing as one half-dissolved in her mouth before she could swallow it. Sarah sipped at her coffee, wary of the heat but needing to take away the aftertaste of the tablets. She drank it standing looking out of the window into the garden, doing everything she could to stop herself from thinking.

Sarah grabbed the vodka bottle by its neck and unscrewed the cap. She lifted it to her lips and the overpowering smell of alcohol forced her to remember how she had felt when she'd woken up. Using every ounce of willpower she had, she walked over to the sink and emptied the bottle. The smell reached out for her and her mouth cramped with desire, but luckily the liquid was already working its way down the pipes.

Although wishing that she had emptied the bottle down her throat, Sarah remained pleased about what she had done and made herself another strong coffee.

Around midday, she got restless and went for a walk. Her initial reaction was to go right, but that would take her past

Serena's, and she didn't feel ready for that yet. So instead she turned left.

The warm August breeze brought the scents of a dozen different flowers to her. She had a glimpse of a barely remembered dream, and then it was gone but she was left feeling shaky and cold. She looked behind her, for some reason expecting to see herself in the midst of couples. She felt confused and disorientated when she saw the deserted road. Suddenly, for no reason, Sarah felt scared and wanted to go home. But she was far too stubborn to let an undefinable feeling send her running home like a child.

She walked on the right-hand side of the road towards possible oncoming traffic as she'd been taught by her mother, walking past nothing but fields. She began to slow down, and as she relaxed the brilliance began to return to the day.

Halfway towards town, she walked past a house, with only one visible difference to her own – it had a for sale sign planted in the front garden.

She looked at it deeply, as if she'd never seen such a sign before. After a few moments, Sarah continued walking, her mind whirring.

The idea of moving away, of just packing up and going, had occurred to her before. But the idea of selling her parents' home was unimaginable, and she had dismissed the whole thing. It was only while passing her neighbour's home that it struck her. She didn't need to sell her house so that she could move. She had more than enough money to live on.

Although she took a couple of months to come to any conscious decision, the matter was really decided the second that she had seen that sign.

*Jack tried to keep his mind on the job at hand, but he wasn't finding it easy. He kept thinking about Sarah, and her decision to move. Had she been moving on, or running away? Or both?*

*He saw Maggie, and thoughts of Sarah Fletcher were driven from his mind. For a moment, he was overwhelmed by a longing for her, to just hold her and touch her. To hear her say that she still loved him. In that moment he would have given up everything for her, including Sarah Fletcher.*

*But as she moved away from him, the feeling passed and he began to move through the crowds after her. He followed her as she browsed in shop windows. He followed her as she wandered down aisles, and when she treated herself to a bacon roll Jack was four steps behind her, pretending to browse in a bookshop window.*

*He was partly relieved and partly frustrated when she walked over to the bus stop and stepped under the shelter. He waited for a few minutes, still hoping that he would glimpse Maggie's bit on the side. After seeing nothing of interest he turned and walked away, As he walked back through the streets his mind wandered back to Sarah (although it had never been too far away). It was forty-five minutes later when he came back to himself and went home.*

*They lay together under the covers, just enjoying the closeness of each other, the warmth. Her hand rested on his chest, while his fingers stroked her bare shoulder. She knew that she should get dressed and go home to her husband, but all she could feel was Rob's gentleness as he touched her, as he loved her. The idea of going back to a man who was obsessed with a book written by a serial killer made her feel sick. All she wanted to do was stay in the arms of her lover.*

*"I'm getting paranoid," Rob said, still stroking her shoulder. "I was sure I saw Jack earlier when I picked you up."*

*Startled, Maggie looked at him. "Was it Jack?"*

*Rob laughed. "No, can't have been. Like I said, I'm getting paranoid. It's this dangerous lifestyle of mine."*

*Maggie's own smile was forced. The idea that Rob had seen her husband just felt too right.*

# Chapter Sixteen

Sarah looked around the living room for the last time, feeling less unhappy than she'd expected. And without shedding a tear (as she'd believed she would), without even a lump in her throat (as she'd known she would), she locked the front door behind her. Getting in the car and driving away felt the same as it had always done, as if she was only nipping to the shops.

Using her road atlas she'd already planned her route the night before. She was going to try a change of scenery for a while, try to lose herself in the crowds. Each mile she drove was a mile further away from Jack Daniels and his investigations, and she felt freer.

An hour and a half later found her exactly where she wanted to be. It was a decent sized town, a place where she could be comfortably anonymous without being crushed to death.

She found the hotel she was looking for, and as she drove into the car park she tried, unsuccessfully, to repress a smile. "The girls are early workers around here."

Outside the front doors of the hotel stood a group of three women. 'Working girls' was the kindest term for them that Sarah had heard. But a prostitute was still a prostitute. They were dressed more or less the same – knee-high boots, short skirts and small tops despite the chill, and a bit too much makeup.

Sarah carried her bags towards the entrance, making sure that she wasn't staring but also making sure that she wasn't ignorant of them either.

They all turned to watch her approach, and Sarah felt a good-natured smile form on her lips. One of the blonde-haired women smiled back. That smile, Sarah saw, turned her pretty face into a beautiful one.

She walked into the hotel and to the main desk, wiping the three women from her mind.

"May I help you?"

Sarah looked at the stuck up men behind the desk. "Reservation for Sarah Fletcher."

"You expecting him again today, Em?"

"Huh?" Emma Kelly looked at her friend.

"Your regular. It's usually Thursdays he shows up, in't it?"

Emma smiled. "Yeah, hopefully. Usually around six."

It would be nice if he showed up. It was always good to know your punter – it usually meant the same old stuff, no nasty surprises. Plus she liked him. He was the only one she used a condom with, anyway.

They chatted the December hours away without interruptions. At about half past five Emma saw the familiar red Escort pull up. The car stopped and she automatically got in, relishing the warmth inside. They exchanged a quick smile before the car moved on.

He wasn't bad looking, but not conventionally handsome either. His nose was a bit too crooked, his chin a bit too soft, but still she liked him, enough to make the job a bit easier.

They stopped at the usual place, and she led him down the usual alley. At the bottom on the left-hand side was a nook that she didn't think anyone else knew of. It was small and cramped, little more than a hole in the wall, but good enough. In the three and a half years since their arrangement began they had never been discovered yet.

She pushed her whole body against his, feeling him grow against her groin. Her hand reached inside her handbag and retrieved the sleeve of condoms.

"Choose your coat, sweetheart."

He pushed her outstretched hand away from him. "Not this time, all right."

Smiling, Emma gave his penis a gentle squeeze with her free hand. "You know the rules. No coat, no fun." Again, she tried to move the condoms towards him.

Violently, he pushed her against the opposite wall, and spoke *at* her rather than to her, filling her face with the brandy fumes that she hadn't noticed before. "I said not this time! Do you understand? You're the whore, I'm the client. *I* pay *you*! I'll decide how things'll happen. Got it?"

Shaken, but trying not to show it, Emma nodded in the dark. "Whatever you say, hon."

Emma walked straight home instead of going back to her spot. She'd had enough for one day.

It was dark, helping to conceal the worst, but the people she passed on the street still stared. She ignored the laughter that they didn't try to hide – she'd heard it all before.

A middle-aged woman passed by with her fiancé, and stopped to watch the woman walk away from them. "Poor girl."

Her partner turned around and looked at the woman's disappearing figure. "She shouldn't be too surprised, though. Not in her line of work." He started to walk away and, after another moment watching the hobbling shadow retreating, she followed him.

Emma unlocked the door to her dark flat, walked in and closed the door against all the sniggers and prejudices. Her shoulders were sore as she stripped off her top, and she tried not to imagine the bruises that were probably appearing there. It took longer than necessary to take off the bottom half of her outfit – she just didn't have the courage to do it. He'd hurt her down there, she knew it, but she wasn't looking forward to finding out how badly.

With her eyes closed she removed her boots, then her skirt, and finally her knickers. Standing in just her black bra, Emma opened her eyes, took a deep breath, and looked down at herself.

Thick lines of blood had trickled down her thighs and calves, and had dried on to her skin. Hands trembling badly, she touched the inside of her thighs, wincing at the tenderness there. Dreading it, but needing to know, she moved her fingertips further, biting her lip to hold in a whimper. Tears slipped down her cheeks, and she whispered to herself. "Bastard."

She raised her hand to her face and saw that there was no fresh blood on her fingers, only dried flakes. She hoped that it was a good sign.

Shaking all over, shock beginning to set in, she unlatched her bra and slipped it off, then walked to the bathroom. She switched on the shower and when it was warm enough she stepped under the spray.

An hour later, Emma walked back into her living room, and sat in the only chair. Unmindful of the pain across her shoulder blades she stretched down next to the chair and picked up the bottle of rum.

Tears of shame and hatred prickled her eyes, but she didn't even try to fight them or hold them back; she just let them fall. She swallowed a mouthful of rum, her own personal painkiller. "Serves him right if he catches it."

She'd contracted HIV when she was eighteen. Walking home from a night out with friends, on a street that she had used for years, she'd been attacked. The man had wrestled her to the ground behind a bus shelter, and had raped her.

While he raped her, he'd kept his hand over her mouth, and she'd fixed her gaze on the band of gold on his finger. As long as she looked at that, she could pretend that it wasn't happening, even when the pain overwhelmed her. After all, married men didn't rape.

He'd run off as soon as he'd finished, and she'd lain still, not knowing what to do, too stunned to move. Eventually, staggering with pain with every step, Emma had made her way home. When she walked into the living room where her parents sat watching TV, her mum had taken one look at her, and had uttered a small shriek before rushing to her. She'd sat Emma down and had tried to find out exactly what had happened.

While his wife had been fussing, Emma's father had left the room to call the police. He'd stood by the front door waiting for them to arrive, not wanting to see the state of his daughter, feeling totally useless.

Even with her mother's arms around her, she could feel his hands on her, one smothering her, the other moving over her body.

But for Emma the most humiliating part was the examination. Her clothes were taken for forensics, and her injuries photographed. Even when she'd been allowed to have a shower, she still didn't feel clean. Every time she closed her eyes, the image of his wedding ring floated in front of her.

Washed, but still dirty, dressed but still feeling naked, the interview had been made as comfortable as possible, but it was still terrible. Emma had to go over everything, giving them every little detail: how he'd touched her, how it had made her feel – everything.

Her nightmare, which as far as she was concerned couldn't get any worse, continued with the results of the HIV tests three months later.

Her parents did what they could, but they couldn't help. The counsellors she saw didn't help – no matter what they said, they couldn't take the disease from her, couldn't undo what he'd done to her. No matter what she did she couldn't feel clean, and she began to notice people looking at her, staring at her. Their eyes told her that she was soiled, and Emma began to believe them.

The first time she'd stood on the corner of a street, the first time she'd taken a punter, she'd been petrified. And when he began to insist that no condoms be used she nearly told him. But the look in his eyes helped her decide: it was his choice.

Emma looked at the bottle in her hand, fighting her way out of her memories, and screwed the lid back on. "His choice," she whispered. She went into the bathroom and turned the taps, hoping that a bath would make her feel better.

Moss was a lot bigger than Millsbury, and Sarah wandered along the streets, taking in as much as she could. Among the shops that she recognised – chain stores and catalogue shops – were dozens of smaller ones. She gazed in all of the windows, not looking for anything in particular, just getting an idea of what was there, a feel for the area. She bought a copy of the local paper and went into the friendliest-looking pub. It was brightly lit and inviting, and the faces behind the bar were smiling. Sarah got her drink and sat down at a table in the corner.

She glanced at the paper, trying not to take in the news of violence, theft, and vandalism. Her stomach turned when she got to a piece about a gay blessing being held in a church. Her parents had taught her the proper way to have relationships, and she still agreed with them. "Disgusting."

She spent a few moments contemplating how sick she thought it all was before turning to the property pages, taking the time to read them properly. There were a few houses for rent, and a couple of them actually sounded decent.

Sarah finished her drink and left the pub, again taking her time as she window-shopped, strolling back to the hotel.

*Jack closed the diary, put the book and photos in the drawer and locked it. He stood and walked away from his desk, wanting to return to it, to return to Sarah's world, but he wouldn't let himself. On an impulse he couldn't explain, something he'd never done before – hadn't even thought of doing before – Jack locked his office door behind him.*

*The hallway was colder than his office had been, and he shivered. Suddenly, he looked over his shoulder, half-expecting to see the ghost of Sarah Fletcher, and laughed at his foolish actions. He walked closer to the front door and looked up the stairs. No sign of Maggie. He picked up the phone and dialled the number from memory. It rang twice before being answered.*

*"Hi, it's me. I was wondering if it was all right for me to come 'round for a chat." He looked upstairs again. "No, just me. Half an hour? See you then. Bye."*

*Jack walked up a couple of stairs. "Maggie. I'm off out for a bit."*

*After a few seconds a reply came. "Will you be long?"*

*He glanced at the phone. "Not too sure."*

*"Oh, well. Doesn't matter. See you later."*

*A little hurt at her carefree attitude, Jack left the house, got into his car and drove away.*

*Maggie watched him go, her stomach turning, but still determined, damn the consequences. She was going to end it.*

*She quickly ran downstairs, wanting to get things over and done with before Jack came home. Maggie bypassed the phone, allowing herself only a quick glance. She was tempted to call Rob, but decided against it: he'd only do what he could to talk her out of it, and would probably succeed.*

*She stopped outside Jack's study and breathed deeply to calm herself. Her hand, which seemed to be a mile away from her body, moved towards the handle, and she pushed it downwards.*

*It refused to budge.*

*"Shit."*

# Chapter Seventeen

Saturdays were Emma's best days. They were the only evenings that she actually felt like a human being. She stood in front of her full-length mirror and looked at herself closely. It was amazing what a bit of makeup and some stylish clothes could do. She wore a dark blue trouser suit, and black ankle boots. Her short blonde hair was fixed behind her ears, and the light shades of makeup brought out her blue eyes. Looking at her reflection she could almost believe that she had a respectable job, that she wasn't just a twenty-five-year-old prostitute.

After another quick check over, she grabbed her handbag, put her coat on, and left the flat.

One of the main reasons she always felt better on Saturdays was the difference in people's reactions. People who would ordinarily taunt her and stare at her when she was in her street clothes, nodded and wished her a good evening.

She walked slowly, enjoying the breeze in her face, knowing that her cheeks would soon be red without the aid of any blusher. It was refreshing, and she wished that she could just carry on walking, could just walk away from the disaster that was her life.

The Grande Hotel came into view and, despite how good it felt to be walking, Emma had no intention of not going in. She had to earn her money somehow.

In the plush lobby, she was almost overwhelmed by the warmth. She saw Garry Handforth behind the desk dealing with a customer, and she gave him a quick wave. He waved back as she turned into the bar.

Sarah stepped out of the lift and walked towards the bar. Almost everyone was dressed smartly, and she felt conspicuous in her jeans and plain black T-shirt. She ordered her drink though, and sat on a stool at the bar.

Glancing around, she saw a blonde also sitting at the bar that she thought she recognised. After deciding that she must be wrong – she hadn't been in the area long enough to know anyone – it came to her. She was one of the prostitutes who had been outside the main doors on the day she'd checked in.

Sarah watched as a man in a navy-blue business suit approached the woman. She looked hastily away and smiled to herself. Quickly, she drained her drink and stood. After a few seconds of searching she saw the door across the lobby leading to the ladies' toilets, and walked over to it.

Emma saw the glint of gold on his finger and smiled. She wasn't going to feel guilty about this one. It would, in fact, be a pleasure.

Gently, she squeezed the man's thigh and smiled sweetly up at him. "I'll be back in a minute, sweetheart. I'm just gonna go and freshen up."

She walked across the lobby floor, listening to the sound her heels made on the wood, and over to the main desk. When Garry was finished with the customer, she stepped closer to the desk, leaning slightly over it.

"How's it hanging, Garry?"

He smiled widely. "Not too bad, Emma. How's things with you?"

She started to look through her handbag. "Not bad. Business has been good." She took out a plain white envelope and handed it over.

"Thanks, Em. This'll come in handy."

She grinned. "It always does." Lightly, she hit the desk and pushed herself away from it. "See ya later."

"Yeah, see ya."

The door to the ladies' toilets squeaked as it opened, and Emma waited until it had closed again before walking over to the full-length mirror. As she checked her hair and makeup, a cramp bit into her lower stomach. The colour drained from her face, leaving her skin grey, and she groaned, stamping her foot in annoyance. "I don't fucking believe it."

She felt the wet warmth flow out of her and rushed quickly into one of the cubicles.

Sarah laughed to herself as she flushed the toilet and straightened her clothes before opening the door. Whoever she'd heard it was obvious what was wrong, and Sarah knew exactly how it felt.

Still smiling, she washed her hands, glancing up into the mirror as a cubicle behind her opened.

Their eyes met for only a split second, but Sarah still saw a glimpse of the monster that was behind the blonde woman's face. Black veins pulsed under the skin, turning her beautiful face into something grotesque. Her eyes burned red, and the same black lines polluted the whites of the eyes. The woman passed to another sink and Sarah dropped her eyes back to her shaking hands.

"You all right, darlin'? You've gone awfully pale."

Sarah looked up, mindful not to look towards the mirror. Almost painfully, she managed a small smile. "Fine. Period pain. Always comes on suddenly."

Emma returned the smile. "It's a bitch, ain't it?"

Sarah nodded.

Emma walked to the door, leaving Sarah leaning over the sink. Before walking out, she turned back. "You sure you're okay?"

"Yeah, fine."

Holding her stomach, Emma walked across the lobby floor and straight through the main doors, ignoring Garry's puzzled gaze. She wrapped her coat around her, and buttoned it up.

The pain in her stomach increased and she kept her hand pressed against her abdomen. She couldn't believe that she was going to lose a whole week's worth of work – she wasn't even due on yet.

She wondered again how badly that bastard had hurt her.

Instead of going back into the bar as she'd planned, Sarah made her way to the lift. She was still shaking, her legs felt like rubber and her stomach felt queasy. As she waited for the lift doors to open, she consciously stopped her eyes from closing, knowing that if they did she was bound to see the blonde woman with the black veins that pulsed beneath.

Finally, the doors opened and she stumbled inside, grateful that no one else was around. She stabbed at the buttons and only hit the right one after the fourth try. She leant against the glass panels wanting to forget what she had seen. The lift eventually stopped on the right floor and she got out, digging in her pockets for the key card. She staggered along the hall, and it took three swipes of her card before the door would unlock.

She went straight to the minibar and opened it. Instead of taking one of the small bottles supplied by the hotel she took out the litre bottle that she had bought earlier.

Once on the bed, she spun the cap off and gulped it down quickly. With the alcohol burning down her throat she started to feel human again. In reflex, Sarah closed her eyes, and was instantly plagued by the image she'd seen. Her eyes snapped open, and her stomach lurched upwards. She jumped off the bed and rushed into the en suite just in time, as the alcohol forced itself back up. Sweat running down her face, tears running from her eyes, she stayed over the toilet even when her stomach was empty. When the smell started to make her feel worse, Sarah flushed away the mess, leaning against the bath. As soon as the black spots in front of her eyes had disappeared and her legs felt less like water, she stood up and walked back to her room. Knowing it wasn't a good idea, Sarah picked up the vodka bottle again.

Emma tested the water with her hand and turned the taps off. It burnt her feet as she got into the bath, and she eased herself down, allowing the heat to soothe her. Her stomach cramped up instantly, but the muscles relaxed as the water worked on them.

Six days. Six days if it followed the usual pattern. No work for almost a week. Well, it wasn't as if she'd starve. Her rent was paid for the next three months, and she had money in the flat, locked securely in a cash box hidden under a loose floorboard.

She'd been stashing money away for two years – her 'running money'. It had been the plan to save ten thousand pounds. Ten grand and then quit, just pack up and get a proper job. She had more than that, though. At last count, she had just over fifteen.

She could afford to quit, could give it up easily, but there were two problems. Firstly, she was used to the lifestyle. The idea of working a nine-to-five in an office scared the hell out of her. It just seemed so boring. Secondly (and closer to the truth) she enjoyed her own brand of revenge. She liked infecting men, liked knowing that they were being punished for cheating on their wives or partners. She wouldn't let herself consider the fact that she was probably infecting the partners as well. It wasn't something that would help her sleep at night.

Emma closed her eyes, meaning only to relax. Within a minute she was asleep.

*"God, it was totally nuts." She rested her head on her hands and looked at Rob across the table. Her cheeks were flushed, but it wasn't just the embarrassment of what she had told him: Maggie felt like a teenager around Rob.*

*"That was yesterday. You might as well forget about it." He smiled and took her hand into his own. "And, anyway, even if the door had opened, you wouldn't have done anything." But he realised that he didn't honestly believe that.*

*Neither did Maggie. "The way I was feeling, Rob, I would have, I'd have destroyed that bloody diary."*

*Although he felt sick at the thought, he managed to keep his smile natural. "Good job that the door* was *locked then."*

*Maggie smiled weakly, still unable to believe her actions yesterday. It was so unlike her. "Do you know something? I don't even know why."*

*He raised his eyebrows and looked at her deeply. "What do you mean?"*

*"I mean, I don't know why." She could feel her cheeks burning, but she wasn't going to stop. She was going to have her say. "Why should it bother me? Wrapping this up is so important to Jack; it's keeping him occupied, which means I don't have to worry about him getting suspicious." Gently, she squeezed his hand. "It's also giving me an excuse to put off telling him about us."*

*Rob pulled back a little. "Are you having second thoughts?"*

*"Good God, no. I'm in love with you, Rob, and I want to be with you." She smiled at the relief on his face. "But thirty-four years is a long time and no matter what, I don't want to hurt him. I* do *care for him; it's just not the same anymore."*

*He kissed her fingers. "I don't want to hurt him either, Maggie. But you've said it yourself, there's no point in staying in a marriage just for that. If you still loved him, I'd tell you to work at it. Caring for him, though, it just isn't enough."*

*She nodded. "Yeah, I know. It just doesn't make things any easier."*

*"Life is never easy."*

She walked around the shops, dressed in normal clothes: jeans, jumper and jacket. For December, it was almost warm, and Emma was taking advantage of the turn in the weather. Her stomach still hurt, but she'd had worse, and could cope with it. What she couldn't cope with was that she'd fallen asleep in the bath the night before. She'd woken up an hour and a half later, the bath full of cold water, and looking like a prune.

She stopped to admire an evening dress in a shop window, so she didn't notice the pretty brunette that walked past her, and probably wouldn't have cared even if she had. With one last longing look at the black dress, she walked home, glad that she had at least been out.

Once inside, the first thing she did was to start to fill her bath up – this time she planned to enjoy it. She rechecked the door, making sure it was securely locked, and then undressed. Feeling unusually wary and unsafe, Emma slipped into her black silk dressing gown, pulling it tightly around her body. It was weird – she'd never felt unprotected in her own home before.

In the living room, she pulled back a corner of the navy carpet, exposing the floor beneath. Using a hole in one of the boards, she pried up half of the wood and took out the metal cash box from underneath.

She sat on the sofa, legs tucked up next to her, and opened the box. One by one, Emma removed the bags of money. The bags were coin bags from the bank, and she had five hundred pounds in notes in each bag. So far, she had thirty-one full bags, and a loose hundred pounds.

She looked up as someone knocked on her front door. "Shit. Who the fuck's that?" Closing the box and leaving it on the sofa, she got up and walked over to the door. She looked through the peephole before opening it.

"Hi."

It only took a second for Emma to recognise the woman at her door from the hotel yesterday.

"Hi."

The woman uttered a shy little laugh. "I was looking for..." She drifted off, looking past Emma and into the flat. "Have you got a leak? I can hear water."

Emma's face dropped in surprise. "Shit! My bath!"

As the prostitute ran back into her flat, Sarah smiled, walked in and closed the door. She followed the woman into the bathroom and watched as the blonde turned off the taps. Water had run over the sides, and the carpet looked a little spongy.

Emma looked over her shoulder at her visitor, shrugged her shoulders and laughed. “You’d have thought I’d have learnt by now, the amount of times I’ve done this.” She rolled her sleeve up, preparing to pull out the plug.

Quickly, before the woman had a chance to react, Sarah grabbed the blonde hair by the roots and slammed the head that was attached against the bath.

Black stars danced in front of Emma’s eyes, and the pain in her head was accompanied by a sticky warmth that she immediately recognised as blood. Almost immediately afterwards, she felt herself being lifted.

Hot water splashed over Sarah as she dropped the woman into the bath.

Emma floundered in the scalding water, trying to keep her head above the water level, but she wasn’t even sure which way was up. Whichever way she moved, she seemed to meet resistance, unable to find the air that her lungs needed.

There was pressure on the side of her head, and her brain managed to tell the rest of her that it was the woman; it was the brunette holding her head under the water, stopping her from getting up. But at least it let her know which way she had to go, and she pushed upwards. She tried to grip the sides of the bath to help, but everything was wet and she couldn’t find any purchase. Blackness clouded her vision once again, and she tried to fight against it, tried to elevate the pressure from her chest. It ached, felt as if her lungs were being torn apart, and her head was spinning.

But for some reason, it didn’t actually *hurt*. She was in pain, she knew she was, but somehow the pain was distant.

Sarah held her under for a lot longer than she really needed to, just to make sure that it was really over. The blonde woman had stopped struggling a few minutes previously, and the only thing moving in the bath was the woman’s short hair. Slowly, Sarah removed her scalded hand from the water and felt ill when the woman's head appeared to follow it up, bobbing on the surface.

She moved back a little and bumped her hip on the sink. A lipstick rolled into the basin and Sarah picked it up. Her feet felt as if they were being sucked down by the carpet, and she hated the wet sound they made as she moved. Kneeling beside the white bath, water soaking into the bottom half of her jeans, she used the lipstick as a pen.

Passing through the living room, she saw the cash box and thought of taking it. But, while a brunette with wet patches on her jeans might not draw too much attention, a brunette with wet jeans carrying a cash box probably would. It was a chance she wasn't going to take, especially for money she didn't need.

Without further thought, she left the flat, closing the door behind her.

*Jack closed the journal, quickly put it to one side, and brought out the photographs from the drawer. He knew he was right, but wanted to make sure. He flicked through them, looking for a picture of the woman he had just read about. After going through them twice, he allowed himself to admit that there wasn't a photo of the prostitute amongst them.*

*He looked at his clock, and picked up the journal again. Instead of opening it, he got up and walked to the phone in the hallway. His fingers punched in the numbers and he waited for the other end to be picked up.*

*"Carter."*

*"John, it's Jack Daniels."*

*"Jacky-boy!" Carter sounded thrilled to be hearing from him. "How's it going?"*

*"Not too bad. Listen, I need a favour."*

*"Sure. No problem."*

*Jack ran a hand through his dark hair. "I need you to do a check on your murder files for me. December, two years ago, blonde-haired prostitute."*

*"The Fletcher case?"*

*"Yeah. Same MO."*

*"I'll have a look, and call you back."*

*"Cheers, John, I appreciate it." He hung up and stood still, looking at the phone.*

*"Who was that?"*

*Jack looked up at Maggie at the top of her stairs. "Just someone I needed to talk to." Without waiting for any kind of response, he walked back into his office, and closed the door.*

*He wanted to continue with Sarah's diary, wanted to dive back into her world, but he knew better. What he wanted didn't matter, it was what he* needed *that did. He* needed *to wait until he heard from John, needed to verify it.*

*Jack paced around his office, looking at the books, picking one up here, one up there, flicking through them, before putting them back. He looked out of the window, seeing nothing. He almost sprinted out of the office when the phone started to ring.*

*"Jack. I think I've found it."*

*"Yeah, already?" Jack said, even though it felt as though he rang John hours ago.*

*"Yeah. Look, I've been planning a visit for a while. I think now's as good a time as any. How you fixed for meeting up tomorrow?"*

*"Just tell me where and when."*

*"I'll tell you what, I'll give you a bell tomorrow, and we'll sort it out then."*

*"Great. See you then, John. And thanks."*

*"No probs."*

*Jack put the phone down and walked into the kitchen. There was no way he was going to carry on reading until he knew everything he had to know.*

*He spent the rest of that evening back in his office, ignoring the diary as best he could, going over his notes.*

# Chapter Eighteen

*John walked over to the table, set his drink down, sat on the chair, and finally said hello to Jack. They shook hands over the table, and Jack studied his friend's face.*

*"Looks like you're finally losing the colour from your 'tache, John."*

*"Yeah, I know." He ran his fingers over his short moustache. "Typical, ain't it. All my life I've hated my ginger hair, and now that it's being overrun with grey I wish it was as bright as it used to be."*

*"How's the missus?" Jack had a sip of his pint, wishing that he hadn't asked as he saw John's face fall.*

*"Not too good. Her sister's taken her out for the day, that's why I was able to come down."*

*"Cancer spreading?"*

*"No. Well, not that fast. She's just always in a lot of pain. Usually doped up."*

*"Have you tried again to get her to have treatment?"*

*John laughed bitterly, drinking half his scotch in one go. "She refuses. You've got no idea how stubborn she is. As far as she's concerned, the cure's worse than the disease." He raked a hand through his hair. "Not that I blame her. This is the third time, and she's been told that there's a high chance she won't survive it. Why should she spend what time she has left throwing up and losing her hair again?" He looked at Jack, his green eyes dull. "No, I don't blame her."*

*They drank in a silence that was both companionable and uncomfortable.*

*"Well," John said, putting his empty glass on the table. "Enough of this depressing shite, Jack. Down to business." He picked up the case from beside his seat. "Let's have a look at the goodies I've brought you." The sparkle had come back into his eyes. He took out a dark blue folder. While Jack continued with his drink, John went through the details of the file.*

*"Emma Kelly, twenty-five years old. Well known as a local walker,*

*killed December eleventh, two years ago, drowned in her bath tub. Her downstairs neighbour had water coming through her ceiling, went up to complain and found her." John brought out another piece of paper, with a printed image on it.*

*"This was on the lipstick that was used. What do you think?"*

*Jack took the offered piece of paper and studied it carefully before taking another piece out of his own folder, placing them on the table and turning them so that his colleague could see. "See for yourself."*

*John looked at the two pictures of a fingerprint on the table in front of him. "Identical."*

*"That one," Jack said, pointing to the one on John's left. "Was taken from Jackie Austin's bedroom window."*

*John looked at the prints for a couple of seconds before pushing them aside. "If it wasn't enough, we've got another connection." Delving into the case again, he looked up as Jack stood.*

*"Refill?"*

*"You know me, Jack. I never turn down a drink." While Jack got the drinks, John put two photographs on the table and turned them towards Jack's chair.*

*He was almost sitting down before he saw the pictures, and he dropped the last few inches in a rush. "Shit," he muttered, no more than a slight exhale of air.*

*"Yeah, shit." John swallowed a gulp of his fresh drink. Pointing at the first photograph, he said, "That one was taken about half an hour after the neighbour called it in; they think she'd been dead about two hours at that point. And the other one is what was written on the side of the bath."*

*"And what, they thought it was a punter?"*

*"Yeah. That or someone who just didn't like pros."*

*"Can I have a copy of that file?"*

*"What're you talking about, Jack? This* is *your copy."*

*"Thanks, John."*

*"No problem, amigo." John looked at the solemn expression on his friend's face. "Looks like your girl was busier than we thought."*

*"Yeah. Looks that way."*

*One more photograph. One more photograph to add to the other ten, one more for him to add to memory. The reports were laid out on the desk in front of him, and although he'd only read them twice he already knew the details. Eleven. Not ten killed, eleven. John was right, she'd been busier than any of them had thought. He'd already added to his notes, notes that would eventually be sorted out to make his final report.*

*As he thought of that, his heart filled with apprehension. Sarah Fletcher had been a part of his life for so long that nothing seemed to have existed before her. And life after the case just seemed unimaginable.*

*"Dad came round to see me the other day, Mum." Sarah picked up her cigarettes and lit one, then passed the pack to her mother.*

*"Yeah? He never said anything to me."*

*Sarah looked at her mum closely, trying to understand how she could look both happy and sad at the same time. "He said that you've been out a lot lately."*

*"I've been busy. Plus your dad is still reading that thing for work." Maggie stood and started to walk to her daughter's kitchen. "I'll put the kettle on; make us both a nice drink."*

*Angrily, Sarah stubbed out her cigarette, half-smoked, as she listened to her mum clattering around in the kitchen. She put her head in her hands as her mum started to talk again.*

*"I spoke to your Auntie Maureen today. Your Uncle Frank's still talking about selling the shop and buying a farm. He still thinks he can make a success out of it, but that's your Uncle Frank, always—"*

*"Are you having an affair?"*

*Both the voice directly behind her and the words that were spoken resulted in Maggie dropping the cup when she jumped. She turned around and looked at her daughter, her eyes wide.*

*"That's what Dad thinks. He thinks you're seeing someone else. So? Are you?"*

*One second Maggie was trying to think of a way to lie to Sarah, and the next she had burst into tears.*

The paper had been delivered with her breakfast, and still covered her tray. She hadn't felt like eating since she'd killed the prostitute. It hadn't helped that yesterday she'd read about the woman's death in the local paper. They'd jumped to conclusions, speculating that it was probably a disgruntled client. The reporter had also gone into details of the woman's health before she'd been killed. At the end of the report, the journalist had pleaded for all of the woman's customers to get themselves checked out at clinics as soon as possible.

The thing that sickened Sarah the most was that the woman had probably infected hundreds of men. And *she'd known*. That was the worst thing: she'd had the results for years, and had known that she was passing the disease on.

Slowly, she shook open the paper and turned straight to the properties for rent. For the last two days, Sarah hadn't ventured outside her room, had taken all of her meals (without being able to eat them) in there, and she knew that if she stayed within these walls much longer she would go crazy.

Using a red pen, she marked the houses that caught her eye, but only ones that were fully furnished – she had no intention of furnishing someone else's house. When she'd marked all of the properties of interest, Sarah opened the curtains for the first time in days. As she opened the window to let out the stale smoke, she saw movement in a window across the street.

Watching the window, she saw someone with a pair of binoculars, which hadn't been focussed on her window but now were. She watched the man lower them and, even from the distance, Sarah could see the smile on his face. Slowly, he moved away from the window and a curtain was drawn across it.

Sarah turned and slumped down against the wall, heart hammering away in her chest. Having done what she'd done, she didn't want *anyone* watching her. As she always found herself doing lately, she went straight to the minibar, hoping that she had missed something. But when she looked inside, what she already knew was confirmed – it was empty.

"Bollocks!"

The idea of going down to the bar for a couple – or a dozen – passed through her mind, but the thought of sitting there amongst all those people, with them all watching exactly what she did, wasn't appealing. No, she preferred to drink alone. She'd just have to go to the off-licence down the road and pick up a few bottles.

She closed the curtains again so she could dress, picked up her breakfast tray and left the room. Outside with the do-not-disturb sign securely on the door and the tray left next to it, Sarah walked down the stairs and out through the lobby.

Feeling exposed, she hurried as quickly as she could to the off-licence, wanting to get back to the safety of her room as soon as possible.

With the door safely locked, the curtains still closed, Sarah sat on the bed, facing the television. She switched it on and, with the bags of drink by her feet, uncapped the first of the bottles, choosing it at random.

The early morning sun bleached her room a cold yellow, and the furniture around her was just shadows. It was warm in her room, but Sarah still felt goose bumps rising on her flesh. There was something wrong, something had changed. Nothing was missing, nothing had been added, and nothing was out of place, yet Sarah *knew*, could feel it in every part of her body, that something was wrong.

She moved the quilt and got out of bed. Picking the white cotton dressing gown up off the floor, she kept her eyes moving everywhere still trying to pinpoint what was wrong.

Quickly, refusing to keep checking over her shoulder like she wanted to, she walked across the floor and pulled open the curtains. She expected to see the man across the street staring towards her again. Relieved when she no one, she breathed out the air that her lungs had been holding.

Despite being obviously cold outside, Sarah thought that she'd never seen such a fresh day. The clouds were moving quickly, so she knew that there was a decent wind blowing, the kind that would sting your cheeks and ears but leave you feeling totally alive, the kind that would blow away all of the cobwebs.

Apart from the clouds in the sky and the odd bird flying, the street appeared deserted, no movement. She found herself looking at the window across the street and hated herself for it.

A door opened further down the street and a figure stepped onto the pavement from the newsagents, and her heart jumped into her throat.

Even when he stepped onto the street properly, where the faint light should have shown all the details of his face, it was nothing but a dark shadow. While every inch of her screamed at her to turn away, not to look, Sarah watched his progress towards the hotel. Opposite her, only twenty feet below the pervert's window, the figure stopped and turned towards the hotel.

Although there was no way she could know for sure, Sarah thought that their eyes had caught each other's. She was terrified, yet not exactly surprised, when he lifted a hand and pointed at her. After a moment, he lowered it again.

His head shifted slightly, and raised his hand again. Something in the tilt of his head told Sarah that he wasn't pointing at her, but pointing *behind* her. That he was warning her.

Slowly, Sarah turned around. The man from the window across the street stood behind her, the leering grin on his face, his hands reaching for her.

Sarah screamed as loud as she could.

She woke up. Sweat covered her body, and she could feel that the sheet beneath her had absorbed plenty as well. Five days before her twenty-first birthday, Sarah let a sense of déjà vu flood over her.

Cold light filled the room, and goose bumps rose on her body despite the warmth. As in her dream, she was filled with the sense that something was wrong in her room. Knowing that she was following the pattern on her dream, but helpless not to, Sarah lifted the quilt from her body and stepped out of bed. As she had before, she reached for her dressing gown and wrapped it around her body, holding it tightly at the front. She crossed to the window, drew the curtains and peered out. It seemed to Sarah that the same cloud formations floated in the sky, that the same birds flew the same paths.

Instead of looking across the street, Sarah kept her eyes on the newsagents, waiting for the man to emerge. The door opened, and she almost screamed again. Almost hysterically, she started to laugh as a slim-hipped brunette walked out with a pint of milk in her hand.

Remembering that the figure had pointed behind her, Sarah turned quickly, relieved when her eyes confirmed that she was alone in her room. Shaking her head, still laughing, she turned back to the window and looked across the street. The laughter stuck in her throat as she saw the man lowering his binoculars and raised his spare hand in a wave.

Quickly, she closed the curtains, heart hammering in her chest once more. With her back to the window, she spoke to the empty room. "And I thought I had nothing to worry about now I'm away from that copper."

Something clicked in her head. Her mind's eye showed her a picture of DC Daniels in her own living room, comparing it to the shadowy figure she saw in her dreams. What it revealed was that they were the same person.

Without being sure that she was actually moving, Sarah

walked over to the bed. She didn't actually sit down, rather fell, like her legs had been kicked out from underneath her.

"Holy shit!"

She bent down and picked up the bottle she had almost emptied the night before. The mouthful she took burnt the daze away, and she quickly hunted out her journal, unaware that this was not a new revelation.

*Jack slammed the book, closed, onto his desk, his heart jumping unsteadily. Perspiration dotted his forehead and he was aware of a couple of beads working their way down the bridge of his nose.*

*The idea that he was the figure haunting Sarah Fletcher before she'd first met him, following her everywhere she went, appearing in her dreams, both unnerved him and felt completely right.*

*She'd written about it earlier in her journal, but had seemed to forget everything she had known about the shadow that was haunting her. How that was possible, Jack had no idea, but he suspected – strongly suspected – that it had something to do with how much she'd been drinking.*

*He found himself sure, absolutely* positive, *that she had, in fact, had visions of him. After all, hadn't he had a vision of* her *at her house?*

*"Imagination. That's all it was." Yet the words he spoke to the empty room failed to convince him.*

*"So, how long?"*

*Maggie looked at the floor beneath her feet, unable to meet her daughter's eyes. "A while." Although she'd stopped crying about five minutes before, her eyes were still red and sore, and the odd tear still escaped.*

*"Who?"*

*Maggie managed to look at her face for a few seconds before looking away again. "Rob Donnelly."*

*"Rob?!"*

*She heard the disgust in her daughter's voice, and the floodgates opened once more.*

*"What the fuck are you playing at, Mum? I mean, Christ, Dad's best mate? Are you completely insane?!"*

*"No, I'm in love." The words were spoken softly.*

*"I still love your father, Sarah. But I'm also still human. I need more than to simply care for someone."*

*"Do you plan to tell him?"*

*Maggie nodded, her eyes still lowered. "Just as soon as he's finished the case."*

*"Make sure you do." Sarah walked out of the living room, unable to stay in her mother's company any longer.*

"You wanted to see me, Miss Fletcher?"

Sarah looked up at the man in front of her. From his smart appearance, and from the slightly arrogant air that surrounded him, she figured that he was the manager. "Mr Brett. Thank you for seeing me."

They shook hands, and he sat on the chair opposite her.

It was empty in the restaurant, they had the whole room to themselves, yet Sarah was sure that she could feel someone watching her.

"That's quite all right. How can I help?"

Sarah gathered herself together the best she could. "Well, it's actually quite embarrassing."

Simon Brett didn't prompt her. He'd found that when people complained, no matter how they did it, it was best to just leave them to get on with it.

"There's a man in the building opposite, and every time I open my curtains he's there with binoculars staring into my window." As she watched, he seemed to look more amused than surprised.

"Can you describe him?"

Sarah, who could picture him clearly in her mind, nearly laughed, but the thought of him watching her stifled any laughter. "Chubby, light brown hair."

Simon was nodding, his bald head lightly bouncing the lights as they reflected down, not feeling surprised at all. It wasn't as if he hadn't expected it. "That would be Kyle Marsden."

He smiled good-naturedly at her obvious shock. "We've had more than a few female customers report him to us over the last few months. And I know that at least one of them has reported him to the police."

"Wow." Sarah was amazed. "That I was *not* expecting."

"I know it's probably not what you wanted to hear. What we can do is move you to another room, but it wouldn't be for a couple of days, I'm afraid. "We're totally booked up."

The relief she had started to feel was completely washed away. "No, that's okay. I can live with the curtains closed for a while."

She stood up to go, and the manager followed suit. "If you choose to make a report to the police, I'd be more than happy to help in any way possible."

For a second, Sarah actually considered calling the police. She saw herself in a police station identical to the one in Millsbury, saw herself making a statement. But when she pictured the officers, every one of them was Jack Daniels.

"No, that's okay. No real harm done."

"Let me know if you change your mind."

"Lenny! Come on."

He walked away from the doors leading from the kitchen into the dining room, picked up his knife and continued preparing the salad. "Who's that talking to the boss-man? Another employee?"

Joe Walker laughed heartily, his brown eyes sparkling inside his dark brown face. "Forget it, Lenny. She's in one of the rooms and, unfortunately for you, means she's off-limits."

Smiling, a light building in his blue-grey eyes, Lenny Peterson shook his head. "Don't know what you're talking about."

"Course you don't, Lenny. Course you don't."

A plan had already formed in Sarah's mind by the time she walked down the burgundy hall to her room. It was risky, she didn't know if she'd be able to get away with it, and it was most definitely stupid. Her mind was set by the time she reached the window and pulled open the curtains. She had things planned so perfectly in her mind that she was almost disappointed when there was no one standing at the window opposite.

On the dresser Sarah saw one of her bottles and grabbed it. She took a long swig, eyes closed. When the heat wasn't quite as intense, she opened her eyes again. As the alcohol worked its way through her system, as the tension started to leave her, she started to feel grateful.

Yeah, her plan probably would have worked – *probably* – but it would have put her in too much danger. Was it really worth it? She could, after all, just do as she'd already said and keep the curtains closed.

Relieved that she had come to her senses, Sarah put the bottle back, and turned back to the window. The smile froze on her face as she saw the brown-haired figure in the window. No binoculars this time, and she could see his grin clearly. She felt sick to her stomach when he raised his hand and gave a brief wave, and she fought hard to hold the alcohol in her stomach.

While her mind was busy telling her what a huge mistake it was, that she shouldn't be encouraging him, her hand was chopping the air in a return wave.

# Chapter Nineteen

The house was already furnished, the utilities were all connected, her mail was being redirected there, and in a couple of days she would move out of the hotel and at last have her own space. But first she had to deal with Kyle.

She'd thought deeply about cancelling the date with him, of just moving into the house she was renting, and forgetting that the creepy man ever existed. But she hadn't been able to sleep properly since the first time she'd caught him watching her; she'd hardly eaten, had gone through eight large bottles of alcohol. The bin in her hotel room was full of empty cigarette cartons, and the whole room stank of stale smoke.

One more check in the mirror, a glance into her handbag to make sure that she had what she needed, and then she left.

Kyle watched from his usual spot at the window as she put on her jacket, grabbed her handbag, did something to her hair and then walked out of view. He ran a hand through his thick brown hair, still watching the window. After a few moments spent looking at her empty room, he figured that she must be on her way, and quickly closed his bedroom curtains.

They'd met in the street – well, he'd watched her leave her room and had waited in his doorway until she'd stepped out onto the street. Then he'd made his move.

She hadn't recognised him, he was sure, otherwise, why would she have agreed to have dinner with him. In his *house*!

His mum had gone away for a couple of days, visiting her sister, and for that he was grateful. It was a little awkward trying to get a woman into bed with his mum bringing them milk and cookies! Sure, it made things a bit difficult with the girls, but there were plenty of upsides. The money he earned at the video store was his own, food was bought for him, his washing was always done, and his meals were always waiting for him when he finished work.

His room was a total bachelor pad. Silk sheets covered his bed, and his red walls were dotted with mirrors. Everywhere he looked he was confronted by his reflection, and seeing his face looking back at him always made him happy. He tucked his shirt into his jeans, and unbuttoned it at the collar, exposing the heavy gold chain around his neck.

As he opened the bedroom door, the phone downstairs started to ring. Quickly, he rushed downstairs, narrowly escaping a twisted ankle and a bad fall, and into the living room.

He grabbed the phone. "Hello?"

"Hi, Baby. Everything okay?"

"Hi, Mum. Yeah, everything's great." Without knowing it, he dropped about fifteen years as he always did when he spoke to her. "Got a girl coming over for dinner."

Her voice grew disapproving as it usually did when they discussed his love life. "Well, make sure you clean up after your meal, and don't stay up too late – you know how you get when you're overtired. What's she like?"

"She's really nice. Really pretty. Her name's Carol."

She grunted, non-committedly, down the phone.

"I gotta go and get ready, so give my love to Aunt Mel, and have a good time."

"Okay, Baby. Love you."

"Love you too, Mum. Bye."

Hanging up, he felt partly saddened. His mother always had that effect on him, making him feel like a little kid that couldn't look after himself, but also as if he needed her to look after him.

The doorbell rang and he rushed to answer it, the leering grin changing his handsome face into something repulsive.

Sarah waited on the doorstep, thinking that she still had time to walk away. Then she heard footsteps from inside and that chance flew away. The door opened, and she found herself looking into the face she despised.

"Glad you could make it," he said, stepping aside so she could enter.

He'd only just left her enough room, and she felt her skin crawl under her clothes as she had to brush past him. The stink of his aftershave filled her nose, but she could still detect the underlying scent of body-odour. She had no idea how she was going to get through the evening.

The actual meal was a pleasant surprise. Steak, chips and vegetables were followed by apple crumble and custard. She enjoyed the food, but felt like gagging every time she looked up to find him staring at her. Small talk came easily, though, and they chatted about movies, books, and the latest celebrity gossip. A few times, Sarah found herself actually enjoying his company, but the leer on his face and the gleam in his eyes always brought her back to reality.

With the meal finished, they took their drinks into the living room. Sarah looked around with honest wonder. It was obviously not a man's home. Covering the walls were photographs of Kyle, in various stages of his life, with a woman in her sixties. Her first instinct was that it was his grandmother; but then she saw the look in Kyle's eyes as he glanced at one of the photographs. His eyes seemed to soften and harden at the same time, and Sarah became sure that it was his mother.

A cloud of doubt formed in her mind as she looked at him, and she placed her glass of wine (her first of the evening) on a coaster on the coffee table. "Where's the bathroom, Kyle? I need to freshen up."

"Top of the stairs. Second door on the right." He was distant, his eyes still focussed on the nearest photo of his mother.

Before she climbed up Sarah grabbed her handbag from the coat rack. As she did, she saw a mirror positioned on the wall at the top. She ignored it, not wanting to see herself, not wanting to see the doubt in her own eyes. Down the hall, she opened the second door in the right and walked in.

It was worse than she'd expected, even after seeing the decor downstairs. The whole room was done in rose pink, including the porcelain. The pink walls were covered in thousands of tiny white flowers, and pink fluffy rugs were set on the floor. Sarah groaned aloud when she saw the matching toilet lid cover.

Resting her bag on the sink, she reached in and brought out the small perfume bottle. She looked at it for a second, and put it in her trouser pocket. She closed the bag up, and left the bathroom with a sigh of relief.

Using the compass in her head, Sarah found the room that faced the hotel.

Her eyes opened wider as they took in his bedroom. It was so different to the rest of the house. Whereas the cream walls of the living room had been decorated with photographs, the dark red walls were decorated with mirrors. "Man," she whispered. "This guy's got some *serious* problems."

With a glance over her shoulder, she walked over to the window. The first thing she saw was the set of binoculars on the window ledge, along with a camera with zoom lens attached, and any sympathy she had for Kyle dissipated. It was bad enough that he'd been watching her, but the camera seemed evidence enough that he'd also been photographing her.

Heart set, she walked from the bedroom and back down the hall. On the wall directly in front of her, at a right angle to the mirror, was a portrait picture of Kyle and his mother.

Shaking her head, she muttered once again. "Serious problems."

As she turned to go back down the stairs, she was stopped by Kyle walking up.

"Thought you got lost up here," he said, his eyes seeming a little guarded.

Sarah faked a smile. "I was just admiring the portrait."

The caution left his eyes, and he glanced towards the picture. "Nice, isn't it."

Sarah followed his gaze, but instead of the picture, she found herself staring at the mirror. Although he wasn't looking at the mirror, wasn't even looking in the *direction* of the mirror, the reflection still began to change. Hoping that the portrait would continue to hold his interest as the photo downstairs had, Sarah watched.

The flesh seemed to slide from his face, melting until very little remained. The skin he did have began to shrink around his face. Lines began to form, some deepening into small furrows. His eyeballs also began to melt and run, the blue irises blending with the corneas. The whole mess began to run from the hollows of his eye sockets, down the shrunken face, and dripped from his now prominent chin. The lined skin on his face began to yellow and crack and, while Sarah watched, his nose caved in. She found herself looking at something that could have been found in a tomb next to Tutankhamun.

"Yeah, it is nice."

His voice broke her concentration on the mirror and, as she looked away, from the corner of her eyes she saw Kyle's reflection jump back to its original image.

She looked at him but, for a second, she was still seeing his mirror image overlaying him, like two photographs developed on top of each other. Purposefully, she blinked, and when she opened her eyes again, she was relieved to find the vision gone.

He turned back to face her, and Sarah forced a smile on to her face, hoping that it looked natural. "So, were you just coming to find me?"

He smiled, and she shivered inwardly. "No. Gotta go freshen up myself." He looked at her almost slyly. "I don't suppose you could fix us a couple of drinks?"

It was a better opportunity than she could have hoped for. "Just tell me what, and where everything is."

Kyle told her everything she needed to know, and watched as she walked down the stairs. Not wanting to waste any time, he hurried to the bathroom.

Sarah made the drinks in record time, despite the fact that she kept looking over her shoulder, expecting him to be stood there watching her. After another check, she pulled out the small bottle from her pocket.

She unscrewed the lid and quickly dumped the contents into his vodka. Quickly, Sarah wafted the glass under her nose, grateful that she'd bought odourless bleach. Even if it had smelt, Sarah didn't think it would have been noticeable, not with the amount of vodka she'd poured into his glass. Still alone, her luck having held, she opened her bag and dropped the perfume bottle inside. There were two others and she put one in each trouser pocket before closing her bag again. She picked up the drinks and hurried into the living room, just as Kyle was walking down the stairs. Sarah looked up at him. "Perfect timing."

They sat down together on the cream sofa, and she handed him his drink. "Cheers."

Watching him all the way, she drank her drink in one go, her own a nice refreshing glass of water. He followed suit and placed his empty glass on the coffee table.

He put a hand to his throat and laughed shakily. "Christ – that burns."

Satisfied, Sarah smiled at him.

Back in her own room, Sarah closed the door behind her, locked it, and breathed a sigh of relief. Without hesitation, she walked over to the window and closed the curtains. With that done, she stripped out of her clothes, leaving them where they dropped, and rushed into the bathroom. Sarah switched the shower on and stepped into the cascading water, her skin screaming at her to turn the temperature up. What she wanted was to feel clean, not warm.

Wrapped in her dressing gown, hair wrapped in a towel, she walked back into her room. From the floor, she picked up her bag and removed the three bottles, all empty.

On her way over to the window she dropped the bottles into the bin, smiling as she heard one of them smash. She opened the curtains a tiny bit, and looked across the street. The lights were on, and Sarah stayed there watching until they went out.

Kyle woke up three times in the night, not really sure what was wrong. His stomach kept cramping up, and his mouth and throat constantly felt dry and sore. He'd drunk over six pints of water, hoping to lubricate his tongue, but it didn't work. He only felt better while he was drinking, but as soon as he took the glass from his lips he felt worse than before.

On his last trip to the bathroom, half hoping that he'd be sick because it might make him feel better and half hoping that he wouldn't because he knew that it would be painful, he caught sight of himself in the bathroom mirror and – until his body cramped up once more – had marvelled at his skin. Although it was probably a trick of the light, to Kyle it looked yellow and strained. And, impossibly, it looked as though he'd lost weight.

During the worst of it he called out for his mother and couldn't understand why she didn't reply.

*Jack looked through the reports on Kyle Marsden. His mother had found him three days after his death, and officers at the scene had said that the smell, as bad as it was, was nothing compared to the body itself.*

*The fact he would have been in a lot of pain, was something beyond dispute. The lining of his stomach had been almost completely eaten away, and the doctor that performed the autopsy had assured them that most of it had gone* before *Marsden had died. Burns and sores had covered his mouth and oesophagus, most of them open.*

*Near the end, he had lost all control over his body, and his mattress had been covered in vomit at one end, and faeces at the other. An astounding amount of blood had been found in both. The doctor was noted as saying that, although it had been poison that had caused his body to react, it was his heart that had killed him. It just couldn't cope, and had simply gave out.*

*Jack didn't want to read one more account of another murder. But, he needed to know the details and, although he hated himself for it, he sympathised with her.*

*Maggie had just told Rob that her daughter knew about them, and that she thought they'd better just cool it a little. Just until Jack's suspicions had calmed a little.*

*"Will she tell him?"*

*Deep down, Maggie had hoped that Sarah would; at least then the responsibility would be taken out of her hands. But Sarah had promised that she wouldn't say anything. Not yet, anyway. Slowly, she shook her head. "No. She won't tell him."*

*Rob nodded, unconsciously running his finger along the scar above his lip. "So what do you want to do now? Not see each other until he hands his report in at work?"*

*Tears were welling up in her eyes, but Maggie refused to give in to them. "No, it's not what I* want. *But I do think it's the way it has to be. The one thing I* don't *want is for Jack to see us together. I don't want him to find out like that."*

*"So we cool things down until you feel ready to tell him." He heard the anger in his voice, but couldn't hide it. It was obvious that she didn't want to tell Jack, that she didn't want to hurt him. But neither did he. He was just sick of coming second best to a man who hardly knew that she was alive anymore.*

*"Please, Rob, don't make this harder for me!"*

*"Why not, Maggie?" He didn't want to cross the line and knew that he was getting close to it. It was as if he was being catapulted towards an irreversible argument. "Why should I make it easier on you, when you seem determined to make it as hard as possible on me?"*

*Looking shocked, Maggie stood. Softly, she said, "I think I'd better go."*

*He was unresponsive when she kissed his lips, and watched silently as she collected her things, knowing that he should do something to stop her from going. Knowing that he shouldn't let her leave like this, he sat and watched her go.*

"Looks like you don't have to worry about being stared at any longer, Miss Fletcher."

Holding the mail she had just been handed, Sarah looked at the manager, watching his eyes for any signs of suspicion. Seeing only the joy of passing on a bit of juicy gossip, she asked him what he meant.

"The man across the street, the one who was always watching the guests, was found dead."

Sarah did her best to look startled. "Wow! What happened?"

"Not sure of the details yet. But at least you can open your curtains again."

She nodded sadly. "Not exactly how I would have wanted it, though."

After a few minutes she was able to escape, waiting until she was a suitable distance away from the reception, in the closed elevator, before she started to smile.

Of course she had known that he had been found. For the last couple of days all she had done was look out of the window, at first waiting to see if he'd appear, then waiting for him to be found. It happened, just later than she'd expected.

Three days after their 'date', Sarah had seen a woman walk up to the front door. She looked slightly younger than in the pictures, but Sarah still recognised Kyle's mother.

Half an hour after she had gone into the house, two police cars had turned up. That was when Sarah had closed her curtains again. If her luck was going to hold, it would hold. If not, she'd deal with it.

Now that it was over with, she decided tonight was going to

be her last night in the hotel. In the solace of her room, Sarah opened a bottle of whiskey to celebrate.

In the morning, despite her hangover, Sarah felt refreshed. She walked down the stairs and over to the reception desk, registering the well-built, olive-skinned man also heading that way.

She was surprised to see the manager himself behind the desk, the bright lights bouncing off his bald head. Sarah took a wickedly funny moment to wonder if he waxed it to get it that shiny.

"Miss Fletcher. What can I do for you today?"

The cheerfulness in his voice was infectious and Sarah's face broke out into a smile. "I'll be checking out today, Mr Brett."

"Oh, what a shame. Moving onto better things?"

Realising that the black-haired man was listening, Sarah blushed slightly. "Not totally. I'm renting a house in town, so I'll still be around."

"In that case then," he leant closer and dropped her a friendly wink. "I won't overcharge you."

Sarah laughed and, after filling out the checkout book, walked back to her room to pack.

"Fancy your chances, do you, Lenny?"

Lenny, who had turned to watch the brunette walk towards the stairs, turned back to his boss, a smile on his face. "Well, I wouldn't be breaking any rules, would I? Now that she's signed out?"

Simon laughed. "Maybe she'll need a hand with her luggage. If she does, I'll make sure I give you a shout."

"Cheers, Simon." Lenny turned to go.

"Did you want anything, Lenny, or were you just skiving again?" Simon asked with a grin on his face.

"Huh?"

"Well, you must've been after something."

Realization dawned on Lenny's face. "Oh, shit." He walked back to the desk and leant on it, shaking his head. "We're gonna need some more staff for tomorrow. We've had half a dozen call in sick today, and it'll probably be worse tomorrow."

"Skiving?"

"Not sure. I'll be able to find out when they all come back."

"No problem. I'll get it sorted."

"Cheers, Simon. Appreciate it." He started to walk away again. "I don't know what's wrong with me."

"Talking to yourself," Simon said, shaking his head sarcastically. "It's a sure sign. Must be love."

Still walking, Lenny looked back, a blush working its way up his cheeks.

Sarah loaded her car quickly, and walked back inside to hand back her key card and to pay the bill.

"Do you need any help with your luggage?"

Sarah couldn't understand the glint in the manager's eyes. "No, that's okay. Already done."

They said goodbye, and Sarah walked away. To himself, Simon said, "Well, Lenny, I tried."

# Chapter Twenty

Sarah had unpacked what belongings she had, yet she still felt out of place. The house didn't belong to her, she hadn't picked out the wallpaper or the furniture. Everywhere she looked, she was reminded that she didn't belong there, and she hated Jack Daniels for forcing her to it.

Her twenty-first birthday was celebrated alone, bundled up in warm clothes, and sitting outside in the garden, the one place that she did feel comfortable. The ground around her feet was scattered with cigarette butts, and she had a bottle of whiskey by her side.

The cold kept her mind fresh and clear and, rather than thinking of the year ahead, Sarah's mind stayed firmly on the year gone. She toasted Serena's memory more than once, wishing that things had turned out differently. But, other than the death of her friend, Sarah felt no real regrets. Everything she had done she had had to do – she'd done nothing wrong.

Sitting on the green plastic chair, she looked at the houses to her left and at the house on her right. Both had Christmas lights up, and the one on her left even had fake snow at the bottom of each window. Sarah's, in comparison, looked desolate and unwelcoming.

But with only three days to go, and with no one to share it with, Sarah had no inclination to celebrate. She supposed it would be different if she believed in it, if she was a Christian, but she wasn't, so it was really pointless. Looking at the Christmas lights, knowing that inside those houses were couples and families, maybe laughing together or maybe arguing together, but nonetheless *together*, she was filled with loneliness. It made her think of not having someone to share it with, no one to buy presents for and to receive presents from. Someone just to be with.

Sarah started to dwell on a single thought. Her last, first, and only, partner had been Tony, and that had been nearly three and a half years ago. Three and a half years with no one to hold her, no one to sleep next to.

Not exactly drunk but pleasantly numb, Sarah laughed to herself. "Shit. I think I've taken a vow of celibacy."

Fed up with her own company, she decided that some action was required.

The local pub was a ten-minute walk from her new home, and walking along the seething streets sobered her up completely. People pushed past her, one of them almost knocking her to the ground, and it made her remember why she hated this time of the year. The season of good will! As far as Sarah was concerned it was a load of crap. People always seemed to be in a bad mood, there was always pushing and shoving in the shops, buyers making sure that they had everything they needed for kids or partners. It turned usually pleasant people into irritable idiots, and she wondered what the point was.

By the time she reached the pub her cheeks, nose, and ears were red, she was tired, in need of a drink and a cigarette, but actually feeling happier.

While the landlord got her drink Sarah glanced around, and her heart started to thump in her chest as she saw one of the pub's occupants.

He was sitting alone, staring into his pint as if seeing something within. His short, black hair was complimented by his olive skin, and she felt her stomach flutter when she saw his eyes. Blue-grey eyes, dark and mysterious, the kind that she could easily imagine drowning in.

She looked back at the barman to find him waiting to be paid, her drink in front of her. She ignored his slightly hard gaze and gave him the money. She took her glass and, passing the man from the hotel, walked to a table in the corner, noticing that he turned to watch where she sat.

Her cheeks flushed, but she made no acknowledgement that she had seen him – talking to strangers wasn't exactly a hobby of hers, and she wasn't comfortable with it. Thinking about it, she realised that the only time she *was* any good at meeting people was just before she killed them, and she had a feeling that that kind of behaviour wasn't going to lead to a long-lasting relationship.

She lit a cigarette and stared into her own drink. Halfway through both, Sarah became aware that someone was hovering over her. Looking up, her breath caught in her throat.

"All right if I sit down?"

It seemed to be a rhetorical question as he was already lowering himself into the seat, but she nodded anyway.

"So," he said, putting his drink down and turning those eyes to her. "What have you been doing since you moved out of the fleapit?"

Sarah smiled, feeling at a complete loss. "Not much really. Just getting used to the area, figuring out where everything is."

"Planning on sticking around?"

Those eyes! Her mind didn't feel as though it was functioning properly, and it was because of those eyes. "Well, I'm not planning on leaving anytime soon."

The night went downhill. Loneliness, guilt, and alcohol all played their parts, but the result was more important than the reason.

They'd spent the evening talking, nothing important, just small talk. Lenny asked Sarah if she had any friends in the area, and she'd said no. No, she had no friends.

Badly drunk, Sarah had begun to talk about Serena, explaining how she had been raped and beaten by her husband, about how, after his death, they'd found out that he was a paedophile. She told him about finding Serena hanging from the window.

Lenny had done what he could, but he couldn't stop her from

crying. Realising that it had a lot to do with the drink, he did the only thing he could think of – he took her home.

Getting back took longer than it really should have, partly because Sarah couldn't stop crying but mainly because she was drunk and had trouble remembering where it was that she was living now, let alone how to get there.

Finally, he got her home and, as it had earlier that day, the walk had sobered her up a lot and the tears were gone. She was, however, totally exhausted, both mentally and physically, and extremely embarrassed.

Lenny had started to make them both a coffee when Sarah apologised. "I'm sorry, Lenny, but I'm totally knackered. I need to go to sleep. You can stay and finish you drink if you want. I'm sorry." Too drained to worry about leaving a man that she didn't know in her home, especially while she slept, Sarah walked upstairs. A few minutes later she was changed and in bed, warm under the quilt, with the TV on. She was drifting off to sleep when Lenny walked in, carrying two cups. Her mind was numb, but she caught the sight of the concern on his face.

"Are you sure you're all right, Sarah?" He set the drinks on the bedside table nearest the door, and perched on the edge of the bed.

"Just tired." Her mind was drifting away.

"Do you want me to go?"

His voice, as lovely as it was, was heard only from a distance as Sarah fell deeper. She was barely awake as she shook her head.

The television was switched off when she woke up, and it was dark in the bedroom. Her eyes adjusted to the night, and when she looked to the side of her she saw Lenny asleep beside her on the bed. Relief flooded through her when she saw that he was fully clothed and lying on top of the quilt. A tired smile touched her lips as she noticed that he was holding her hand.

Smiling contently, Sarah drifted back to sleep, her own hand now closed around his.

A short time later, darkness still covering her part of the world, she opened her eyes again. Totally awake, Sarah removed her hand from Lenny's, and went downstairs to the kitchen to get a drink. Despite not having been there for long, she already knew her way around the furniture in the dark.

The curtains in the kitchen had been left open, so Sarah could see out over the moonlit garden. It wasn't as big as her own in Millsbury, and apart from a few borders it was all lawn, but in the moonlight it still looked spectacular.

Although it was the middle of December and she was dressed only in a nightshirt, she unlocked the back door and went outside. She knew that it was cold, *had* to be cold, but her body didn't seem to notice. In fact, her body seemed warm and she was sweating.

Not feeling in control, feeling as if someone was leading her, Sarah walked over the dew-dampened grass in her bare feet to the flowerbeds at the bottom of the garden. With the dew reflecting the moonbeams, it looked like she was walking through a garden filled with diamonds.

Lined along the rear fence, trimmed neatly, were dozens of rose bushes, miraculously in bloom. Sarah walked over to the one in front of her and picked one of the white flowers from it, taking only an inch of stalk. Carefully, she plucked the few thorns from it, and then held it to her face.

Its aroma was strong, and she was sure that she had never smelt anything quite so sweet. Slowly she stroked the rose down her cheek, the velvet petals gentle against her skin. Unknown to Sarah, it preceded a single tear.

Still not feeling the cold, she took her time walking back to the house, still holding the rose to her cheek. Her feet were damp, blades of grass sticking to her soles, but she didn't rush. She was walking in a magical moonlit world, and had no intention of making it end sooner than it had to.

Inside, she dried her feet with one of the tea towels, and just dropped it onto the floor. After locking the door she went back to the window, hoping that she would still be able to glimpse that world.

Her eyes were focussed on the rosebush from which she'd picked her flower, but she still saw the movement.

A woman was walking towards the rear of the garden, the white dress she was wearing moving loosely around her legs. Held to her shoulder, a dark-haired baby looked towards the house, one small hand curled around the woman's throat, the other playing with a lock of the woman's dark-red hair. She was about Sarah's height and maybe twenty pounds or so heavier.

Sarah raised her hand to knock on the window so she could find out who the woman was (her mind not wondering about how she could have gotten into an enclosed garden), when the baby raised its own chubby hand and waved, its fingers hitting its palm repeatedly.

Just watching that tiny movement made Sarah's heart cramp, and a smile broke out on her face. She started to wave back just as the woman reached the rose bushes, and her hand froze with the smile curdling on her face as the twosome passed through the fence.

After a few minutes of convincing herself that she was dreaming on her feet again, she walked back to bed and slipped under the covers. She thought about taking Lenny's hand but decided against it. Instead, she turned away from him and closed her eyes.

A moment later, the white rose slipped from her hand and gently hit the floor.

She woke up with the winter light filling the room, and noticed that the other half of the bed was empty. Wondering what time Lenny had left, she was surprised when she heard footsteps mounting the stairs. Smiling again, she watched as he walked in with two cups of coffee, as he had done the night before.

"Thought you'd like a drink."

He brought the cups over to her side of the bed and put them on the table. As he brought his hand away, Sarah caught sight of a flash of white. "I also found this on the floor."

She felt herself blush as he handed her the rose. "Thanks." It deepened when he wouldn't drop his eyes, and Sarah felt herself falling, those blue-grey eyes catching and holding her.

*The front door opened and closed, signalling that Maggie's return. He'd been totally relaxed reading Sarah's diary, even though it was filled with murder, but knowing that his own wife was in the house made him angry.*

*Jack left the office and went into the kitchen, where Maggie was unpacking a couple of bags of shopping. When she glanced around at him, he saw that her eyes were red and puffy. "What's wrong?"*

*"Nothing. What do you want for tea?"*

*Jack ignored her question and asked one of his own. "Why have you been crying?"*

*In answer, Maggie just shook her head and continued unpacking.*

*"For Christ's sake, Maggie!" Jack stood directly behind her, doing what he could not to lose his temper and not succeeding. "What the hell's wrong?!"*

*She shrank away from his shout, tins of food clattering noisily as she slammed them onto the worktop. "Nothing." It was uttered as a whisper, more to herself than to him, but she heard his annoyance when he sighed.*

*"Who the fuck do you think you're kidding, Maggie? Now, tell me what's wrong!"*

*Suddenly, with an anger that was totally uncommon to her, Maggie whirled on him, venom in her eyes. "Trust me, Jack. You* don't *want to know, not really. And even if I did tell you, how much would you actually* hear? *How much would actually get past Sarah Fletcher and all of that fucking shit?! How much would you* let *get past?!" Tears started falling quickly, and she wiped them away with the back of her hand, then picked up one of the tins to put away.*

*Still angry, Jack spoke up again. "Maggie, what the fuck are you—"*

*He ducked quickly as the tin went flying over his head, and turned to watch its progress. He winced as it hit the clock on the wall behind him, wincing again when the clock fell off its hook and smashed on the floor.*

*Crying harder than ever, Maggie ran down the hall and out of the front door.*

*She stepped off the bus, conscious of the people staring at her blood-shot eyes and puffy cheeks, but not particularly bothered. Like a woman in a dream, Maggie walked down familiar streets, and found herself outside Rob's home. For a second, she thought about walking away, but the idea of being alone to cope with everything terrified her – she needed his support, but more importantly, she needed his love.*

*He answered the door while she was still knocking, took one look at her face, and folded her into his arms.*

They lay together, and Sarah was surprised at how comfortable it felt. She was also surprised at herself. With Tony she'd waited months before actually having sex with him, yet she'd waited only two days with Lenny. It terrified and amazed her at the same time – she never thought she'd feel right about sleeping with anyone so quickly.

He had his arm around her shoulders, and his fingers gently caressed her upper arm, marvelling at how smooth it was. Although Sarah probably wouldn't believe him if he told her, Lenny had also been shocked at how soon it had happened. He wasn't a ladies' man, or the sort to sleep around.

Without knowing he was even tired, Lenny closed his eyes and was soon snoring by Sarah's side. Sarah stayed awake, trying to figure out if she'd ever been as happy.

# Chapter Twenty-One

*Jack closed the book quickly, disturbed by the change in her writing. On one page she'd written about the first time they had made love, and on the next page she's written that she hated him.*

*It was a mood swing that he wasn't prepared for, and he dealt with it the same way that Sarah had – he opened a bottle of vodka and began to drink.*

"Sarah? What the hell are you talking about?"

She stared at him, hate in her eyes, hair hanging lankly around her face, separated where she had continuously run her fingers through it. Her cheeks were flushed, and she was breathing heavily. "I saw you, Lenny. At work. Today."

What Sarah had seen, and misinterpreted, had been innocent enough. On the front steps of the hotel, while waiting for Joe, the chef, to finish up and give him a lift over to Sarah's, Lenny had gotten talking to one of the waitresses. While they had stood together smoking, laughing, and joking, Sarah had driven by. What she'd seen was two people getting acquainted, finding out enough about each other so that they could work well together. What she *thought* she had witnessed was the gorgeous, thin, blonde woman chatting up her boyfriend, and her boyfriend enjoying every minute of it. She had gone home and paced the kitchen floor, smoking one cigarette after another, half expecting him not to come over. When he had walked in, at the exact time he'd told her he would, Sarah had started yelling straight away.

"Sarah," he said, trying to keep his voice calm. "What are you talking about? What do you think you saw today?"

The calmness of his voice infuriated her even more, and she just stared at him. How could he act as if it didn't matter? How could he be so unaffected? "You and the blonde!" she spat out. "So? Who was chatting whom up?"

Lenny's mouth dropped open, and he consciously had to stop himself from laughing in surprise as he realised to what she was referring. In her present state, he didn't think it would go down too well. "You mean today, on the steps of the hotel? Me *talking* to Stacey? Is that what you're going on about?"

In answer, she just stared at him.

"Oh, for fuck's sake, Sarah!" In disgust, Lenny threw his arms up and turned away from her.

"What's wrong, Lenny?" she asked, sounding childish, knowing that she should probably keep her mouth shut, *should* just keep her mouth shut, but not quite able to. "Can't listen to the truth?"

Suddenly, Lenny whirled on her, his face no longer calm and passive, but filled with anger. When he spoke, it was more like a yell. "Truth? Is that what you want to talk about, Sarah? Truth?"

He walked over to her and grabbed her arm, pulling her up the stairs after him. She gasped as he pulled her and, although he knew he was gripping her too hard, he couldn't let up.

First, he took her into the bathroom. Still holding her with one hand he used the other to take the top off the toilet tank. "It wasn't refilling very quickly last week so I thought I'd take a look." Putting his hand in the water he pulled out a half-empty bottle of vodka wrapped in a sealed plastic bag. "Truth, Sarah?"

He threw the bottle into the bath, where it smashed.

Sarah's face had drained of all colour, and tears had collected in her eyes, but looking at her only made him more angry. He pulled her into the bedroom and let go of her arm.

She backed away from him and stood against the back wall, watching as he went through her things.

From her underwear drawer Lenny brought out two bottles of whiskey. "Truth?" he asked as he threw them onto the bed. He moved onto the drawer that held her jeans and trousers, bringing out a bottle of Tequila. "Truth?" he asked, holding it up before dropping it onto the bed to join the two others.

From the wardrobe, a bottle of rum and two more bottles of vodka. "Truth?" From the small desk in a corner, a half bottle of vodka. "Truth?" From the bedside cabinet, another two bottles of whiskey. "Truth?"

He looked at her, feeling no sympathy as he saw the tears on her face. "You want truth, Sarah? There's nine bottles on the bed, plus the one I found in the toilet. That makes ten. Ten bottles I've found in one week." He noticed the guilty glance she gave him. "How many more have you got, Sarah? How many more have you got stashed away?"

Slowly he walked to the bedroom door, and looked back. His rage had departed, leaving him once again compassionate towards the woman he loved. "Want a bit more truth, Sarah? You need to get some help."

She stayed where she was, unable to move as Lenny walked out on the last six months together. She stayed where she was, staring at the bottles on the bed, until she heard the front door open and close. The second she heard it she moved quickly to the bed and grabbed a bottle at random.

Sarah made as if to open it, but stopped before she did. In her mind, she saw the look on his face, and could hear the tone of his voice as he held up the bottle from the bathroom. *"Truth, Sarah?"*

In rage, sadness and despair, Sarah screamed and threw the bottle at the wall. Crying, she collapsed onto the floor beside the bed and wrapped her arms around herself.

*Jack did the maths in his head. She would have been about a month pregnant, maybe a little less. Had she known? No, he didn't think she had. For a start, she probably would have written about it in her journal if she had known. Plus, he didn't think that she would have let things get as bad as they had with Lenny if she'd been aware. So, no, he didn't think she had known about the baby then. At that point she hadn't known that in approximately nine months she'd be found dead by Jack Daniels and his crew.*

*Doing the math again, comparing it with his notes just to be sure, he realised that Andrew Dean would be killed a matter days after Sarah had broken up with Lenny.*

*Jack sat back, hands laced behind his head, thinking. Andrew Dean, the most important of Sarah's kills. Andrew Dean, the man who had helped them connect Sarah to the rest of the killings. Andrew Dean, a complete bastard, but a very useful one after his death.*

He gathered his greasy hair up into a ponytail and secured it with a rubber band. Looking at his reflection in the grimy cracked mirror in the bathroom, noticing that a new collection of zits had appeared during the course of the night, Andy was, at least, pleased to see that the bruise on his cheek bone was still visible. He wore them like a badge, thinking that they made him look harder. His friends were too kind to tell him that, with his scrawny frame, he just looked more like a wimp than usual.

"Come on, Andy. Hurry the fuck up!"

"Hold your fucking horses, Stuart!"

Another quick glance, and he grabbed his keys and bolted down the stairs to the front door, trying not to trip over all the junk that was thrown everywhere. Stuart and Carl were holding the door open. Not that it would matter if they let it shut – the catch was broken so it wouldn't lock, anyway.

Picking up the padlock from a dent in the wall, knocking out a bit more of the crumbled brickwork, his mates went outside.

"How can you live in that shithole?" Carl asked, trying to keep his tone light.

"It's cheap," he said, securing the door with the padlock.

They stopped by an off-licence, and then went and sat on the steps of the magistrates' court, drinking and watching the world go by.

As Andy sat there, he saw the perfect opportunity walking on their side of the street.

The man walked with his head up, dark skin almost glowing

in the streetlights. Andy, knowing that his friends had the same hatred that he did, decided to impress them a bit.

"Oi, Paki!" He saw Carl and Stuart look at each other, and assumed that it was a look of admiration. What he didn't see were the frowns on their foreheads, and Stuart shaking his head at Carl's raised eyebrows.

"Why don't you fuck off back home?" He smiled, but the smile was soon dropped.

Without missing a beat, with a sincere smile on his face, he turned to face the spotty kid, and copied his parent's Nigerian accent perfectly. "When you know the difference between a Paki and a nigger, then say it to me again, kid."

This brought a large scattering of shocked laughter, and even a spate of applause from the few people who had been close enough to hear, and even Carl smiled. "What the fuck are you staring at?" Andy barked at a brunette who was stood staring at him.

In a slurred voice, obviously drunk, she said, "Just a pathetic Hitler-wannabe." She continued to stare for another moment and then walked on.

"Come on, Andy." Stuart stood up, followed by Carl, and finally by Andy. "We'll go by the pub. See if we can pick anyone up."

Andy looked at the man who'd shown him up, watched him walk down the street as if he had the *right*, before finally turning and following his friends.

Although she knew that she was still drunk, her mind was now clear, focussed. It was seeing that spotty, greasy-haired idiot thinking that he was so hard, mouthing off to the black bloke.

One moment, she'd been swaying down the street, hardly aware of anything. The next, she'd been listening to that idiot having a go. It had filled her heart with joy when the black man had said what he had.

She knew that the reason for her head clearing the way it did was that something was pointing him out to her. Something was telling her that the scrawny white bloke had to be sorted out.

They ended up back at Andy's after a four-hour pub-crawl, staggering back in the dark. Carl thought that he was either very drunk or else someone had spiked his drink with LSD or something, because he was sure that they were being followed. Upstairs in Andy's bedroom, Carl looked out of the window, searching the streets below for the trim brunette. The streetlights created too many shadows and Carl couldn't tell if anyone was there or not. He thought that he saw one particular shadow across the street, directly opposite, move slightly, but he just shook his head. It was probably just him swaying.

When he went downstairs, ignoring the putrid smell that attacked him from the entire house, he found Andy and Stuart passed out on the floor. "To hell with this." Pissed off as well as just as pissed, Carl walked out of the house, using the string where the door-handle should have been to close the door properly. "Shithole," he muttered as he walked home.

She watched the skinhead from the shadows of the alleyway – watched him as he looked out of the window. He was the one that had scared the hell out of her when she was following them, by constantly looking over his shoulder.

If she hadn't seen the man with the long hair shouting at the black man, she would have assumed that it was one of the skinheads. An inaccurate prejudice, she knew, and, she should know better than anyone not to accept anything at face value.

From her hiding place in the dark, she watched as he walked from the house and do something to the door before walking away. As soon as he was no longer in sight, and after another look at the window to make sure no one else was watching, Sarah crossed the road and walked up to the door.

She laughed when she was how the door was closed, and shook her head in disbelief.

On her walk home, Sarah thought about how she was going to deal with the idiot with the long hair. She was sure going to enjoy it!

It was hard for her to get to sleep that night, her stomach was churning in anticipation and a smile seemed permanently fixed on her face.

Lenny Peterson couldn't have been further from her mind.

Andy woke up – well, came around was a lot closer to the truth – to find himself alone, both Stuart and Carl gone, which was nothing unusual. He paid a quick visit to the bathroom, and then picked himself up another can of beer from the hallway before going back to the living room. Dust flew up as he dropped down onto the sofa, and he waved a hand in front of his face to clear the worst of it.

There was only one picture on the damp walls, and it was of him and his father. Actually, it was a photo of him, his father, *and* his mother, if you allowed for the fact that her head had been cut out of it.

She'd walked out on them when Andy was only four, although she claimed that she'd only walked out on his father, not on him. On the few occasions the he had seen her, she'd tried to turn him against his dad, trying to fill his head with crap, saying that his father had used to beat her. But, even at a young age, he wasn't buying it. Sure, his dad *had* hit her, but only when she'd deserved it, the same way that Andy had been hit when he did something wrong. Only when it was deserved. So, his dad had cut her out of all the photographs and, after his initial shock, Andy had joined him.

So Alan had brought up his son alone, explaining everything the way it had been explained to him – everything was the blacks' fault. No jobs around, it was down to the blacks. Not enough food or money, down to the blacks. Generally having a bad day, it was *their* fault.

By the time that Andy hit thirteen, he'd started targeting anyone who wasn't white. Throwing eggs at windows, spray-painting doors, hurling abuse at any one younger or smaller than himself, anyone who couldn't fight back. Because at the bottom of it all, he was a coward and wouldn't do anything if there was the slightest chance of being caught.

Spilling the rest of the can onto the floor as his hand relaxed, Andy slept and dreamed, as he usually did, of his mother telling him to get away from his father, before his dad completely ruined his life. As always, the dream ended with his father running after his mother with a baseball bat.

Sarah woke up with dawn light starting to spill through her window, and rushed to the bathroom. She barely made it in time. After being sick, she continued to kneel before the toilet to make sure that there wasn't going to be a repeat performance. When she was sure that she was okay, she wiped her mouth and flushed the whole mess away.

She stood up slowly, fighting against a wave of dizziness that flooded over her. Quickly, she brushed her teeth to try to get rid of the taste of bile, and then walked downstairs to the kitchen.

Instead of a cup of coffee, she found her bottle of vodka and took a quick mouthful (a little something extra to clear the horrible taste away) and then made herself a coffee. She began to sip it as soon as it was made, burning away the still-lingering taste.

Sarah thought back to her actions the previous night, and her smile resurfaced. Sure that she was going to be able to deal with him the way she wanted to, she purposefully turned her thoughts away.

Looking into the garden, she thought how wonderful it looked in the June dawn, how warm, even at five in the morning.

With her cup still in hand, she unlocked the back door and stepped out.

Her nightshirt was short sleeved and reached just above her knees and she wore nothing on her feet but she was still hot. She knew that in a few hours' time the heat would become unbearable.

The grass was dry under her feet, but loose blades still became stuck to the soles of her feet as she walked away from the house. Nearing the back fence, Sarah began to get cold, and she sipped her coffee to try to warm up again. In shock, she spat out what had been in her mouth. The liquid wasn't even warm, it was cold, as if it had spent a few hours in the fridge.

She moved to the edge of the flower border where she stopped, her toes resting on the soil. She looked at the rose bush in front of her. Her eyes glanced down at what she was wearing, and her mind shrank away from the thought of the damage that could have been inflicted by the rose bush if she hadn't have stopped. Her toes wiggled in the dirt, and she watched as the dry grains scattered. As she watched, all of the soil in the border began to jump and vibrate violently. For a second, she considered the possibility of an earthquake, but rejected it. An earthquake would make everything move, not just the dirt in a flowerbed.

Slowly, mounds of dirt began to rise in the border, small hills forming. Sarah tried to back away, to get her toes as far from those hillocks as possible, but her body wouldn't obey her commands.

With no other option, she watched as fingers began sprouting from the tips of the mounds, followed quickly by hands as they rose upwards. In front of the rose bushes, half a dozen pairs of hands waved gently from side to side, like malformed plants caught in a strong wind.

Suddenly, they stopped swaying and began to reach towards the sun-bleached sky again, straining hard against the confines of the earth. Hands rose upwards, arms now exposed to elbows.

No matter what she tried she could not get away from those stretching arms. The arms stretched higher, and she knew that soon whoever owned those arms would also appear.

"You should have been more careful, Sarah."

Now that she didn't want to move, her body turned around so that her back was to the moving arms, and she found herself looking at the familiar shape of Jack Daniels.

The sun was rising in the sky, and nothing was in shadows, yet his entire being was. As was customary with his visitation, no matter how hard she tried, Sarah could see nothing but his shape.

"You've let your standards slip, and now you'll pay." His image faded in front of her until he was no longer there.

Sarah felt her breath stop in her throat. It was expelled in a scream as hands grabbed her ankles and began to pull her over.

Her eyes rolled up into the back of her head as she fainted, Jack's words following her into the darkness. *You should have been more careful.*

Sweat dripping from her body, Sarah woke up in bed, her throat hoarse. Her head rested on her pillows and she breathed deeply, trying to regulate her breathing and slow the thudding of her heart.

Despite how real it had been, after a few moments she managed to convince herself that it had just been a dream. Sarah flicked off the covers and felt herself freeze again. Covering her feet was a mixture of dirt and grass.

*Jack snapped the book closed, his own heart beating frantically in his chest, and for a second was sure that he was going to have a heart attack.*

*The first time that he'd been to that house after Sarah had killed Andrew Dean, after the connections had been made – and after she'd gotten away from him – he'd walked into the garden. Straight to the rose bushes.*

*He'd stopped about three feet from the edge of the flower beds and had uttered those exact words, meaning Andrew Dean's death.*

*She* had *been too sloppy, leaving too many things for them to find at the scene of Andrew's attack. The things that she had used, especially the matches, were covered in her fingerprints, as was the letter she'd sent to Andrew to lure him out. Plus there was the matter of the letter that she had sent to the police.*

*Yet with all of her sloppiness, she'd still managed to get away.*

*As soon as he had uttered those words, as if they were some sort of incantation to bring her there, he'd glimpsed her. For a split second, and* only *a split second, Jack had seen Sarah, barely dressed, turning towards him, a look of fright on her face. Then she was gone. He'd managed to persuade himself at the time that he'd seen her because he'd* wanted *to see her. That he'd been tracking her for so long that his mind had shown him exactly what he'd wanted to see.*

*Again, he felt it, that connection between the two of them, as he had at Sarah's home when he had seen her at the window.*

*He took out the notes he'd been making on the contents of the diary, unsure as to whether to add that part or not. After an uncertain moment, he quickly jotted it down. He could always keep it out of his final report. Jack also jotted down his theory about why they had found so much proof – her drinking.*

*He had proof in her diary that she had been an alcoholic: the bottles that she'd hidden around the house to be later found by Lenny; the jealous behaviour; the swearing; the drinking first thing in the morning; and the tendency to grab a bottle the second that something went wrong.*

*Reading about the planning of the Andrew Dean attack worried him. She was beginning to enjoy it, to take pleasure from it. He wondered if he could blame that on her drinking as well, but strongly doubted that that was the cause.*

# Chapter Twenty-Two

"Can you believe this shit?" Andy passed the note to Stuart.

Stuart read it aloud. "'Ignorant dimwit. To get things sorted, meet me under the bridge on Wood Lane at twelve tonight. Don't think you will, but you should if you're man enough. Figured out the difference between a Paki and a nigger yet?'" A smile erupted on his face. "Looks like you made a new friend, Andy." Still grinning, he passed the note to Carl.

After reading it twice, Carl burst into laughter. "Holy shit. A stand-off. Don't hear about them except in old Western films."

Andy tried to smile, tried to laugh it off as if they were, but he couldn't. The idea that the black fucker had found out where he lived was bad enough. But that he wanted Andy to fight things out, the whole thing terrified him. And if he was man enough? Christ, he'd never felt like more of a child. At any moment he fully expected himself to fill both sides of his trousers.

"So, what d'ya think?" He looked at Stuart and Carl, his face turning red as his voice cracked. "For real, or set up?"

"Probably both," Stuart said, taking the note again. He glanced at Andy, grinning. "So, you gonna show?"

"Course I'm gonna! What d'ya think I'm gonna do? Bottle out?" God, he wished that he didn't sound quite so defensive, that he could at least *sound* as laid back as the other two were.

Stuart raised his hands in mock surrender, trying to keep a straight face as Carl suffered another fit of laughter. "Chill, man, chill. Just wanted to know if you wanted a bit of help."

Andy again thought that he was going to wet himself, this time in relief. He did what he could to keep the relief from his voice, and didn't do a very good job. "If you want."

"How long we got?"

"If we're going to do it," Stuart said, instinctively taking over. "I want to get there as soon as it's dark." He glanced at his watch.

"That gives us about five and a half hours." He turned back to Andy, smiling at the pallor of his skin. "Looks like we got a date tonight."

The bridge Sarah had chosen was one that Lenny had shown her. It didn't have any purpose, didn't cover a river or track, but it looked nice. It was in a private garden, a metal chain-link fence confining the entire property, but Lenny had taken her through a gap that was near the base of the bridge. It had been brilliant just to lie there that night, with his arm wrapped around her shoulders, fifteen feet closer to the stars.

She felt a pang of regret, a need for her ex-lover again, but forced it away. Concentrating on what she was doing helped her, and she set up her things, getting everything ready.

It was a quarter to six, four hours and fifteen minutes before they were supposed to arrive, but she'd rather be too early than too late. And besides, she didn't mind the wait.

"No sign of anyone." Andy was perched on top of the metal fence, and spoke at his normal loud volume.

"Shut the fuck up!" Stuart whispered fiercely, casting anxious glances towards the house three hundred yards from where they were. "And can you hurry the fuck up, and get over the fucking fence!"

In the dark, Andy flushed a deep crimson, but obediently jumped down on the other side. Immediately, before Carl and Stuart started to climb over, he began to search for the bats that Stuart had bought along.

Stuart jumped down beside him first, followed closely by Carl. Andy handed one of the two bats to Carl, and tried to hand the other to Stuart.

"No thanks, pal. Don't need one." He walked towards the bridge, his eyes searching for signs that anyone was nearby.

Carl and Andy followed, both carrying the baseball bats.

Andy kept his eyes forward, not bothering to check anywhere, content to let Carl and Stuart look after him.

Carl, on the other hand, wasn't searching. He was scanning. His eyesight was perfect, and he had no problems seeing in the dark once his eyes were adjusted. While his friend looked mainly around the fences and the house, basically trying to look everywhere at once, Carl concentrated on the bridge, knowing instinctively that the bridge was the best place to hide – full of shadows and raised walls.

Glancing at the top, he thought he saw a woman's face peering down at them. But when he blinked, the image was gone. And anyway, the face had been white, so nothing to worry about there.

Coming up to the bridge, Carl glanced to his left and stopped abruptly. A leering smile appeared on his face. "Oi, Stu."

Stuart stopped a few feet from the bridge, Andy half underneath it, and looked at Carl questioningly.

Using the bat, he pointed to the row of mirrors. "Looks like someone's into kinky sex."

Stuart smiled, and then carried on until he had joined Andy under the bridge. "Never understood it meself. Sex is sex."

Carl glanced up as he walked underneath. He couldn't shake the idea that someone was up there, and was thinking of checking it out. He walked to where Stuart and Andy stood and leant against the inside of the bridge, getting caught up with what was being said.

"You think he'll show?"

In the dark, and without even having to see Andy's face, Carl and Stuart could see that he was shitting himself. And without having to see Stuart's face, Carl knew that he was trying to wind Andy up even more.

"It's a possibility."

"So, what are we going to do to him?"

Stuart scoffed lightly. "What's this 'we' shit?" He got himself into a more comfortable position against the wall. "Me and Carl will only get involved if *his* mates get involved."

He suppressed a smile, trying to keep his tone serious, when he heard Andy's rough intake of breath. It was one of his few pleasures in life, winding Andy up. "You *can* handle one on his own, can't you, Andy? You don't need help with *one*, do you?"

"Course I fucking don't." He blushed even harder, knowing that Stuart was just messing with him, but unable not to rise to it.

Despite where they were and what they were waiting to do, Stuart and Carl still exploded into loud laughter.

"Shit!" she muttered under her breath. She'd had the perfect opportunity to get him, the other two away from the bridge, and that greasy-haired prat had been under her, *directly under her*, and she hadn't been quick enough.

So now she had to wait, to just sit patiently and wait, peeking over the side and hoping that he'd walk out again.

She heard laughter from below and looked down. She'd almost forgotten that she'd put them there, but when a car swept around a nearby corner she found herself staring at a dozen images. The car was gone, taking its headlights with it, but Sarah could still see the images in the mirrors, repeated over and over.

The thing she saw was dead. Its skin was green, mould growing on its decaying cheeks. Its eyeballs were no longer white: they had turned a green-black and were slowly escaping from their sockets. To Sarah, it looked very similar to the creatures that George A. Romero had created, and she fully expected to see it start munching on an arm or leg.

Just when she thought that her luck was never going to get any better, he stepped out from the cover of the bridge. And she raised the can of petrol.

He was getting fed up with them always taking the piss,

constantly. Walking away from their laughter, a car swept around behind him, and he saw his reflection staring back at him, before the lights disappeared again.

Out from underneath the bridge, he felt rain fall heavily on his head and shoulders and looked up. In the dark, he saw fire raining down on him.

His screams stopped their laughter instantly. In an explosion of light, they watched as he fell, looked at each other and rushed over to him. Andy was writhing on the ground, his face plus the top half of his clothes were on fire. Smoke wafted up from him, and they couldn't get any closer, the heat from his burning body forcing them to keep away.

Carl looked up as he moved out from the safety of the bridge, expecting to see half a dozen black faces peering down at him, ready to attack again. Instead, he saw the face of a white woman staring back at him. Smiling.

He watched as she bolted away from the edge, reappearing on the ground and disappearing through a hole in the fence.

"Can't you shut him up, Stu?" Carl said, turning back to look at both Andy, writhing on the ground in agony, and Stuart, who looked scared and uncertain for the first time since Carl had known him.

Stuart just looked back at him, unable to speak.

"Let's just get out of here, Stu!" Carl grabbed his arm and tried to drag his friend away from the screaming form.

It seemed to wake Stuart from whatever daze had captured him, and he looked at Carl in disgust. He shook his arm free. "What the fuck are you talking about?" He looked down at Andy, trying not to gag on the smell of burning flesh.

"Go to the house, Carl. Tell them to call an ambulance."

"No." Carl shook his head. "No! How do we explain it. We're on private property, Stu, we're—"

"Shut up, Carl! Go and get an ambulance!" Violently, he

pushed Carl towards the house, and there was no way for him to argue.

Noting the lights coming on inside the house, Carl began to sprint away as Stuart tried to extinguish the flames.

Sarah sneaked up to the greasy-haired bloke's house with two cans of spray paint, black and red. When she had finished, she walked away without looking back.

Carefully they collected the things from the top of the bridge, light from the cars making the job a little easier.

The lad had been taken to the hospital, burnt badly, his clothes melted onto his body. So far, they hadn't heard how he was doing, but the look on the faces of the paramedics as they had loaded him into the ambulance hadn't been very encouraging.

John Carter was immediately set upon when he arrived at the scene. The owners of the property, two self-righteous idiots in his mind, wanted all three of them, including the one currently at the hospital, arrested for trespassing.

He ran a hand over his moustache, knowing that the first few threads of grey were beginning to creep in, and then did something he'd never done before in his whole career – he lost it.

"A boy is lying in hospital, and you want him *arrested*?! What the fuck is wrong with you two?!" Seeing them cringe slightly didn't help his temper, neither did the momentary look of fear in the woman's eyes.

"John?"

After a moment's hesitation, staring at the couple in an extra effort to get his meaning across, John looked around at the uniformed officer that had called to him, and walked over.

"You all right?"

Mixed in with the curiosity was genuine concern, and it managed to unarm him. "Not really." He was looking at the officer, but also looking through him. "Paula had a hospital appointment today. The cancer's not responding to the treatment."

"Shit, John. I'm sorry."

"Thanks." Mentally, he shook himself. "So, we got anything?"

"I'll say so." They walked on the direction of the bridge. Even with the bad light and at the distance, John could see the area of burnt grass.

"We got a couple of things that look promising. A petrol can, a couple of boxes of matches, all with, what might be, very good fingerprints." Here he stopped and faced John directly, a small smile on his face. "And we do have a definite."

For some reason, it shocked him. He'd assumed that for something so well planned the perpetrator would have been a bit more careful. "On what?"

"They saw her running through the gap in the fence. She wasn't too quick."

"Great!" John said, nodding. "That's really good—" He replayed what he'd just heard and stared at his companion with fresh amazement. "*She*? Did you say, '*She*'?"

Laughing, he nodded. "Yep. One of the lads, Carl Gradey, said he saw a woman running from the top of the bridge and through the fence."

"Gets better and better." He shook his head, trying to separate the important and the not-so-important. "Right. I want them both interviewed, and I want you to get Andrew Dean's address."

"No problem, boss."

John walked, smiling to himself as the other officer walked away and started barking orders at everyone else, and then his smile faded as thoughts of his wife began to crowd in again.

Seven o'clock the next morning, Sarah sat in the living room, a bottle of vodka by her side, cigarettes and ashtray also close by. As she watched the news on the television, she once again began to smile before turning her attention back to the letter. When the news was finished, and the letter in an envelope ready to send, she felt amazingly pleased with herself. She got her journal, opened it, and began to write.

The first sign Jack had of the death of Andrew Dean was the seven o'clock news. He'd had another restless night and was awake early. The report had come on, about a twenty-year-old white male who had died in the hospital, burnt alive.

For some reason, it caught his attention, and he put his paper down and watched the report a bit more closely. His heart began to pound a strange rhythm in his chest when he saw the door behind the reporter.

Spray-painted in black, with a red circle around it and red line passing through it, was a swastika. And underneath it was the word he had gotten used to seeing over the years: EVIL.

After hearing the name of the town, Jack rushed to the telephone. Once he had made sure that he wouldn't be stepping on anyone's toes, he arranged to speak to a fellow DC in Moss, a John Carter. And then he gathered the things he may need, left a note for his wife and then left the house.

Just over an hour later, he was introduced to John, and shook the man's hand. "I'm DC Jack Daniels."

At the mention of his name, John raised his eyebrows. "You're Jack Daniels?"

Jack nodded. "Yeah. Do we know each other already?" He was taken aback when the man in front of him uttered a short sharp burst of laughter.

"No. But someone does." Indicating for Jack to follow, John walked into his office and started to go through a folder on his desk. He pulled out a piece of paper in a clear evidence bag and handed it to Jack. "See what you think."

That's one less racist thug you have to worry about. No real need to thank me.

Give my regards to Jack Daniels and tell him I said hi.

Sarah

He looked up at John. "The killer's a woman?!" He looked at the handwriting again, knowing that it was the same as the other letters that had been received. "And she even signed her name. If it is her real name."

"I've got a couple of officers digging around to see if there's any more murders with the same MO, have had since your call. Nothing yet."

Jack nodded. He was feeling embarrassed. How could he have assumed that it was a man? "Have you got a decent canteen, somewhere we can get a drink. I think we need to fill each other in."

It was two hours later that Jack left the police station and he was finally able to ring Maggie. There was no answer at the house, but he wasn't overly concerned. He found a B & B, a place named 'The Sleep And Eat', in the centre of town, and got himself booked in. It was small, but surprisingly clean. He was getting settled in when his mobile phone rang.

John gave him the details of another murder, and the directions to the house opposite an up street hotel called The Grande. After a few wrong turns, Jack managed to work his way there.

Telling the woman who answered the door that he was doing a follow-up on the murder of her son, he managed to find out all of the details, but after ascertaining that there was nothing that wasn't in the files that John had, he thanked her and left.

Despite the fact that things still weren't looking up for him, he felt a sudden cramp of hunger, his appetite having reappeared from the vacation it had taken once he had seen the news. Down the road, he saw a newsagents, and his stomach craved a bar of chocolate so he made his way to it.

Walking around the shop put him off buying anything to eat,

at least from there. The dust on the bottles of juice and all available surfaces didn't fill him with optimism. But he always felt guilty if he'd walked around a shop and didn't buy anything. So before he left he bought a newspaper, rolling it into a tube so that it was easier to carry.

He started to walk back down the street, glancing at the hotel. When he was directly opposite, in front of the Marsden house, he turned to look at the hotel properly.

Instead of climbing the building, his eyes went straight to a window three stories up and immediately found himself meeting the eyes of a woman looking out at him.

Not knowing why, not in control, he raised his empty hand and pointed at her. After a few seconds he dropped his hand, seriously embarrassed, and more than a little freaked out.

Although he couldn't see her clearly, her features a little distorted, he saw movement in the room behind her, and goose bumps broke out all over his body. Behind her, a monster stood, its face rotten and decaying, with its arms stretched out towards her. Alarmed, he raised his hand again, pointing at the thing behind her, hoping that she'd understand.

Relieved, he watched as she turned around, and felt his breathing stop momentarily as both figures disappeared. He blinked repeatedly, but nothing he did would bring them back, nor make him feel any better. Although he didn't know it then, he'd just suffered his first vision of the woman he was chasing.

As soon as his legs felt like they could cope, Jack tracked his way back to the B & B, trying Maggie on his phone, again and again, with no success. He woke early the next day and went out to get better acquainted with the streets, taking time to stand in front of the hotel, daring his eyes to recapture what he'd seen the day before.

Slowly, taking his time and enjoying the peace and quiet, Jack walked along the streets. The silence was broken by the shrill ringing of his mobile phone, and he hurried to free it from his jacket pocket, hating to have the quiet spoiled.

"Hello?"

"Jack?" Maggie sounded a mixture of worried and annoyed. "Jack, where the hell are you?"

He felt like hitting his head against a brick wall. "I tried ringing you a couple of times last night! You weren't in!"

He explained quickly, his excitement at the breaks in the case not shared by his wife, which dampened his own.

"Just as long as I know, Jack." She sighed deeply. "When will you be back?"

"I don't know. I'll call you later tonight, let you know what I'm doing."

She said goodbye and hung up.

Jack continued with his walk, clearing his head of all the useless crap, and concentrating on the case. With his mind working on what it had to, Jack felt better.

Completely in his own world, he didn't see the woman walking towards him, didn't see her shifting her brown hair out of her eyes.

She wasn't watching where she was going, and they collided. They both apologised, and Jack had only a second to notice the terrified look on her face before she rushed away. He watched her as she turned the corner, wondering why she had been so startled. As he tried to commit her face to memory, it occurred to him that he knew her. Her best friend had been attacked by her own husband, and then the husband had been found dead. What had his name been? Daniels? Davis? Dawes? That was it, Dawes, Henry Dawes! One of the men killed in the case he was working on.

Suddenly everything clicked in his head, and he quickly followed her steps, but he had left it too long, and there was no longer any sign of her. Sweat seeping from every inch of his body, Jack cross-referenced her with the description they'd received from the boy at the bridge. As far as he could tell, it was a perfect match.

Plus there was the letter that the local cops had received, signed by a Sarah. Wasn't *her* name Sarah? Sarah Fletcher? He thought it was. Without hesitating any more, Jack pulled out his phone again, and rang John Carter.

*Thinking back, Jack could still remember how it had felt, how it had felt to have everything fall into place in his head. After all the years of searching, of hunting, of hoping, and she had literally bumped into him.*

*Hearing the front door open and close, he sat back and waited to see if his wife would walk in.*

*Maggie closed the door as quietly as she could, but knew from experience that there was no way to close it silently. With the confidence of finally having made a decision, she pulled her suitcase out from underneath the bed, and opened it ready to pack.*

She hadn't been able to sleep, no matter what she tried. Drinking hadn't helped, neither had writing in her diary. Also, she'd been throwing up almost constantly, and just hadn't been able to relax.

Even though watching the news that next morning had cheered her up, knowing that her handiwork had paid off, she just couldn't unwind. There was something in the back of her mind, something telling her that it was time to run again, to hide before she got caught.

It was her nerves telling her to run, but her head told her not to worry, that there was no way she was going to get caught, she was far too clever. Maybe if she'd laid off the booze she might have trusted her instincts, but the drink had made her more confident, more stupid – like signing her name on the note to the cops. So, because of the alcohol, she sided with her head.

Early the next morning, after no sleep at all, she went out for a walk, hoping that the exercise and fresh air would help tire her out. It was warm, and the air only woke her up more.

A part of her hoped that she'd run into Lenny, so that maybe things would sort themselves out. So she walked through the streets in a daydream where she and Lenny patched things up.

The first sign she had that someone was walking towards her was when they bumped into each other.

"Sorry," she apologised, hearing him say the same thing, and looked up. As her mind registered the face looking back at her, she first thought that she was having another vision. But her head corrected her – mainly due to the fact that she could see his face. This was the *real* Jack Daniels.

As soon as she was able, Sarah rushed away, fighting hard against the impulse to look over her shoulder to see if he was looking at her or, worse, following. Not sure where it went, Sarah turned right down a side street, praying that it wouldn't be a dead end.

Sarah managed to track her way home. For the third time in ten months, she packed her things to move.

# Chapter Twenty-Three

It was a bit of a dump, it was smaller than she was used to and she had to share a bathroom with another couple, but she thought that it would do short term.

Again, she ignored the advice of her gut instinct to run as far as she could, to just get away from the man who was following her. Instead, she'd rented a room on the other side of town. There was no furniture apart from a double bed, a desk and chair, and a full-length mirror. With nowhere to unpack her clothes into, she pushed them under the bed, still in the suitcases. But, she paid cash, no lease to be signed, no rent book, no credit or reference checks – so in that respect it was perfect.

In her head, Sarah kept replaying the instant that she had bumped into the officer, seeing the look on his face and, more importantly, the look in his eyes, searching her memory for anything out of place, any hint of recognition. She found nothing that made her worry – she told herself that moving was just a precaution. She had posted the key to the house through the front door, notifying no one of her new address. On her drive back to her new home, she bought a hair-dye pack from a chemist.

Driving away from the town centre, Sarah felt her unease and anxiousness flowing out of her body, the muscles relaxing one by one. She turned down a side road and continued along the back roads, enjoying the peace and serenity of the countryside. She had the windows down, the slight breeze across the fields bringing the scent of rapeseed into the car.

After half an hour of driving Sarah pulled into a passing-place and got out of the car.

It was hot outside, and the breeze did little to alleviate the humidity. Instead of enjoying being outside, she found the air hard to swallow and the heat hurt her head, so she decided to cut short her impulsive stop. A little annoyed, Sarah jumped back into her car and, as quickly as she could manage it, she got her car up to speed, making the air rush through the windows.

Glancing across the fields, Sarah caught sight of a quick flash of colour, and after a few seconds was able to pinpoint it. To be safe, not knowing why it was all so important, Sarah pulled the car over again so that she could find the source.

Her surety that the heat was making her hallucinate was stolen from her as she saw a woman running along a stretch of road around a bend.

She had light brown hair, a little shorted than her own, and Sarah could see that the woman's cheeks were flushed from running. Every other step, she was turning around and looking behind her, constantly checking over her shoulder. Sarah continued to watch her from across the fields.

Just when she was about to shrug it off as nothing, something happened that nearly stopped Sarah's heart – a car appeared from nowhere, about thirty feet behind the woman. Sarah blinked a few times, trying to get her head around the small silver car that had arrived out of thin air. Not taking her eyes away from the moving figure, she started the car up. With the handbrake off, she put the car into gear. Her foot slipped off the clutch, causing the car to lurch forward and stall, as she saw the silver car rush forwards and hit the running woman.

Even from the distance, Sarah saw the fine spray of blood that flew upwards when the woman was knocked into the air. Before she could see the body hit the ground, she turned forward and started the car again, driving as quickly as she could towards the injured woman.

Part of her wanted to turn away, to just drive off and forget that she'd seen the incident, but the rest of her forced her to keep moving. Nearing the place where the woman had been hit, Sarah locked her doors, just another precaution. After all, she didn't know *who* was in the other car, or why they'd run the woman over. Thinking about it, was she so sure that she wanted to get involved? Too late now, Sarah was nearing the car. She slowed to a crawl, peering through the windows of the other car. It was hard to believe, but it looked to be empty.

She drove alongside it, glancing at it from the corner of her eye. She slammed her foot on the brake, dipping the clutch just in time to prevent it from stalling again, turning fully to look at the car. Or, rather, where the car *had* been. Sarah found herself staring at the empty road – the car was no longer there.

Two feet away from the still body, Sarah stepped out of the car, and was struck again by the heat outside, leaving the door open. Her legs felt rubbery as she took steps towards the woman, not sure if she could handle knowing that the woman had been hit by a car that had first miraculously appeared and then disappeared. Eyes fixed firmly on the ground, she could see red dots on the tarmac, and she tried to convince herself that it wasn't what she thought it was, that it wasn't blood, but her tired mind refused to be lied to.

At first, she thought that the woman was dead, but the uneven rise and fall of the woman's chest below her bright red top convinced her otherwise. Sarah rushed back to her car and took her mobile phone from the glove compartment and walked back to the wounded woman.

Sarah would have preferred it if the woman had been face down on the ground, or at least if her hair had covered her face, but she was unlucky enough to be able to see the woman's brown eyes. One was filled with blood, some of it trickling down her cheek. Speckles of blood covered her face and Sarah saw an alarming amount of grit embedded in her flesh.

She looked down at her phone and started to punch in 999 on the keypad. Before she could put in the last digit, something came over her and she switched the phone off.

The woman at her feet was fully conscious, and was looking at Sarah through a red mist. Her lips opened, and Sarah watched a bubble of blood form on her lips, and then burst, red splatters falling over the woman's face.

"I'm sorry, Melasand. I'm sorry."

From her own lips, Sarah heard another's voice, slightly lighter and more musical than her own. "It's over now, Karen."

Feeling control coming back to her, Sarah watched as the woman stopped breathing. Watching closely, she saw lesions beginning to rise on the woman's forehead. She screamed. It was all too much now and she ran back to her car as she saw the word that she used to mark her kills form, embossed on the woman's skin.

Quickly, she drove around her. As she drove away, Sarah began to rationalise her actions – if she was to phone the police, she'd be implicated in the death, and it wouldn't take long for them to connect her to the murders. There was no way that she was going to let that happen, especially on behalf of a dead woman that she hadn't even killed!

Her drive back to her new home was the most terrifying thing she'd ever gone through. Her tired, overwrought mind saw too many silver cars travelling on the roads behind her, and once when she looked in the rear-view mirror she was sure that she had seen a pretty, blonde-haired woman with grey eyes sitting behind her.

It was a relief when she got back to her tiny excuse for a flat and locked the door securely behind her. Then she buried her face into her hands and started to cry.

When the crying fit eventually stopped, Sarah wiped her eyes and picked up the box of hair dye that she had purchased earlier. Hoping that the people across the hall wouldn't want to use the bathroom, Sarah went back into the hall and into the bathroom with her towels in hand.

She read the instructions and put on the disposable gloves. Hoping that she wouldn't end up with bright red hair (her mind called up the image of the dead-woman's shirt), she applied the dye. The smell made her a bit queasy, but it wasn't until she looked into the mirror that she was physically sick. With it rubbed into her hair, the dye didn't look as bright as she'd feared, but it still unnerved her. It looked as though it had been marinated in blood.

Falling quickly to her knees, she leant over the toilet bowl and was sick, using her arms to support her and trying not to let her hands touch anything. Her hair hung over her face, and she could feel the dye going onto her skin.

She sat up, still feeling queasy, and removed the gloves. Efficiently, she wrapped a towel around her shoulders, hoping that not too much of the dye had gotten onto her T-shirt, and then proceeded to wash the mess from her skin.

Confident that it was all gone, and after making sure the bathroom was clean, she walked back to her room.

With nothing else to do but wait for her hair to absorb the colour, Sarah sat at her desk and pulled out her journal.

*It had been easy enough to track down the house that she had rented. Her bank manager had been a character reference on her application to rent, and she'd had her mail redirected from her old home.*

*He'd taken it personally, he remembered that; that she'd managed to fool him! He'd also blamed himself for letting her get away. Not just once, but twice. Other people didn't blame him, he* knew *that, but he was angry enough at himself.*

*Jack wasn't sure what to make of what he'd just read from Sarah's diary. Cars disappearing into thin air after hitting and killing someone? It just wasn't possible. Doubt started to creep into his mind however, just as he'd managed to assure himself that it was an impossibility. Why would she lie about that murder when she had been so honest about the others? The journal was for her benefit, he knew, so writing something down that wasn't true would have no purpose. Unless her delusions had reached a new level.*

*He closed his eyes, hoping to clear his mind so he could look at things clearly again, but the sound of Maggie moving around above his head stopped him from relaxing. He didn't know what she was doing up there, but he wished that she'd stop.*

*What Maggie was doing was packing. She had two suitcases full of clothes and a small bag for her makeup and toiletries. Maggie was packing slower than she could have, even now putting off telling him. It was going to hurt both of them. She knew it was for the best, but it was still going to hurt.*

*When she'd packed all the things that she needed, when there was nothing else she* could *pack, when it couldn't be put off any longer, Maggie picked up her cases and bag and walked downstairs.*

*A deep breath, putting her bags down by the front door, she then walked down the hallway to her husband's study. After another moment's hesitation, she knocked on the door.*

*"Come in."*

*Another deep breath, then Maggie walked into the lion's den.*

Now with dark red hair, Sarah walked into the chemist, and bought two items. The first was a pair of low-prescription reading glasses, which she put on as soon as she got outside. The second item, in a small white paper bag with the chemist logo printed in blue, she carried to the small room she was renting.

Before taking her second purchase out of its bag, she looked at herself in the mirror.

The brunette with the soft features was no longer there. Instead was a redhead in glasses, which made her look more intelligent, but also somehow hardened. She looked like a distant cousin of the brown-haired woman.

After following the instructions on the pregnancy test box she went back to her room. Sitting on her bed, she waited two minutes before looking at the result window on the thin stick.

She saw the two blue lines in the middle of the second window, and lifted the instruction leaflet up next to it, just to confirm the result.

Pete Carter was on his way to work. He rode his bike down the middle of the road, making sure that no cars could overtake him. By the time he pulled onto the dirt track, with the sound of horns sending him on his way, there were eighteen cars behind him.

He steered his pushbike through small puddles instead of avoiding them, throwing dirt up onto his trousers. Although it was brilliant sunshine, Pete wore a thick winter coat, not really noticing the sweat that ran down his face.

In the road in front of him, Pete saw a bird. It had been injured, its wing broken by flying into a car, yet it still tried to fly away when it felt the vibrations of the bike getting closer.

If he'd continued to move in a straight line, he would have missed the bird by a good few inches. But instead he swerved towards it, aiming for it. He felt a great amount of satisfaction when he heard and felt the birds tiny bones break beneath the wheel. The moment of joy was quickly forgotten, as if it had never happened, and Pete continued down the thin road.

He entered the work site, disregarding the one-way rules, and parked his bike in its usual place inside the bike shed. With his coat still on, his bag still on his back, and the mud starting to dry on his trousers, Pete walked to the entrance of the factory.

As he moved closer to the doors, his whole personality started to change. He finally noticed that his coat was on and that he was sweating, and he took it off, carrying it the rest of the way. He noticed the mud on his trousers and frowned as he tried to remember how they had gotten so dirty. A bird hopped across his path and he smiled when he saw it, swerving away from it so that he wouldn't scare it.

He walked into the changing area, using his swipe-card to clock in, and was greeted by the usual welcome.

"Hiya, Freddy," someone shouted, and half a dozen others broke into an off-key rendition of Queen's 'I Want to Break Free'.

Pete no longer minded being constantly compared to Freddy Mercury – he did, after all, look a lot like him, and it was an image that he now did everything to encourage. He had the eyes, the hair, even the moustache. At one time, he'd thought about shaving the moustache off, but this idea had been met by shock.

Pete laughed at them and walked straight to his locker. Carefully, he hung up his coat and bag, and then walked out to the laundry room. He selected his overalls, took them back to his locker, changed his shoes, and then put the overalls on.

With half an hour to go before work started, he put on his hair net and hat, and went and sat in the canteen.

The buzzer signalling the change of shifts rang out loudly through the entire factory, and the canteen emptied rapidly. Pete walked with the rest of his shift onto the factory floor and, like the rest of his colleagues, found it a little disturbing how easily it was to fall back into the same routine.

He had a normal working relationship with everyone: jokes were shared, he bitched about the bitchiness within the factory, and he worked on the machines as he did every day.

His shift was supposed to finish at eleven o'clock that evening, but they were running late with the orders, and Pete didn't clock out until nearly one in the morning. He said his goodbyes to everyone and walked over to his bike.

With his coat on and his bag over his shoulder once more, he swung his leg over the frame and started to pedal. Although it was pitch black, Pete had no lights on his bike, and felt no real need for them – anybody driving would have their headlights on and would see him in plenty of time.

As it had on his way across the factory grounds, his personality started to change, reverting back to the way it had been before he'd started work. He moved his bike out to the centre of the road, and didn't even bother stopping at the junction – he just rode out onto the main road, regardless of any other road users.

At first he was just disappointed that there weren't any

animals to hit, but he soon started to become angry. He began to pedal faster, pumping out his aggression, and gradually began to swerve his bike all over the road, including the wrong side, as if he was drunk. For some reason, he didn't consider his actions dangerous, especially so early in the morning. For Pete, no one else existed.

When he reached home, he stood his bike up against the wall next to his window, and unlocked the communal door. At the door to his room he noticed an envelope taped to it, he took it off and carried it into his room, not noticing the stench.

He opened the letter in the dark and then switched on the light to read it. His room was a mess. Newspapers were strewn everywhere, over the furniture and over the floors, take-away boxes littered the room, and food rotted inside.

He only glanced at the letter, its contents – 'sort out the stink!' – wasn't of any interest, and it soon joined the rest of the rubbish. Boxes stood piled up against one wall, but his mind didn't register the tiny white maggots that crawled over them. All his mind saw were the boxes with his pets inside.

She hadn't slept very well, had spent most of the night staring up at the ceiling or looking out of the window. At about two o'clock, she heard the main door open and close and one of the rooms below open and close. From the squeak of the door, she thought it was probably the dark-haired bloke with the moustache. Then things remained quiet.

Gradually, light began to filter through the thin curtains and Sarah watched as patterns were made on the walls and ceiling, feeling the room starting to warm up.

At six o'clock, over an hour and a half after the sun had begun its ascent, Sarah left the building.

Walking around the outside, she barely avoided tripping up over a bicycle that had fallen onto the path. She picked it up and set it against the wall before walking off.

At the shop, Sarah bought herself a carton of cigarettes, a large bottle of whiskey so that she could celebrate getting pregnant, and a newspaper. She didn't glance at it until she got home, but as soon as she did, she lit a cigarette and opened the new bottle, laying the paper on the bed so that she could read it and keep her hands free.

SERIAL KILLER KILLED BY SERIAL KILLER?
Report by Sally Coles

The body of twenty-nine year old Karen Thompson was found yesterday evening in the middle of a South Yorkshire back road. According to a police source, the single woman was struck by a vehicle, which caused fatal internal injuries.

On investigation of her home, police found evidence that she had committed several hit-and-runs in the past three years, leading to numerous deaths.

Even stranger, is the fact that Thompson's death is being linked to *another serial killer*, although police refuse to officially comment on the status of their investigations.

Her eyes kept going back to the headline, her mind refusing to grasp it entirely. *Serial killer? She's a serial killer? Christ,* she thought, the whiskey burning her throat. *Is that what I am?*

She walked over to the window and pitched her cigarette outside, watching the small arc of embers as it fell. Once it had hit the ground, erupting another small spill of embers, Sarah grabbed her journal from the desk and sat back on the bed. Carefully, she ripped the page from the rest of the newspaper, folded it up and put it in the back of her journal.

Then, despite how sick she felt, regardless of the part of her telling her that it was bad for the baby, Sarah concentrated on getting drunk, only half-conscious when she was sick beside the bed half an hour later.

"She is wanted in connection with the murder of seven people. Police ask that anyone with any knowledge of her whereabouts contact them immediately. She is considered dangerous, and anyone who spots her should not approach, but contact the police immediately.

"That bulletin again.

"Police are asking for any information about the possible whereabouts of Sarah Caroline Fletcher, twenty-one years old. She is approximately five feet tall, brown hair..."

Pete turned the television off, shutting the woman off in mid-sentence, feeling puzzled. The photograph that had been shown had seemed familiar to him, but he wasn't sure why. After a goodbye glance at his boxes, he picked up his bag and left. He slowly cycled a couple of miles down the road, and then turned onto a footpath. Two minutes later, he was in his usual spot, deep in the woods. It was public property, but in the four years that he had been going, he had never seen another soul there. He was glad: other people just got in the way.

He leant his bike against and old oak and unzipped his large bag. Not bothering to be cautious, knowing that he wouldn't be disturbed, he took out the air rifle and box of pellets. He put one in straight away, and simply started to walk.

Although he'd only had five hours sleep, he felt wide awake and rested. It was another reason that he liked to go shooting early in the morning, the fresh air always seemed to revive him, no matter how down he felt. Plus it seemed to bring the animals out.

Birds were singing in the trees, flying from one branch to another, but shooting birds didn't appeal to him that morning. A couple of grey squirrels darted in front of him before running up the truck of a fir. But he wasn't in a squirrel mood either. A flash of red caught his eye, and he smiled as he saw the red brush of a fox disappearing into the woods. It had been a long time since he'd seen a fox, let alone hunted one, and Pete knew in an instant that it was definitely a fox day.

Being as quiet as he could, he started moving after the animal, breathing slowly and calmly so as not to lose control and get overexcited. His heart was beating quickly, and he could feel the blood pumping through his veins, filling him with purpose.

The fox had stopped by a fallen tree, its tongue lolling out as it panted, and looked straight at Pete, its eyes showing no fear. It didn't move as Pete slowly raised the air rifle and rested the butt against his shoulder. Nor did it move as Pete looked through the sight mounted on top of the staff. Only when Pete fired did it move, thrown instantaneously against a tree with a sharp yelp.

He walked over to it slowly, loading another pellet into the gun.

Using his rifle, he prodded the fox to see if it would react, still amazed at the burnt-red of its coat. With no reaction, no movement, Pete squatted beside it and turned it over with his hands. Its head was covered in blood, still flowing from the hole in the centre, in between the eyes. A greyish substance had also trickled out, but Pete saw this no more than he saw the blood – for him, the fox was asleep, and the idea that he had shot it, despite the gun he still held, was ridiculous.

He picked the fox up by its tail, swinging it gently as he walked back towards his bike, blood flowing with each arc. Without ceremony, Pete stuffed the fox into his bag, pushing his rifle in on top. Slinging it over his shoulder, he mounted the bike and started home.

She woke up three hours after drinking herself to sleep, totally disgusted with herself for the mess she'd made beside the bed. After cleaning it up, Sarah looked at the remainder of the whiskey longingly, but forced herself not to – she felt ill enough as it was. Instead, she went to the bathroom and freshened herself up, then walked downstairs and out through the main entrance. Walking past a window, she happened to glance in.

Her mouth dropped open, and she gagged without realising it, as she saw the man in the centre of the room. She'd seen him a few times since she'd moved in, and he'd looked decent enough. Now, holding an obviously dead fox by the tail, he looked like a waxwork creation for the Chamber of Horrors section at Madame Tussauds. Blood covered his chest, and if Sarah had looked through the window a second earlier, she would have seen him cuddling the animal like a stuffed toy.

Sickened, but unable to stop her unintentional surveillance, Sarah watched as he placed the animal into a shoebox on his bed. He dressed quickly and left the room, and Sarah ducked around the corner of the building as he walked outside. She watched as he swung a bag over his shoulder, got onto his bike and pedalled away.

Sick morbid curiosity stole over her, and standing outside his room, Sarah could smell something.

When she was thirteen, her parents had taken her on a trip to the south of France. After a brilliant week away, they'd returned home to find that the freezer had broken in their absence. The smell that had welcomed them that summer when they had opened the freezer was brought back to her as she stood there. And, believing it to be one of the stupidest things she'd even done, she opened the unlocked door and walked inside.

The smell was worse than she'd expected, and bile immediately started to rise in her throat. She fought it back down and looked around the room in disbelief. The mess on the floor – clothes, paper, food cartons with mouldy bits inside – was bad, but it didn't explain the intensity of the stench. She looked at the bed and saw the shoebox that he'd put the fox in.

All of her skin began to itch as she saw the plump maggots that were already crawling over the box, and it felt as though they were crawling over her as she saw the amount that covered the bed. Now that she'd seen them, she realised that they were everywhere: they moved amongst the mess on the floor, crawling in and out of the boxes, crawling over clothes. Looking around, her eyes noticed where the majority of the maggots were. Lined up underneath the window, Sarah counted forty-three shoeboxes, very much like the one on the bed.

"Oh, Christ. They're all full of—" Instead of finishing, Sarah rushed out of the room, closing the door, and out into the fresh air just in time. The door closed behind her, and supporting herself against the wall, Sarah vomited bile, the thick yellow substance pooling by her feet.

As soon as she was able, she whispered to herself. "Sick fucker." Even as she vomited, she started planning the way that she was going to kill him.

*It was a technicality for her now. Looking back through his notes, Jack saw that the first four murders – not including Anthony Freeman – had all been committed after she'd seen their true images. But the deaths of Marsden, Dean, and Carter had all been planned before.*

*She was starting to use it as an excuse to herself, giving herself permission to kill those people. But coming to that conclusion only puzzled him more. If she was using it as an excuse, then that would only work if it was real.* If she thought it was real, *his mind amended.* If she truly believed that she was seeing something that wasn't – *couldn't have been* – there, she would be able to convince herself that she was doing it for one reason and one reason only.

*It was quiet in the rest of the house. Jack could feel the stillness pressing against him, but didn't feel awkward about it, the stillness wasn't in the least oppressive. He was actually quite glad he was alone – at least it meant that he could concentrate on the journal, could stay in Sarah's world without any distraction.*

*Pretending to himself that he didn't mind that she was gone, didn't mind that she'd lied to him, didn't mind that she was probably on her way to live with her bit on the side, Jack continued with his work. Yet the issue of his wife wasn't very far from the front of his mind.*

*She couldn't stop herself from replaying it all in her head as she rode the bus with her luggage at her feet. Half of her found it impossible that she could just have walked out on her husband, on her marriage, as easily as she had. But here she was sitting on a bus, travelling to her lover's home with suitcases full of clothes. The other half of her rejoiced, sang, celebrated the fact that she'd done it, actually* done it! *All the times she'd thought* Next argument, I'll tell him, *and* that's his last chance. *She was finally free to be happy.*

*She hated herself for lying though. As she'd walked down the hall towards Jack's study, she'd promised herself that she would do what she could to make it painless for the both of them, but that she would also be totally honest with him. But as soon as she'd seen him looking at her, the journal open in his hands, she'd become dejected. As quickly as she could get the words out of her mouth, Maggie had told him that she'd had enough, and that she was going to stay at a friend's until he had finished reading that damned book. She'd told him that she would have her mobile phone with her, and that, when he had finished working they could sort things out then. She'd left his study before he'd had the chance to respond.*

*Maggie got off the bus and walked to Rob's flat. She frowned as she saw the red car parked in front of Rob's, blocking it in the drive. Puzzled, she carried her bags up to the front door and rang the bell.*

*She waited for a few moments and was reaching for the bell again when the door was opened.*

*Rob looked drawn and pale – looked, for the first time since she'd known him, his age. He held a cigarette by his side, and Maggie saw that his hand was shaking severely. He looked upset.*

*Feeling her joy fading quickly, she tried to recapture it by pointing to her suitcases. "I've finally done it, Rob." Her smile failed as she saw his lack of response.*

*He managed a wan smile and stepped aside, dropping the cigarette onto the pavement. "That's real good, Maggie," he said, picking up her suitcases. He nodded inside. "You'd better go in, honey."*

*Frowning again and feeling unusually nervous, she stepped*

*through the door. Rob followed her in and left the suitcases by the door, closing it with his foot.*

*"We've got a visitor."*

*With thoughts of Jack having beaten her, Maggie walked down the hall, ready to finally face the music. She pushed the door open and looked at the figure seated on the sofa. The relief that she should have felt at not seeing her husband wasn't there. If possible, she felt even worse.*

*She blew smoke out of her lungs and looked steadily at Maggie, getting gracefully to her feet. "Hello, Mum."*

*Maggie knew that Rob had joined her in the doorway, but his presence did nothing to comfort her. Unable to speak, all she could do was look at her daughter.*

*"So, you've left Dad?" The hurt and anger were plain in her voice.*

*Maggie nodded.*

*"Does he know about Rob? Does he know you're here?" She already knew the answer.*

*Tears falling down her cheeks, Maggie looked at the floor and shook her head.*

*Sarah nodded expectantly and walked past them out of the living room, without speaking. The front door opened and closed quietly.*

*Realisation set in, and Maggie sank to the floor and cried.*

# Chapter Twenty-Four

She drove down the narrow roads, mindful of the ditches on either side, keeping her speed slow. It was all slowly being planned in her mind, everything almost worked out. She'd followed him for the past four days, working out his routines. At first she thought about killing him on his way back from work, and although the routes he took were secluded enough at that time of night if anyone saw her car they would probably remember it. So she'd decided on the stretch of wood that he hunted in: it seemed like the perfect place. Now she just needed to put the finishing touches to it all.

Pulling out of the junction, Sarah saw a police car pull someone over, and a grin surfaced. When she had passed, she watched them out of her rear-view mirror, and then had to pull over onto the side of road herself the smile falling from her face.

Her car. *Her car!* Sarah's hands were shaking as she switched off the ignition, and she kept her eyes trained on the mirror, watching the police car. Now that the idea had occurred to her, she expected to be followed instantly.

How could she have been so stupid? She'd been so careful – changing addresses, moving to the other side of town. But she'd failed to cover the obvious. If Jack Daniels knew the details of her car, all he had do to was put it on the system and she'd be screwed!

Realising that it could look a little suspicious if she stayed where she was, Sarah started the engine again and drove away, watching in her mirrors until the police car was out of sight. Even when she could no longer see it, she still couldn't relax. She was expecting to be caught at every turn of the road.

When she got home, she parked her car around the back of the building instead of the front. She was now expecting a battalion of police officers, led of course by Jack Daniels, to walk around the corner and arrest her.

Quickly, she walked to the newsagents and bought the two local papers. At home, she grabbed the pages that were filled with adverts of cars for sale and disregarded the rest.

She saw two adverts that looked ideal and, using her mobile phone, began to make arrangements.

An hour later, she was knocking on the door of a semi-detached house, sunglasses covering her eyes. It opened and a young man, no older than eighteen, stood looking at her. Well, looking at her cleavage.

Amused, Sarah smiled. "I'm Serena Davis. I rang about the car."

He looked up, a red fever sweeping up his face, and rubbed the back of his neck. Flustered, he pointed to the car on the road. "I'll go and get the keys."

Still smiling, Sarah walked back to the road and looked at the car without any real interest, but she *did* look – if she bought it without barely a glance it could look a little odd.

It was a light-blue B reg Escort, and she was surprised that it was still standing. With all the rust that was creeping upwards from underneath, it looked as though the only thing holding it together was the flaky paint. The seats were in bad condition, almost worn through to the stuffing in places, and cigarette burns everywhere. Even with two months MOT left on it and four months tax, it wasn't worth the hundred and fifty pounds he was asking for it, but for convenience sake it was worth that and more.

Five minutes later, having asked a few questions just to make it look sincere, Sarah sat behind the wheel, her receipt and two sections of the V5 form on the seat beside her. She'd wound the window down, hoping that the air outside would take away the musty smell. Strangely curious about what would happen, she started the car.

The loud backfire she'd expected didn't happen, and she was

pleasantly surprised. Yet it was still a relief to know that she wouldn't be driving it for long.

The ride home took a little longer than necessary, but Sarah wasn't too sure about the brakes and had no urge to find out if they would work in an emergency. Glad that the short ride was over, she pulled into the parking space next to her other car.

When she got out – images of the door falling off as she pushed to open it – she stood in front of both cars, comparing them. One old, one new (well, fairly); one almost entirely eaten by rust, the other without a speck on it. It was really unthinkable that she was seriously contemplating choosing the rust-bucket over her own.

With a shake of her head, she made a quick trip to her room and grabbed the bag that she had prepared earlier. Hurrying back down the stairs the bottles of alcohol clinked together inside the carry-all.

Inside her own car, realising that she could still smell the musty stink from the Escort, she checked her bag and its contents, taking her mobile phone out and putting it in the door's side-compartment.

She'd planned it all out, and had picked out the best place to go – somewhere quiet, but not completely deserted, with a small but powerful stream nearby. Before driving out of town, Sarah stopped at a cash machine. For the second time that day, she withdrew three hundred pounds, not quite sure why, just following her instincts.

She drove for half an hour, sticking mainly to back roads, feeling comfortable with the reactions of the car. It was going to be difficult for her to get used to driving the Escort.

On a blind bend, Sarah stopped the car and got out. From the bag she took out the bottle of vodka and the half-empty bottle of whiskey. The vodka, she just dropped into the passenger side foot well, glad when the glass didn't break. She opened the whiskey and took one last mouthful from it – purely as a bit of

Dutch courage – then poured what was left over the seats, dropping the open bottle into the driver's foot well.

She put her mobile phone into her jeans pocket, and took the second-to-last item out of the bag, swinging the bag onto her shoulder.

Using the button, she pushed the blade of the retractable knife out, squinting as the sun reflected off the metal and directly into her eyes. Leaning back into the car, she held the blade next to the skin of her hand.

Gently, much too gently to break the skin, she moved the knife over the fleshy pad of her hand, her stomach clenching at the idea of pain. She tried again, pressing a little harder, but she still couldn't bear to do it. She thought about all the people she'd killed, trying to summon up the hate she'd felt for them, trying to invoke a reaction within herself, trying to work herself up to do it. She nearly managed it – she actually made a slight cut before losing her nerve.

Just as she was telling herself that it didn't matter, that her plan would work without the blood, a car drove by, the driver blasting his horn and, not surprisingly, Sarah jumped. The blade of the knife was thrust forwards, not across her skin as she'd planned, but *into* her hand.

She screamed in surprise as well as in pain, and she didn't hear the driver cursing her for parking next to a blind corner as he drove off. She felt dizzy as she removed the blade from her hand, not because of the blood, but because of the pain. But her mind was still functioning properly. Before too much blood was wasted, Sarah stuck her hand back into the car, and rubbed her bleeding hand across the seatbelt and dashboard and then held her hand over the side of the door, ignoring the stinging as best as she could.

As soon as she was satisfied, she walked around the bend and up the road a little, in the direction of the nearby rivulet, moving purposefully from side to side, her hand held out as if for balance, blood dripping onto the road.

Moving onto a public footbath that stretched across an empty field towards the river, she walked another couple of yards and then stopped. She swung her bag from her shoulder, still holding her hand out. When a decent sized puddle of blood had formed on the ground, Sarah took the first aid kit from the bag. Using a large plaster and covering it with a tightly-bound bandage, she dressed her wound. It stung like hell, and blood was already seeping out from beneath the plaster, soaking into the bandage. Still it was better than nothing.

Following the trail of blood, she went back to her car and unwound the driver's side window. She leant in the open door, checked that the gear stick was in first and took off the handbrake. Then she got out and closed the door.

Her head swam momentarily as she walked to the back of her car, resting against it, eyes closed. Breathing slowly, she felt began to feel normal again and after a moments rest she started to push against the car, fighting the sickness that tried to overpower her. After the initial effort, the vehicle started to move smoothly.

As the car went down the steep ditch, Sarah had to stand quickly, again fighting dizziness, to avoid falling flat on her back. She had an idea that if she did that, she'd never get back up again.

When the car had stopped moving, Sarah saw that both doors had jammed shut, the passenger side on a rock and the driver's side on the incline of the ditch. Carefully she worked her way down the ditch, trying to maintain control over her weakening body. She moved awkwardly through the open window, feeling claustrophobic as soon as her whole body was inside. It took a lot of courage to close the window, to shut herself inside completely, but she managed it. Stealing herself against the noise, she used her elbow to smash the glass. Before climbing out, she tapped out as much glass from the window as she could, but still managed to cut her hands a couple of times as she boosted herself out.

She walked the way she had driven, in the opposite direction to the trail of blood, leaving the car behind her, hoping that it would look to the police as it looked to her. The midday sun started to press down hard on her.

For over an hour, Sarah walked under the June sun, passing under any shade when possible. She skirted by two small villages, not stopping. By the time she reached the third, which she was sure was a safe enough distance away from her 'accident', her head was pounding, her body ached, but she wasn't really feeling any of it – her body didn't seem to belong to her anymore. In a daze, she stumbled to the first person she saw.

His strength was tested almost immediately away. The middle-aged man barely managed to catch her as she collapsed forward, the beagle he'd been walking barking excitedly at his ankles. A crowd of people quickly gathered, and an ambulance was soon on its way.

She woke up in a hospital bed, and for a moment had no idea why she could possibly be in a hospital. As she concentrated, hazy half-formed images of walking down roads came to her. Her left hand was sore, and she was shocked to find herself hooked up to an IV drip. Her heart was beginning to race, and she glanced around the room she was in. Across the room, near the window, stood a woman in a nurses uniform.

She looked up and saw Sarah looking at her, and smiled. Instead of relaxing her, for some reason Sarah felt more anxious. Especially when the nurse addressed her by name.

"Hi, Sarah. How are you feeling?" She walked over and perched on the edge of the bed.

Throat feeling sore, Sarah could only speak in a whisper. "How'd you know my name?"

"You were talking in your sleep. Most of what you said was

garbled, but we managed to get your first name."

The idea that she had talked in her sleep, that she could have said *anything*, took Sarah's fear to a whole new level.

Without seeing any of what Sarah was going through, the nurse gently patted Sarah's right hand before standing. "I'll go and get the doctor. He said he wanted a word when you came around."

Sarah was left alone, too many thoughts buzzing around her head. Just thinking about what she could have said made her feel sick. She could have woken up in handcuffs instead of just the hospital's identification bands. A more frightening thought came to her – she might not have woken up *at all*. It could have all ended there.

The nurse returned with a doctor, and he started asking questions about what had happened. Sarah played dumb, simply saying that she couldn't remember.

The nurse smiled sympathetically while the doctor looked unconvinced, but he didn't press her any further. Under his supervision, the IV was removed, and Sarah was allowed a small drink of iced water to refresh her throat.

"We're going to keep you in for a few days, Sarah, to make sure that you and your baby are okay."

Sarah nodded in response, but with no intention of staying in the hospital.

*Jack was impressed, there was no denying it. The blood leading away from the car had been the thing to convince him. He'd believed the same as everyone else, that she'd been drinking while driving and had severely misjudged the bend, had gone into the ditch, then wandered off in a daze. And the possibility that she had wandered to the nearby stream and been carried away was widely accepted. The one thing that he had disagreed with his colleagues about was the assumption that she was dead.*

*But the idea that she had been in the hospital, in easy reach, made him angry. If a proper search had been done then they might have been able to stop her from killing four more people. They might even have been able to stop her from killing herself.*

*And it was that last that really upset him; that Sarah's life might have been saved.*

*"She came around to tell me to stay away from you." He had his arm around her shoulders as they sat on the sofa, trying to calm her.*

*"She's got no right to, though," Maggie said without commitment.*

*Rob laughed, beginning to feel better, just because Maggie was in his arms again. "Maggie, she's your daughter. You've been cheating on her father, with his so-called best mate no less, so she's understandably angry. She's trying to protect her family. And, she's scared that you'll get hurt.* That's *her right."*

*Maggie was getting ready to reply, when a voice interrupted, coming from the living room door.*

*"He's pretty perceptive." Sarah walked into the room, almost smiling herself when she saw Rob remove his arm from her mother's shoulders, like a couple of kids caught fooling around. Then she remembered that this was her* mum *and her mum's bit on the side, and the inclination to smile left very suddenly.*

*"Where'd you go?"*

*Sarah was stunned at the scared trapped animal look in her eyes. It didn't take a genius to work out what her mum was scared of. "No," she said sitting on the chair opposite them both. "I haven't told Dad."*

*The relief on her mum's face, and on Rob's, was obvious. But she couldn't share it. "I wanted to. I phoned him, but the line was engaged." She rose again, unable to stand seeing her mum with Rob. "I'm gonna go."*

*Maggie watched her get up, smiling nervously, beginning to feel slightly more relaxed again.*

*At the door, she turned and looked at her mum, needing to say something but knowing that it would change their relationship completely, that she'd never be able to take it back.*

*"I'm not proud of you, Mum." Before she could truly see the look of pain on her mother's face, she turned again and walked away.*

In the taxi, she brought the knife out of her bag and cut off the two identity bracelets from her wrists, feeling better as they fell away. It had been easy to walk out of the hospital.

Her hand, patched up and bandaged properly, started to throb, and she wished she'd gotten some painkillers before she'd left. But she could deal with it with another type of painkiller.

The taxi dropped her off in town, a couple of miles away from the hospital, and she walked along unfamiliar streets, until she came across a taxi office.

It would have been easier to stay in the first car, but she didn't want to risk the driver recognising her and then being able to tell the police where she lived. Better to be cautious. When she told the woman with the headset on behind the counter where she wanted to go, the woman asked her if she was joking.

"No, I'm not joking."

"It's easily a fifty-minute ride."

Sarah thought of telling the obnoxious, arrogant woman with the headset on that it was, at most, a forty-minute ride, but decided against it. It probably wasn't the best way to keep a low profile. "That's not a problem."

The simple response seemed to annoy her, and she turned her back on Sarah. "Sit down. I'll see if anyone's available."

Sarah smiled as she sat on the uncomfortable plastic chair, wondering if the drivers would also have problems with communication, or if maybe they had gone on attitude adjustment courses.

Still not turning back to face her, the woman called over to her. "Someone will be here in quarter of an hour."

Sarah thought about doing something childish, like making faces behind the woman's back. Instead, she pleasantly said, "Thank you."

After what seemed like hours of looking around the barren walls, but was only twenty-five minutes, a driver finally walked in.

"Call for me, Sheila?"

"Her." She pointed over at Sarah, and then resumed working on her crossword puzzle.

Sarah stood as the bloke walked over to her.

"You the one going to Moss?" His tone was perfectly friendly and, more importantly, his eyes showed nothing that worried her.

She nodded, stood and followed him outside. She sat in the passenger seat and looked straight at the windscreen, focussing on the glass. Not wanting to complicate things but needing to know, she concentrated on his ghostly reflection. After a few moments with no change, she dropped her eyes and relaxed into her seat.

"Don't worry about Godzilla. She can be a little off sometimes."

Sarah was shocked into laughter. "That's her 'off'? Christ, I'd hate to see her in a bad mood."

They laughed together, and Sarah became afraid of his friendly glances, afraid that he may recognise her if asked. From her bag, she got her sunglasses and put them on.

She was dropped off ten minutes away from the room she now lived in, and paid the fare, adding a twenty-pound tip. The idea that he was just as likely to remember her for her generosity didn't occur to her.

When the cabbie was out of sight she began to walk home, wanting to get back so she could take a couple of aspirin with a drink of vodka to try and kill the pain that had become a permanent resident in her hand. Just as she was walking into the car park, coming towards the building from behind, she saw the man from downstairs leaving on his bike. Instead of going straight up to her room, she went to his. As it had been on her last visit, the door was unlocked.

She opened it and walked in, the stink twice as bad as it had been last time. Looking at the boxes stacked underneath the window, she noticed that another couple had been added.

Braver than she had been on her first expedition into the jungles of his room, she walked deeper inside, trying to block out from her mind all of the different things that she could be walking on. Maggots were crawling over everything, but she tried not to think of them bursting under her feet, feeling more than a little queasy.

Lying on the floor in one corner was his air rifle, and Sarah picked it up, her fingers brushing against something furry underneath, revulsion making her cringe away. She was fighting the sickness as she looked at the floor underneath her feet, so she was too busy to notice the figure that stood in the doorway.

"Who are you?"

Sarah whirled around guiltily as he began to walk towards her.

In her bedroom, waiting for the dark to descend, Sarah sat on her bed. She'd had a shower, trying to wash away the feeling of things crawling over her skin as well as washing away his blood, and her wet hair hung down the back of her T-shirt. It was clinging to her back, but that was unimportant. She looked at the air rifle that stood in the corner behind the door.

Her plan to get him in the middle of the woods had gone completely awry – she'd really had no choice. He'd gone at her, it had been self-defence. She'd just swung at him, and the butt of the rifle had connected with his head, and he'd just collapsed.

So now she had to wait, wait for it to get darker, so that she could move him. It was a risk, leaving him there alone – if he came around while she was upstairs moping, he could call the police, and that would be that. But she really had no choice – it was more of a risk to try and move him in daylight. And there was no way that she was willing to stay in that room with him.

Half a bottle of vodka had helped her calm down, but she was still on edge while waiting for the sun to go down. The sky grew darker and she felt her courage beginning to return, helped by the vodka she had consumed. The pain in her hand had decreased to a low continuous throbbing, which also made her feel a little better.

Taking her small cosmetic mirror with her, she walked back downstairs to his room. The door was closed as she'd left it, and she opened it slowly.

Her fears of him jumping out at her proved to be inaccurate. He was still lying where he'd fallen, and Sarah was sickened as she saw maggots crawling over him, as if he were already dead. She quickly walked in and closed the door behind her. Squatting down, her fingers went onto his neck, and she was relieved to find his pulse was strong and regular. She didn't want him to die yet and spoil all of her fun.

As soon as she was sure that it was all clear, she walked outside and brought the rusty car around to the main doors. She switched off the ignition and opened the boot, noticing the musty smell was worse at the back.

Hoping that no one would come out and interfere, she rushed back to his room. Grabbing him under the armpits, she managed to drag him along the hall and outside. Using every ounce of strength she had, she hoisted him up and into the boot, bending his legs so that he was completely inside. She rested her hand in her pocket and felt the mirror. It occurred to her that she didn't know if he was evil or not, didn't know if he truly deserved it or not. She opened the boot again and held the mirror out, capturing the reflection of his face in the glass.

It wasn't really a relief when the image began to distort and change, she realised that it was all too late anyway – she had gone into another person's home, and then used his own rifle to knock him out, self-defence or not.

However, she was looking at an image of a drowned man. His

features remained the same, he still looked like himself. But he also looked as though he'd been submerged in water for a long time. His skin had loosened, and had bleached almost completely white. Bruises, bright purple compared to the whiteness of his flesh, were obvious around his neck and eyes. As Sarah watched, a maggot crawled out of his mouth. She brought the mirror away and started to close the boot again when she saw the maggot crawling over the back of his neck. Hurriedly, she slammed the boot down.

Slowly, so as not to make too much noise, she drove away from the building. Getting onto the main road, she was glad that she hadn't waited any longer. There were enough cars so that she didn't feel too conspicuous, and few enough so that she didn't feel too crowded.

The only time she did feel vulnerable was in the supermarket car park. At eleven at night, it was almost deserted, and although she needed to make sure that no one would interrupt her, she still found it unnerving.

She stopped at the far end of the car park, parking across three spaces, and turned off the engine. As she got out of the driver's side door, leaving the key in the ignition, she contemplated letting him out. But her mind flashed her the image of the reflection, followed swiftly by an image of the stacked boxes. Standing behind the boot, she thought that she heard movement from inside, maybe a cough. But even if she had, what was she going to do? Let him out for a bit of fresh air?!

Using her other keys, she pressed down on the paintwork. Knowing it was stupid, especially after everything that she had put herself through to try to convince people that she was dead, that it would only attract attention to his murder, Sarah wrote her trademark. There were more movements from inside, but she finished and walked away.

By the time Pete came around properly and realised that he was in a lot of trouble, Sarah had walked halfway home. It was dark and there was no one around to hear him banging against the metal coffin that he was in.

By the time she got back, her hand was throbbing again, and she was feeling really light-headed. After making sure that her door was locked, she had a few mouthfuls of vodka to ease the pain in her hand and collapsed onto the bed. A few seconds later she was sound asleep.

For the first time in her life, Sarah was aware of the fact that she was dreaming.

She was kneeling beneath the limbs of the tree in front of her parents' graves, moonlight filtering through the leaves, a slow strobe effect moving on the ground. The reason she knew that she was dreaming was because of the fear that stirred in her when she was looking at the graves. In all the years since their deaths she had never felt scared by them. *For* them and for herself, yes, but never scared *of* them. She tried to get up, to walk away, but her legs refused to obey. Instead, all she could do was to look at the stones in front of her.

Movement to her left caught her attention, but she couldn't move her head for a better look. All she could see was darkness in the moonlight, and trying to track whatever it was from the corner of her eyes was making her head hurt. It was coming closer, and Sarah was finally able to define its shape.

It was Jack Daniels, and he walked over to her, also gazing at the gravestones, looking at them in sorrow. Without glancing at her once, he took a wallet from his jacket pocket and removed a cash-card from it, which he dropped into her lap. "It won't be long now."

Her hands moved of their own accord, and soon held the card up before her face. It was hers; she saw, her own bankcard. At first, Sarah thought he meant that it wouldn't be long before she was caught.

As she gazed at it the card disappeared from her hands, and

she found that she could move her head to look at Jack who know held her cash-card again. A large amount of anger welled up inside as she saw him bending the card repeatedly until it snapped.

"Soon it will be useless." The card was miraculously fixed when he dropped it again into her lap, before disappearing.

Still puzzled, Sarah looked back at the headstones to find that they had been replaced by cash cards standing on their sides. Simultaneously, they cracked open and exploded outwards, and Sarah screamed as maggots were propelled towards her.

She awoke quickly, jumped from her bed and ran down the hall to the shared bathroom. Barely making it, she knelt before the toilet (images of kneeling before her parents' graves momentarily appearing) and was sick. She knocked her injured hand against the bowl and was immediately sick again as pain flooded her body.

She plodded back to her room and got some clean clothes from her bags and went straight back to the bathroom. It felt so good to strip out of the sweat-absorbed clothes that she'd spent the night in.

Although the sun had only just risen in the sky, it was warm already and Sarah knew that it was going to be the hottest day of the summer so far. She wondered briefly how Pete would be feeling, locked inside the metal container, feeling it warm up bit by bit. The idea made her feel queasy again, so she pushed it away.

After finishing the bottle of vodka and lighting up the first cigarette of the day, she went to the shop and bought the local paper.

Within fifteen minutes of getting home, Sarah had arranged to view a G reg white Polo, and a one-bedroom self-contained flat. She went to the toilet, her heart skipping a beat as she saw the few specks of blood in her knickers. But she came to the conclusion that it couldn't be anything to worry about – just a little bit of blood, that was all.

It did put the pregnancy in the front of her mind, and as soon as she got back into her room, she rang the Grande Hotel, hoping to speak to Lenny.

*Like all of the dreams she'd written about, Jack felt uneasy. How had she known? How had she known days, weeks, months, before things happened? And why was it always Jack telling her what was going on?*

*For a moment he thought about leaving the bits about him 'helping' her out of his notes – some people could think that he* really had *helped her. In their minds, it could certainly explain how she'd avoided capture for so long. In addition, Sarah was dead, couldn't be prosecuted, and it was always handy to have a scapegoat. But he knew that he wouldn't leave it out, leave* anything *out. Not that it had anything to do with doing his job – as far as he was concerned it had never been* just *about his job. As strange as it seemed, Jack found that he had a lot of respect for her. And it was out of that respect that he would keep everything in his report. For some reason, he felt like he owed her something.*

*He also felt uneasy about her drinking and its effect on the baby's health, even though he knew the outcome. He wanted to be able to warn her, to help her. Was she even aware that she was drinking excessively? Did she think that there was nothing wrong with it? Jack didn't think that either of those were right. As far as he could see, she just didn't think about it, didn't acknowledge her drinking at all.*

*Walking slowly to the kitchen, he wondered when his respect for Sarah had started to grow, and ignored the silence within the house.*

*It was midnight, yet the curtains had not been closed, and the darkness filled the outside world. The kitchen was clean, but not because Jack had tidied. He just hadn't used anything that needed cleaning.*

*His body tried once more to tell him that he had to eat, but his brain failed to hear it. It tried to tell him that it had been days since he'd eaten, that filling up on coffee and the odd drink of whiskey wasn't nourishing enough, but thoughts of Sarah were drowning everything else out.*

*With his coffee made (and a dash of whiskey added), he looked out of the window, peering into the garden.*

*He switched the outside light on and unlocked the back door. Walking outside, he suffered a huge sense of déjà vu. The day that he and Rob had gone to see Sarah about Serena's suicide he'd walked around Sarah's garden, trying to get a bit of inspiration.*

*Looking at his garden now, it dawned on him that he'd gotten more than a* bit *of inspiration – it was an exact copy of Sarah's, only scaled down to fit the available space. Cup in hand, he walked around the garden, looking at it the way he'd looked at hers, seeing things exactly as he'd seen hers that day.*

*Although Maggie had only been gone for a few hours, in Jack's mind, for the time being at least, she had ceased to exist.*

# Chapter Twenty-Five

He dropped the plates into the sink, most of the kitchen staff jumping as they heard the china smash. And those that weren't already, started to smile as soon as Lenny started to swear.

"Fucking stuck-up arsehole wankers!" He made no attempt to keep his voice low.

Joe untied his apron and slipped it off. Still watching and listening to Lenny, he hung it up on the peg next to the hand sinks. He then gave instructions to a couple of his staff before striding over to the waiter.

"What the hell—" Lenny said as the chef wrapped his big dark hand around the back of Lenny's neck and herded him roughly outside the back door, not responding to the waiter's half-formed question.

In the enclosed yard, Joe dropped his hand from Lenny and walked over to one of the brick walls and leant against it, his arms crossed across his chest simply looking at him.

After a few seconds of silence Lenny threw his hands up in the air in frustration. "What?!"

"What the hell was that about in there?"

He sounded calm and if he hadn't known Joe for so long Lenny might have assumed that it was only an excuse for a skive. But five years was a long time, and there wasn't much that they didn't know about each other. "What was what about?"

"That shit in the kitchen. Who's pissed you off?" He smiled but those who knew Joe as Lenny did would have recognised it as the first sign that he was losing his patience.

"Just the same old shit. I just can't deal with people looking down their noses at me, that's all." He turned away from the chef.

Joe nodded, knowing, perhaps better than Lenny himself, what it was *really* all about. "You haven't spoken to her yet, have you?"

Lenny whirled around, his face filled with thunder, ready to start shouting that he didn't know what the hell Joe was talking about. But the look of honest compassion and concern on his face robbed him of all the aggression. "No. I've come close to ringing a couple of times, but I can't. If she's gonna stop drinking, she's got to do it herself. I can't do it for her."

Below his white hair, Joe's forehead creased in concentration. "She rang yesterday morning. I wasn't sure I should tell you, but now I figure its better you know before you decide anything." He smiled, before adding, "And, I don't think the staff's nerves can deal with you like this." Lightly, Joe pushed himself off the wall, patting Lenny's arm as he passed. Before re-entering the kitchen, he turned back, his smile now completely genuine. "You know, Len, you look a little pale, a little off colour. Food hygiene and all that, I think you'd better go home." He dropped a sly wink. "Probably turn out to be a forty-eight hour thing. You'd better collect your stuff and get off home."

Feeling off balance, Lenny watched as his boss and friend walked back towards the inside. After a few seconds, with things finally straightening out in his head, Lenny walked back through the door, turning left and walking away from the kitchens. In the staff cloakroom, he quickly got his things together, changed out of his uniform and dumped it into the laundry chute. The hotel had its own staff laundry, which suited Lenny fine – the less washing he had to do the better.

In his jeans and T-shirt, Lenny left the hotel via the tradesman entrance. As soon as he was far enough away, he slowed his walking down and lit a cigarette. He took his mobile out from his pocket and flipped the case open. He dialled Sarah's number, and his finger hovered over the button with the picture of a green receiver.

Not sure what he could say, he flipped the casing down and put it back into his pocket. He continued walking, taking no notice of where he was going.

As he had for the last few weeks, he replayed the last time they'd been together, how angry he'd been and how scared and upset she'd looked. His mind kept bringing up the image of those nine bottles lying on the bed, seeing them so clearly that he could almost read the writing on the labels. He kept seeing them no matter where he went, no matter what he looked at, no matter what he did.

Approaching her house, Lenny first though it was an illusion – surely he couldn't have walked over here after all, not without being aware of it. As he neared, he was forced to admit that it had to be real, because there was no way he could have thought *this* one up!

Police tape encircled the front of the property; uniformed and plain-clothed police officers walked around, going inside, coming outside, some taking photographs.

If Lenny had gone with his first instinct and gone over to ask what was going on, things would have turned out a lot differently. He even took a few steps towards the house, but then carried on his way. Whatever it was, he rationalised, he doubted that it could have anything to do with Sarah – she just wasn't the sort to get into any major trouble – and he didn't want to waste their time when they all looked so busy.

Walking away, he didn't see the plain-clothes officer with the big build and short dark hair watching him.

It was a small room, nothing special, but Sarah spent ten minutes cleaning it as best she could. The rifle she had taken from her late neighbour stood propped up against the wall next to the door. And, apart from her journal on the desk, TV and few things that she needed to make the coffees, there was nothing else in sight.

She filled the kettle up and switched it on. While it boiled, she looked around the room again, and relaxed when she saw nothing out of place.

Her eyes *did* focus on something that really should have been hidden, but as she got up to hide it, the knock on the door took all thoughts of the journal from her mind. Butterflies fluttered in her stomach as she walked to the door and opened it.

He hadn't changed at all, and Sarah felt close to tears. In the instant she saw him, all the hurt came back, and her heart began to ache. She hadn't realised how much she needed him until he was standing in front of her again. Not totally sure of how to act, she simply opened the door a little wider and stepped aside.

Lenny also realised how much Sarah needed him. He looked at her clothes and wondered when it was that she had last washed them. Her face was pale, her eyes sunken in the doughy flesh, and was covered in spots. She looked tired and drawn, and there was a bandage on her left hand. The last thing he focussed on was her hair, lank and greasy hanging around her face, but at least it gave him something to say.

"You've dyed your hair. It suits you."

Self-consciously, Sarah put a hand to it, closing the door with the other. "It doesn't look brilliant, but it's not too bad. Do you want a coffee?"

He nodded and watched as she walked over to the desk, and began making the drinks. "So, what's happening over at the house?"

Smiling, Sarah turned to him for a second, not losing her stride. "I'm not too sure. All I know is that it's something to do with the owners." She turned back to what she was doing. "The cops asked me a few questions. You know, had I seen them, had they had any packages delivered, had I noticed anyone watching the house, that sort of thing. But nothing that really gave me any details."

Even though it was right next to her, Sarah didn't see the journal. Lenny had captured her full attention. She picked up the cups and walked over to him. She handed him one, and then sat on the bed next to him.

"How have you been?" Part of her wanted him to say he'd

been okay, but most of her wanted him to utter some cliché about how he'd been lost without her.

Lenny shrugged. "I've survived." He heard the hardness in his own voice, and forced himself to soften it. "I've missed you," he added simply, refusing to look at her.

"I've missed you, too," she said in a choked sob.

He wanted to put his arms around her, but wouldn't allow himself to weaken. If he did, he would be powerless to make it clear that she had to change, and he wasn't about to lose the opportunity. Instead, he got up and walked over to the window, the journal with all of her secrets within only inches from him. "So, who found you this place?" He looked back at her with a smile.

It was what she needed, and she gratefully smiled back. "Short term. I had to move out of the house in a hurry. I'm moving into my new place today though, if you fancy helping me."

"Where is it?" He tried to sound offhand, but inside he was glad. He couldn't imagine her living in this shithole much longer – he'd only been there for two minutes and he was sure that he'd been bitten by something.

"Just up the road. It's more money, but I'll have my own bathroom, so it's worth every penny." She had, in fact, already paid six months up front.

A silence developed between them, both of them drinking their coffees, and an atmosphere began to form. As hard as it was for him to admit, there were still too many questions that hadn't been answered yet for them to simply fall back into the relationship. After a few minutes he had to break the silence. "Why'd you ring me, Sarah?"

She turned to look at him. She had been practicing ever since she had found him, rehearsing the different ways that she could tell him, but with him there, all of her speeches had just fallen out of her head. "I'm pregnant, Lenny."

It sunk in straight away, but he couldn't react, not because he wasn't pleased but because he was surprised – they'd been careful. He could tell by her face that she was waiting for him to react, *needed* him to react. He raked his hand through his hair, shaking slightly. "Wow."

Sarah laughed nervously. "Yeah, that's pretty much what I said." She got up and took both of the empty cups to the desk.

Watching her, Lenny crossed his legs at the ankles, hitting something that was hidden under the bed and recognised the clinking of several bottles. It summoned up the old anger at her, but he also felt disappointed. Although he had expected it, he hadn't wanted it to be true. "Are you still drinking, smoking?"

She turned quickly, and Lenny saw a blush creeping up her cheeks, making her look ill as well as guilty. Sarah turned her back on him again, swiping at her tears with the palm of her hand. "Smoking, yeah, but I'm cutting down gradually."

It was obvious that she was lying, but Lenny wondered if she was lying to the both of them rather than just to him. "How much are you drinking, Sarah?" he asked, trying to remain calm.

Again, she whirled around, her blush instantly confining itself to the areas above her cheekbones, as she shouted at him. "I told you, I'm not drinking anymore!"

"No?" He deliberately kicked the bottles under the bed. "So, if I was to look under here I wouldn't find any bottles, or hip flasks, or anything?"

Colour was filling her face again, and she shook her head. "I'm just going to go to the shop," she said, walking to the door. "I need some more milk for the coffees." She walked out without looking back at Lenny, slamming the door behind her.

He heard her footsteps walking down the hall, and then descending the stairs. After a few moments he heard the main door swinging shut. As soon as he was sure that she was gone, he knelt before the bed and looked underneath. He sighed as he saw the half a dozen bottles hidden there.

Hands curled involuntarily into fists, he turned on the small television set, hoping to find something that could help him to relax. Instead, all he could find was the news, and he left it on for a touch of background noise so that he wasn't in a totally silent room.

Feeling thirsty, he walked over to the desk and put the kettle on once more. Looking down he saw the white leather-bound book and read the two words that were printed upon it. He was reaching for it when he heard the words that the newsreader was saying.

"The search for Sarah Caroline Fletcher, the twenty-one-year-old suspected of being involved in numerous murders, is being intensified today, police revealed, as her car was found crashed into a ditch."

Slowly, as if in a dream, Lenny turned to look at the TV in time to see a photograph of his girlfriend. Not for one moment did he doubt that it was her – the image was just too clear. Although he didn't want to, his mind turned back to that morning at the house; all of those officers, and he heard her speaking inside his head. *I'm not too sure. All I know is that it's something to do with the owners.* Suddenly he felt very sick.

"It is believed that she was drink-driving and tried to take a sharp corner too quickly. Although no body has yet been found, a significant amount of blood was found at the scene, and it is assumed that she has wandered away in a daze after the accident. Police are requesting that anyone with any information come forward as soon as possible, as Fletcher may be severely injured and may need medical attention."

The newsreader went onto another topic, and Lenny found himself recalling the bandage on Sarah's hand. Feeling light-headed, he rested his hand on the desk, helping to support himself as best he could. His hand rested on the journal and he took hold of it. Releasing the desk, he walked back over to the bed and sat down, although it felt more like someone unpinning his legs. Hands shaking, he opened the book.

He scanned the pages, turning them quickly, but not quickly enough. He was so engrossed in what he was reading that he didn't hear the door downstairs close. Nor did he hear the footsteps walking along the hall, or them stop in front of the door.

Startled, he looked up as the door opened, not even thinking about hiding the book. He'd been scared before, but the feeling that consumed him as Sarah walked in went far beyond scared.

As Sarah stepped through, she kicked over the air rifle and bent over to pick it up, not looking at Lenny. Holding it with her finger outside the trigger guard, she stood up and finally looked over at him.

His blue-grey eyes were huge in his face, and she saw that he'd been crying, tear tracks marking his skin. He was looking, she saw, not at her but at the gun she held, and that was when she noticed that *he* was also holding something.

"Sarah?" It was whispered, barely audible.

"What are you doing, Lenny?" Her question was also whispered, but not for the same reason. While he was scared, Sarah was beginning to get angry, her hand gripping the gun getting tighter. Nor was her question important. It was blatantly obvious what he was doing. The only important thing was what he now knew. And she wasn't that good at lying to herself – it was clear that he knew what she'd done, she could see it on his face.

"Why, Sarah?" His tears were falling more freely now. "Jesus Christ, Sarah, why'd you kill that little girl?" Again, he was only half-aware that he'd spoken aloud.

Sarah raised the gun in an empty threat, resting the butt of it on her shoulder. "Put the book down, Lenny, *please*."

Even though he had a gun aimed at him he couldn't drop the book. It was as if his fear had chased away all of his common sense. "How could you do it, Sarah?"

Tears streaming down her own face she squeezed the trigger, hoping that the empty click it would make would scare him. The recoil wasn't very bad, but in the state that she was in it was hard enough. The pellet that Pete had left in from his last hunting trip was thrown from the barrel with a soft pop, and a split-second later was embedded in Lenny's throat.

He wasn't thrown backwards violently, but he did shift backwards as it penetrated, and he dropped the journal to the floor. Automatically, his hands flew to his throat, feeling blood pour over his fingers.

His hands were around his throat, trying to hold in the blood that was flowing out of the hole, covering them with its sticky warmth.

He was looking at Sarah, saw her slowly lower the gun, completely stunned. He tried to open his mouth to tell her that it was all right, he knew that it had been an accident, that she hadn't meant it, but his mouth wouldn't follow orders. He could feel the pellet in his throat, burning like a lump of hot coal.

She was moving towards him slowly, as if wading in water as thick as tar, but his vision was getting worse, too much black snow was drifting in front of him. Before she could reach him, he collapsed backwards upon the bed.

Sarah began to panic, and rushed around packing her things.

*He'd been with John at the house, about half an hour after he'd had the vision of her in the garden, when the call had come in.*

*They'd been standing in the living room of the house that Sarah had occupied for months, and Jack had told John about the man he had seen, about how he had moved a few steps towards the house before changing his mind.*

*"I wish I'd chased him up," he'd said, but John had merely shaken his head.*

*"It would have been a waste of time, Jack, and we've got too much to think about to be chasing after unrealistic possibilities. We've got to*

*deal with the facts we've got, mate."*

*He'd started to reply, his instinct telling him it was a mistake not to go after the man he'd seen, when another plain-clothed officer walked over to them.*

*"We've had a report come in over the radio, John, and I think you'd better get over and take a look-see."*

*The three of them, leaving the house in the capable hands of the other officers, had taken a ride out to the local supermarket. The heat had been extraordinary, that was something else he remembered – it had been boiling.*

*When they had arrived, it hadn't taken long to pinpoint where they were supposed to be. Two uniformed officers were standing between a badly parked panda car and an even worse parked Ford Escort. A small crowd had formed and, while the officers were taking information from a couple of them, they seemed in no rush to disperse the rest.*

*They pulled up next to them, and Jack had gotten out of the car first and approached the two plods. The arrogant-looking twenty-two-year-old, that didn't seem to be doing much of anything, told Jack in a very ignorant way that it was police business and to push off. He'd blushed a very deep scarlet when Jack had flashed his badge.*

*After a few bumbled apologies from the kid, Jack had waved away the situation, and the small crowd of people, and had been filled in on the details.*

*The car had been parked there for two days, and a security tape had shown a dark-haired woman walking calmly away.*

*While walking past, a young couple had smelt something foul from within the car and reported it to the manager of the shop. The manager had then gone outside to investigate himself and had seen the engraving on the boot. He had called in the police immediately.*

*"Anyone opened the boot?"*

*The officer, losing the blush from his cheeks, had shaken his head. "We wanted to wait for forensics before we did anything."*

*Jack looked at John, a small grin on his face. "You feel like waiting?"*

*"Nah." His face had also opened in an identical smile. "Too damned*

*hot. Bust it open."*

*Jack had walked briskly around to the back of the car. "I'm gonna need something to bust the lock open with."*

*"Keys are in the ignition," John said, with an unbelieving shake of his head.*

*"Things keep getting better and better, don't they?"*

*The good humour he felt had disappeared within a second of the boot opening.*

*The heat had been bad, and the result was something that made Jack stagger back from the car. The heat billowed out, also forcing the built up gasses to be thrown out. It was the smell of rotted meat that had been boiled, but it wasn't the only reason that he had moved backwards.*

*What he'd seen had caused that. Pete's pale face had blistered extensively. His moustache covered a few of them, but there were too many elsewhere. Quite a few of them had burst and ruptured: a mixture of blood and pus covering the surrounding skin. The ruptured blisters had turned yellow, had hardened and cracked. His lips were dry and they had cracked severely, blood filling the crevices.*

*At his gasp, the other four officers had gathered around, all but one managing to keep their heads. The ignorant youngster hadn't been one of them – he'd moved away from the car, fallen to his knees and vomited.*

*With the photo of Pete Carter in his hand, it wasn't hard to go back to the moment when they had found him. He was completely there, could feel the sun on his back, and could smell the stench of the cooked body. Then he forced it away, yet sadly not too far.*

*Slowly, he began to replay the interviews with Chris Johnson, the young lad that had sold Sarah the car.*

They sat on the sofa, the boy's parents opposite with Chris off to one side.

"Can you remember what she looked like, Chris?" John asked, trying not to look at the boy's parents, and to remain looking at Chris.

Chris ran a hand through his soft fluffed-up light brown hair, using his finger to push his glasses further up the bridge of his nose. Yet the look on his face wasn't one of concentration, but of someone who is enjoying what he's remembering. "Red hair. She was wearing a pair of sunglasses. Pretty good figure." He smiled a little more than he meant to.

"Red hair? Are you sure it was red?"

Chris nodded at Jack. "Red. Dye-job, by the look." He missed the quick glance shared between the two officers. "Looked a bit too red, if you know what I mean."

They left shortly afterwards, both too excited to talk, too many thoughts and ideas rolling around their heads.

After driving halfway to the station, John turned to Jack. "So, we know it was her. And we know that she's dyed her hair."

Without saying anything, Jack nodded, negotiating the car along the road. They were close behind her, he knew it – he *felt* it.

Several officers walked into Pete Carter's old room at twelve minutes past six that evening. Neither Jack nor John were among them; they were busy doing a door-to-door. It was Jack's idea, just another thing that his instinct was commanding him to do.

On the first floor, after having no luck from anyone on the ground floor, Jack noticed one of the three doors was slightly ajar. After knocking and receiving no reply, he slowly pushed open the door.

The body was sprawled over the bed and Jack rushed over to it.

"Shit, Jack."

He turned around and saw John looking at a TV set that was near the door. Written on it, in what could only be the victim's blood, were two words: NOT EVIL.

Almost incredulously, Jack turned back to the corpse on the bed and got closer so that he could see the face. "Who are you?" he whispered and, in a way, he received an answer – he recognised him!

"From this morning," he said, turning back to John. "I recognise him from this morning. The bloke I was going to chase after, the bloke that looked as if he wanted to talk to us." He could hear the excitement in his own voice and knew that it was severely inappropriate.

"You're sure? It was him from this morning, no doubt?" John also sounded excited, but also uneasy.

He watched as Jack nodded, then continued, making it clear to himself. "So, she killed him, *this morning*, when most people at the station think she's dead. That's it, right?"

Jack whirled around, searching the small room with his eyes, half expecting to see her standing in the doorway. The he faced John again, exhilaration dancing in his eyes. "When did she go, John? Shit, we've only just missed her! Only by a few hours!" He looked back at the dead man on the bed.

"Hello?" Rob was out of breath, and stood in the hallway of his flat, with absolutely nothing on, even though it was still early evening.

"Rob. It's Jack." He was understandably worked up, and his voice showed it. Every word he spoke was barked. "She's still alive, Rob!"

His guilty conscience took a moment to step aside and allow Jack's words to sink in. "Alive? How…"

He had no way of finishing because they were suddenly a million questions to be asked, and he didn't know where to start: What had happened, how did Jack know, had anyone new been hurt? But the most important question had nothing to do with the job – how the hell could he have done that to this best mate?

"I don't know all the answers yet, Rob, but I do know that she's dyed her hair." He laughed shakily. "I think that's the only thing I *do* know." That laugh again, and then he began to focus once more. "Right, what I want you to do, Rob, since you're in the home town, is to go over all the files again. See if there's anything we might have missed."

"Anything in particular?" He was used to Jack ordering him around, so he didn't even notice it anymore. And even if he had, Rob wouldn't have minded. Not under the circumstances.

"I don't know."

A small silence, and Rob knew that Jack was going over everything in his head again, trying to find *something*, some small discrepancy.

"No, I don't know." This time a bit more sure. "But you could do me a huge favour. Tell Maggie I don't know when I'll be back. I've tried ringing, but she's not answering."

Like a snake, Rob's guilt reared up again, but he forced himself to sound normal. "I'll try and track her down." *Shouldn't be too difficult*, he added to himself.

"Cheers, Rob. You're a mate," Jack said and hung up.

"Yeah, some mate," he whispered. With that dagger in his chest, he walked slowly back into his bedroom. He looked at the woman between the sheets of his bed with mixed feelings of lust, love, and despair.

"That was Jack. I've got to track you down and tell you that he doesn't know when he'll be back."

Maggie Daniels looked at him, shocked, for a moment, before cowering beneath the sheets, covering her nakedness, and beginning to cry.

# Chapter Twenty-Six

Six hours after she'd moved in, her flat had a lived-in look, and that was putting it mildly. Her things were scattered across the living room floor and a thick cloud of smoke already hung in the air. She'd already gone through a litre bottle of vodka, and was lying on the sofa working on a second. The ashtray next to her had been emptied into the kitchen sink twice and was close to overflowing again.

Her heart felt as if it was going to burst, her throat had a lump the size of a tennis ball in it, and her chest felt tight. But she had not been able to cry. Sarah wished that she could shed some tears, that she could do something to alleviate the pain, but it didn't matter what she tried, what she thought of, nothing worked.

So she tried to get rid of the pain the only way she knew how – she drank. Yet the alcohol seemed to be having no effect on her at all, she still felt completely sober. As far as her body was concerned she might as well have been drinking water.

There were no curtains up in any of the rooms, and the half-moon shone its light, unfiltered, into the first floor flat, and apart from that, darkness ruled. Sarah hadn't arranged the electricity, the gas, or the water, so she had no choice but to sit in the moonlight. Not that it would have made a difference if she had. Sarah only wanted the darkness.

Continuing to drink, Sarah did not sleep, and saw Lenny standing before her in the light of the moon.

Despite his guilty conscience, or maybe because of it, Rob managed to come through for Jack. As soon as he and Maggie had promised that it wouldn't happen again, he'd gone down to the station and delved into the files again.

He wasn't like Jack, who could remember all the details of everything and who never forgot a face. Once he'd left the office, things were forgotten, *had* to be forgotten, unless he was seriously emotionally involved in the case.

That was another thing that bothered Rob, how emotionally involved Jack had become with the Fletcher business. Even from the start, he'd chased the killer with a passion that had frightened Rob. It was as if he just couldn't let it go. There was a look that Jack got in his eyes when he was talking about the case. Not pride or anything like that, but something. Some sort of bond, as if he was personally tied to the case. And it always made Rob feel more than a little uneasy.

He was unable to get hold of him through the Moss police station, nor could he reach him on his mobile. On the answer phone, he left a message and after hanging up went back to his living room.

Usually a tidy person, he found it uncomfortable to have the papers strewn around, but it served a purpose so he tolerated it. He sat on the sofa and ran his hand across his chin, feeling the beginning of stubble starting to push through, before picking up his notepad.

There were only a couple of notes written there and, although he could have lucked out, Rob felt almost ashamed that he hadn't found more.

Since yesterday evening, he'd gone through the files twice, both times trying to open his mind to it all, trying to read it again as if for the first time, but it hadn't helped.

He'd been in the shower, washing the smell of Maggie's perfume away from his body with regret and relief, when an idea jumped into his head. He didn't rush out of the shower and go running into the living room with nothing on, knowing that he was likely to lose the idea as soon as he stepped out. So, instead, he'd continued to wash, letting the idea develop in his head.

When he was finished and dried, still pondering, he walked back to his living room wearing only his dressing gown. Still not rushing, he sat down with the papers at his feet and lit a cigarette. While he smoked, he let the idea form completely, giving it the time it needed.

It wasn't a magnificent idea, but since it was all he'd been able to get, it was better than nothing.

Jack sat on the bed in John's spare room, one hand supporting him as he leant backwards, the other rubbing the bridge of his nose in between his eyes. Planning to relax for five minutes before heading out again, Jack took his phone from his jacket pocket, meaning to play one of the games.

He looked at the blank screen with an equally blank expression before it dawned on him that he hadn't charged the phone for a few days. Still he tried the on/off button, not surprised when nothing happened. He took the charger from his bag and plugged it in, switching the phone on as soon as it began charging. It uttered its shrill ring as he finished dressing. Quickly, so as not to disturb John and Paula even though he knew that they were both awake, he picked it up and answered it, expecting Rob and hoping for Maggie.

He got neither. In a slightly feminine electronic voice an announcer spoke. "You have one new message. To hear your messages, press one. To save your messages, press—"

Jack cut the voice off by pressing one on his keypad, and placed the phone back to his ear to listen to his message.

"It's Rob. Give me a ring when you get this."

Dialling Rob's number from memory, Jack had no time to speculate about what he may have found, because the phone was answered after the first ring.

"It's Jack. What's up?"

"I've looked through all the files, twice, and no matter how I approach it, there's nothing to find."

"Well, it was worth a—"

"But I *do* have an idea. It's not much, but I don't think it's a bad idea," Rob interrupted. He could almost hear the excitement in Jack's silence. "I started thinking that it was a shame that Sarah's parents weren't still alive, 'cos they'd probably be able to help with whatever's going on in her head."

"Right...?"

"Well, I started thinking back to when we saw her after her friend's suicide, and remembered that she'd said she liked to visit her parents' graves whenever she could."

After a moments silence, Jack said, "Rob, you've lost me completely."

Rob sighed and tried to get his thoughts in order before opening his mouth again. "It's obvious that she loved her parents, and from what she wrote on the TV I'd say that she cared about his bloke as well. Which means that she'd probably be at his funeral if she knew when it was."

Jack rolled it around in his own mind for a few seconds. "I'm not too sure, Rob. It's not like it's anything definite, is it?" But the more he thought about it, the more it seemed like a good idea.

"I know it's nothing concrete, Jack, but be honest. Were you really expecting me to find anything *solid*."

Jack laughed. "No, not really."

Rob laughed as well. "And besides, it's not a *bad* idea. Not to mention, it's the only one we've got. So, we might as well give it a go."

"Yeah, you're right. Oh, I don't suppose you managed to get a hold of Maggie, did you?"

Rob's good mood disappeared instantly. "Yeah, I managed to speak to her last night, told her you'd give her a ring when you get a chance."

"Cheers, I owe you one."

"No problem, mate. Give me a ring when you know what's happening."

"Will do. Speak to you soon, Rob and thanks."

Jack hung up and, alone in a room that wasn't his, he thought about how he could arrange it so that Sarah would know.

He was to be buried on the thirtieth of June, and it wasn't until the evening of the twenty-eighth that Sarah saw the notice in the paper, so Rob Donnelly's plan was almost wasted.

Since his death, Sarah had been unaware of anything. She only moved from her flat when she needed more alcohol or cigarettes, and on one occasion she had nearly done that in her nightclothes. She'd gone as far as the front door before realising.

The flat overlooked a river, and Sarah spent most of her time looking at the light as it danced on the water, moving bottle after bottle to her lips.

It only stopped in the early hours of the twenty-ninth. In a way, it was Jack Daniels that finally made Sarah wake up.

She'd fallen asleep looking at the moonlight on the water, and the next moment she was walking down the street in daylight. Again, she knew that she was dreaming, and her head was totally clear and alert for the first time since Lenny's death, and she began to enjoy the heat and sunshine, the *thereness* of the world, not something half-remembered through alcohol fumes.

She was walking towards a funeral. Trees towered above her, all in rows and, although the heat was wonderful, the shade as she walked beneath was exquisite. She stopped next to one of the trees and rested against it, looking at the group of people gathered around the graveside ahead of her.

As she looked, she recognised a few of the people at the service, the words of the minister drifting over to her, and she finally realised why. It was Lenny's funeral.

She wasn't shocked or upset – in fact, she felt calm and relaxed. It was good to know that so many people had cared for him, that there was such a good turnout. The chef from the hotel was there, so was the manager, and also quite a few of the other staff. There was a man there that Sarah didn't know, quite a big build with ginger hair and moustache, and for some reason she felt a huge amount of loathing for him.

It wasn't until he stepped backwards a little that Sarah had an idea about who he was, because she saw someone else that she recognised: the dark shape of Jack Daniels.

Watching from beneath the shade of the tree, she started to move towards the ceremony. Before she had gotten half way, he turned towards her and shook his head. There was no way she could have deluded herself about the meaning: he was telling her not to get too close. Without any other sign that he had seen her, he turned back to face the minister.

"But it's what I want," she whispered, the tears finally starting to fall.

She was still crying when she woke up, her cheeks damp and sticky. The lump was back in her throat, and this time she did nothing to try to fight it.

"Why do you keep warning me?" she whispered to the empty flat. "I want to get caught. I want it to end. So why do you keep helping me?"

Her trickle of tears turned into a flood, and she ignored her mind's insistence that she needed something to drink. She was finally able to cry for Lenny, as well as for herself.

Walking to the churchyard was exactly as she had experienced in her dream. Despite the reason she was going, she felt serene, mainly because she hadn't had to have a drink just to get herself out of bed.

Her sense of déjà vu increased as she walked into the churchyard, but it didn't make her feel uneasy. In fact, it made her feel comfortable.

The shadows as she walked underneath the trees refreshed her overheated body, and she slowed her pace so that she could enjoy the feeling for a little longer. The words of the minister drifted on the hot air over to her, and added to her sense of familiarity, to her feeling of really belonging in the world again. Adhering herself to the actions of her dream, Sarah stepped beneath the shadow of the trees as soon as the group of mourners came into sight. She was not at all surprised to see that they were exactly the same; same positions around the open grave, same clothes, same stances.

The man from her dream was also there, the one with the ginger hair and moustache, but again it was no real surprise, nor was the feeling of resentment towards him that filled her. As he had in her dream, he stepped backwards, exposing the man beside him.

Seeing Jack Daniels actually in the flesh, Sarah was shocked at the respect she felt for him, especially when compared to the venom that she felt about his colleague.

Remembering what had happened next in her dream, Sarah turned and walked out of the churchyard, keeping to the shade as much as she could, more for camouflage than for relief from the sun, realising as she went that she obviously didn't want to be caught as much as she'd thought.

Knowing that Lenny was being buried properly was enough for Sarah. She could always visit the grave alone for her own private memorial.

The service was fine, he supposed, but Jack had a nagging feeling at the base of his neck that there was something out of place, something that he should be seeing.

John was fidgety and stepped backwards, but Jack didn't look around. He was busy scanning the area directly in front of him, finding nothing. Two seconds after she had disappeared from view, Jack looked over at one of the trees, for some reason expecting to see Sarah standing in its shadow, but there was no one there. Quickly, he scanned the rest of the trees, hoping that maybe he'd just looked at the wrong one, but there was no one standing anywhere near.

When the service was over, with no sign of her, he asked the rest of the team. No one had seen anything.

There had been one person to see Sarah, although he didn't know that that was who he was seeing.

Joe was looking around the churchyard, hoping to find something to fix his attention on to try to stop the tears that were welling up in his eyes. He would cry for the death of his friend – he had no illusions about it being unmanly – but he preferred to do it on his own time.

Under the shelter of one of the trees, he saw a woman with red hair. Small framed sunglasses covered her eyes, and the dark trousers and long-sleeved white shirt gave her an added elegance. Yet he was, after all, here for his friend.

The night after the funeral, Jack lay in bed with his head resting on his arms, thinking about the waste of time it had been. That feeling had returned to the base of his neck, that feeling that there was something he should have seen, that he was meant to have seen. Not able to relax, his mind repeatedly going over the details he wanted to forget for one night so that he could sleep, he gave up and got out of bed, careful to be quiet. In the kitchen, he poured himself a glass of milk, and drank it standing over the sink and looking out of the widow.

The moon was nowhere to be seen in the sky, but the sky was still bright with stars, and Jack was pleasantly surprised to find that he still knew quite a few of the constellations. Looking at a small cluster of stars and trying to figure out the name of that particular group, he saw movement at the bottom of the garden.

In the darkness he could see nothing concrete, but that needle in his neck told him that there was *something* there. He walked through John's office, which had been built next to the kitchen, and out of the back door. Walking away from the bungalow, still holding his glass of milk and only in his boxer shorts, he could still not see anything wrong.

Deeper in the shadows, he neared the bench and saw a figure dressed in white. Dark hair covered her lowered head, and when she lifted her face towards him, it separated to show her face.

While Jack just stood there, unable to move, Sarah rose from the bench, holding something to her chest.

He looked carefully at her, trying to figure out what was different about her other than her hair. His eyes moved to her body and it came to him when he saw the rising bump of her stomach – she was pregnant.

As if to give him an offering, she held her hands out towards him, still holding something between her palms. In one fluid motion, she threw her hands upwards, allowing the items she held to escape.

Jack was caught in a shower of paper, and raised his own empty hand to catch one of the pieces. Before looking at it, he returned his eyes to Sarah to find that she was gone. He didn't waste his time looking around for her, and instead looked at the slip of paper in his hand.

It was a bank statement, with Sarah's address in Millsbury in the top left hand corner, and the account details in the opposite corner. There were no entries on the page, no account balances, only three words typed in bold across the middle of the page. TOO MUCH MONEY.

It hit him like a needle between the eyes. Not a solution, but a means to a solution. Something so simple that he had overlooked it.

All he had to do was to get her accounts frozen.

As Jack was working out his answer, Sarah was sitting on the window ledge looking out onto the dark river. She'd just finished counting the cash that she'd been building up over the past weeks. Every time she'd walked past a cash machine, she'd taken out three hundred pounds, and she was amazed to find that she had over eight thousand pounds. She still had no idea why she was taking the money out of her bank account, but the compulsion wouldn't leave her.

Still at the window hours later after having had no sleep, Sarah watched the day dawning, wonder filling her as she watched the colour of the water change with the sky.

She washed and dressed and left the flat in the early afternoon, and headed straight to the cash machine.

At the ATM she put her card into the slot and waited to punch in her pin number. She waited calmly and felt only amused when a notice flashed up, asking her to contact the bank. After a few moments it was replaced by a notice welcoming her. She was not at all surprised when her card was not returned to her, and simply smiled at the machine. "Clever, Jack," she said in a whisper full of total respect and amusement. Lightly, she trapped the cash machine before walking away. "Very, very clever."

He'd decided to go home, there was really nothing else he could do for the time being in Moss, and he wasn't going to impose on John and Pauline any longer. With her cancer getting worse, they needed all the space they could get.

With his things packed in his Jeep and his goodbyes given to John and his ill wife, he returned to the churchyard, where he went straight to Lenny Peterson's fresh grave.

He took his phone from the inside pocket of his jacket, and started to dial John's number before stopping. They had far too much to cope with, so instead he phoned John's office and told them to get there with forensics.

Feeling tired and wanting to see his wife, Jack left the churchyard, leaving without touching the single white rose that lay on the top of the gravestone, with only one thing beneath it – a piece of paper with INNOCENT written on it.

*Remembering that last trip to the grave, Jack remembered something else: Maggie hadn't been home when he'd returned, which made him wonder if she'd been with her fella then, or if she'd simply been out. Since the acceptance of her affair, doubt over all of her previous activ-*

*ities had crept in.*

*He shook his head, trying to dispel thoughts of his wife and to return to what he was working on, but he found that it wasn't that easy. Now that he'd started to think about her, his mind refused to move on. It was trying to make him admit that his marriage was over, that she'd left him for someone else. No matter how much he'd been hurt, no matter how often he told himself that he hated her, he could not imagine a life without her.*

*Having to force himself to open the journal for the first time since he'd first touched it, Jack began to read again, gradually evicting Maggie from his thoughts.*

*Lying in her lover's arms, Maggie whispered in her sleep. In her dream, feeling wide-awake, looking at the room she was in, she remembered that she had left her husband, and was now staying with his best friend and her lover. As she lay there, eyes open, she smiled. It was the typical story line from all of those shitty soap operas she detested so much.*

*Hearing footsteps moving towards the bedroom door, Maggie tried to wake Rob, tried to pull the cover up to conceal her body, but she couldn't move. Her heart was beating quickly and loudly in her chest, and she could feel the blood pumping strongly in her temples, but she could not move.*

*Her dark green eyes focussed on the bedroom door, watching as the handle started to move. Her mind presented her with the image of her husband, come to either take her home or to take her life, and she stifled a sob as the door slowly began to shift.*

*Her mind was so convinced it would be Jack, for a split second that was who she saw. But she blinked and the image changed.*

*Instead of her husband's huge frame, a small woman stood in a white dress, her red hair looking darker as it fell against the material. She was smiling, not genuinely but arrogantly, and Maggie felt a shiver work its way down her spine.*

*The woman opened her mouth and screamed silently and then simply disappeared.*

*In the room, no sign of her anywhere, Maggie heard a voice in the darkness and knew that the speaker was smiling.*

*"The story's nearly finished now, Maggie. It won't be long.* He *won't be long."*

*Maggie closed her eyes, ready to scream herself, but her dream dissolved into comforting darkness.*

# Chapter Twenty-Seven

She sat up, almost yelling in surprise as pain assaulted the base of her back, just at the top of her buttocks, as if a huge weight was resting there. Carefully, she swung her legs off the bed and slowly stood up, her hands reaching behind her to massage it.

Gradually, the pain began to subside, leaving Sarah to wonder what was going on. As far as she knew it was too early for her to be getting any back pain, but she supposed it could still have something to do with the pregnancy. It was probably better for her to get checked out by a doctor but that was a chance she could not afford to take. And the way she saw it, women thousands of years ago hadn't had doctors on their doorsteps, and things used to go all right. If she was meant to have a baby, she would – she'd just have to do it herself.

She looked longingly at the cigarettes, then grabbed them as she walked out of the bedroom. In the kitchen, she put them in a tin on the window ledge, keeping them out of view. The bottles lined up along the side also looked tempting, and she nearly caved in when she opened the nearest and caught the scent of whiskey. But her nerve held, and she tipped the amber liquid into the sink.

Before the smell got too bad, Sarah went through all of the rooms and opened the windows, wishing that there was a breeze to stir the air inside. Then she returned to the kitchen, and one by one she emptied all of the bottles.

For Sarah, it was a new day, the most important new day of her life, and she intended to make the most of it.

With the alcohol gone and the cigarettes hidden, Sarah found that she seemed to have a lot of time and not an awful lot to do. She thought again of going to the doctors to get some help and advice, patient confidentiality and everything, but again decided against it. If she did go and ended up getting caught, her baby would be taken from her, and there was no way on earth that she was going to allow that to happen.

Beginning to feel excited, truly excited for the first time, about becoming a mother, Sarah took three hundred pounds from her collection of cash and walked out of the flat. Downstairs, she considered taking the car she'd bought before Lenny's death, the white Polo, but chose to walk. She wasn't going to rush, knowing that too much exercise wasn't good for her or the baby but guessing that doing nothing would be just as damaging.

First, she wandered around the shops, looking in the windows, finding her gaze attracted more and more to baby items, especially clothes. In one shop, she bought herself a thick extensive book about pregnancy and a baby's first year.

She then went to the supermarket and did a shop for the month. For a five pound charge, Sarah took advantage of their delivery system, relieved that she wasn't going to have to carry all of the shopping home and up one flight of stairs to her flat.

At home, she sorted out all of her utility bills, giving her name as Serena Dawes, using Serena's previous address as her own. Then she made herself a cup of tea, she perched herself on the window ledge, tucking her legs up onto it. With the water moving swiftly below her window, the sun reflecting off it, she sipped her drink and flicked through her new book. Only a couple of pages in, Sarah was amazed at all the weird and wonderful things that her body was going to be doing in the next months.

Moving carefully, she got off the ledge and retrieved her journal from her bedroom before going back to the window ledge again. Looking through her journal, she worked out the last day of her last period. Using the chart from her new book, she worked out her due date. By the fifteenth on February, if the dates were right, she would have her baby.

The thought terrified her and for a second she longed for a drink a little more substantial than tea. Knowing that as soon as the baby was born she would be responsible for it for the rest of her life, that she would have a life totally dependent upon her, petrified her. She wouldn't be able to just pop out to the shop for half an hour, wouldn't be able to go out on the spur of the moment. Then the terror left her, and she was left feeling exhausted. Her doorbell rang, and she jumped at the unexpected noise, another bout of pain setting at the base of her spine again.

Moving gently, she walked down the concrete stairs to the main doors. She led the two delivery people into her flat, watching silently as they took the bags into the kitchen. When they were finished, she thanked them and saw them to the front door, leaving them to work their own way back downstairs.

She unpacked her shopping slowly, not rushing, putting things where she would be able to reach them without stretching too far: she had to plan for the next few months, had to plan for a huge stomach to get in the way. Now that she was planning for it again, even something as mundane as food shopping, she was getting excited again.

*Jack read her feelings on pregnancy, and wasn't shocked to find that they were similar to the feelings that he'd had when Maggie had told him that she was pregnant. He supposed it was what everybody went through, that conflicting of emotions, but it still seemed to strengthen the connection he felt between them.*

*Unfortunately, thinking about Maggie's pregnancy made him think directly about his wife, and he began to feel angry again. To try to take his mind off his own problems, Jack looked at the picture of Sarah Fletcher, studying the features that he knew so well, feeling that connection stronger than ever.*

*He thought about how much strength it must have taken for her to tip all of the drink away, to turn away from the only thing that had kept her going. And also laying off the cigarettes as well.*

*Jack knew how hard it was to quit smoking – he'd given up the day his daughter had been born, and had only relapsed once. It had been*

*Sarah's first birthday, and Maggie's mother had been trying to take over as usual, trying to tell them both the 'right' way to do everything, and the stress had been too much.*

*He'd gone to his car, an old battered Skoda in those days, and grabbed the half-pack from the glove compartment. Knowing that he was being stupid, knowing he wasn't doing himself any favours, he'd lit up, inhaling the smoke right down to the bottom of his lungs.*

*The cigarette had been stale, and the dry smoke had burnt his throat, making him cough it back up, which hurt even more. It had been so bad, hundreds of black spots dancing in front of him, bent over with his hands resting on his thighs, sure that he was going to pass out or have a heart attack. Or both.*

*After a few moments, the spots had faded to nothing and his chest had felt a little lighter, making it easier for him to breathe again. His throat had still felt like someone had used sandpaper on it, and he had been able to taste a small amount of blood, but he'd still felt better.*

*He'd flicked the burning butt onto the ground, crushing it under his shoe, and nearly threw the remains of the pack into the bin. Instead, he put them back into his glove compartment, a small test for his willpower. But deeper, he knew the* real *reason, and it had nothing to do with willpower – he kept them as a reminder of what happened the last time that particular craving came upon him.*

*Jack smiled as he realised that he still had that same pack after twenty years, had been unconsciously putting it in every new car he'd ever bought, as he did with his maps, and the thought of how they'd tasted made him grimace and laugh at the same time.*

*Feeling considerably brighter, he went back to the journal.*

She lay in her bath, enjoying the relief the warm water brought her. It was a deep bath, and the water covered her entire body, bubbles popping on the surface. Her back had seemed to sigh in bliss once it was enveloped within the water, the gentle movement massaging the base of her back, taking the weight from it.

Breasts that were badly tender were also massaged by the water, and Sarah was instantly relaxed. She closed her eyes and rested her head against the rim of the bath, letting herself drift away.

For the hour that she was immersed, the bubbles having long since disappeared, she fantasised about how it would be, her own child – in her imagination, it was a girl – and how she would care for her, how she look after and protect her always.

Her body registered that she was cold long before her mind came back from her future. Shivering frantically, careful not to slip – it simply wouldn't be good, not in her condition – she stepped out of the bath and towelled herself dry.

Because she had been in the water, the slow loss of blood hadn't been noticed. It hadn't been a lot, nor had any pain accompanied it, so Sarah simply didn't realise that the water was now slightly pink.

Clothed and totally relaxed, she went back to the living room and took her usual place, resting against the wall and perched on the window ledge, and sat staring through the glass at the cloud-blackened sky.

According to the book she'd bought, the sickness she'd been experiencing should be gone in a couple of weeks. She wondered about the person who'd named it 'morning' sickness. As far as she could tell, it had to be a bloke, because any woman would be able to tell him that it was hardly ever just in the morning.

It didn't worry her that she wasn't supposed to be getting back pain yet – as it said in the book, every pregnancy was different. It also said on almost every page that it put the baby in danger if you smoked, and she felt a huge sense of pride for herself – she'd quit, and with no help from anyone.

Not that she didn't *want* one. She'd had no physical cravings, but her mind was still telling her that she was a smoker, that she was supposed to be smoking at least every three hours. But she'd managed to keep away from the packet in the kitchen, and it was getting easier.

She pottered around, tidying things that she really didn't need tidying, and cleaning things that she'd already cleaned, and started feeling tired mid-afternoon. Only wanting to rest for a moment, she sat on the sofa, feeling the cushions moulding around her body, and closed her eyes.

Within seconds, she was asleep and snoring lightly.

In bare feet, she was walking through a forest, feeling the springy ground underneath her toes, not caring as she felt the woodland insects creeping over her skin.

The sun was bright in the skin, although she couldn't pinpoint it she knew that it was up there, and the leaves created a shadow effect on the ground.

She could hear the birds singing, could hear the leaves rustling as animals moved around, and felt at ease. There was someone she had to see, someone she had to meet properly, but Sarah felt no urgency about it. She didn't have to rush, felt that whoever it was would wait for her, no matter how long she took.

The smells of the forest, heated by the sun, came at her with no respite, bombarding her continuously. Overwhelmed, she leant against the trunk of a spruce, her hands resting on her kneecaps, eyes closed. When her head felt a little clearer, Sarah opened her eyes and began to straighten her back. As she did, she became aware of what she was wearing.

It was a white dress, long and flowing, reaching down almost to the ground, moving gently around her ankles. It lay loosely around her figure, draping over her shoulders, the long sleeves widening into bells at the wrist. A round neckline led to a fitted top, and then it just flowed from her bust. Although she generally hated wearing dresses and skirts, she was surprised at how comfortable it felt on her body. After doing a few twirls to notice how it flared up when the air went underneath, stopping when she felt embarrassed and self-conscious, she continued on her way.

The trees ended abruptly and Sarah walked into the clearing, feeling nervous, knowing that this would be where she'd meet the person she had travelled to see. Walking to the other side of the clearing, she looked at the small pool that stood inside a circle of small rocks. It was maybe two metres across, but the darkness of the water told her that it was probably very deep.

Every pool or pond she'd ever seen had always been filled with rubbish: bottles, cans, even the odd bicycle. But this one was clean, there wasn't even a single leaf floating on its surface. Looking on the ground around it, she saw that it was likewise totally clear, not a scrap of litter.

She turned quickly, almost losing her footing and falling into the pool, when she heard branches snapping behind her.

She saw two figures standing in the shade of the trees. Although it wasn't that dark, she was unable to see them clearly. She knew one of them of course, she'd been dreaming of him for years.

But the young child that stood beside him was a complete mystery. Sarah thought the girl was about four years old. At first, she thought that it was Jack's daughter – she knew that he had one – but was sure that his child was close to her own age.

Jack stepped back a few paces further into the shade, and the young girl stepped forward. Light should already have made her features obvious, but Sarah had to watch as the darkness faded from the girl's face a bit at a time. Just before she woke up, Sarah was able to see the beautiful girl, to marvel at the girl's silky brown hair and her dark blue eyes. Just enough time for her to marvel at how much like Lenny the girl looked.

*He'd only been gone half an hour before Maggie peered through the closed curtains for the first time that day.*

*Since her dream, Maggie had become very paranoid and had decided that it must have been some kind of premonition, and that Jack was going to find out where she was. That was, if he didn't know already.*

*In all their years of marriage, through all the arguments and fights, she'd never once been afraid of him. But now that she had walked out on him, she'd changed things. They were no longer in a predictable relationship, if they had been she never would have gotten together with Rob. She didn't know how he'd react when he found out, but she didn't think that he would just let it go. As she watched, a car parked across the street, a non-descript Fiesta, and her heart started to beat quicker, forcing the blood around her body a bit faster. The driver's side opened and Maggie opened her mouth to scream.*

*In her head, things happened as she'd feared. Jack getting out of the car, looking straight at her, his eyes a blank void. Looking at her he walked across the street, getting closer to her. He knocked on the front door once, and then crashed against it. On the second hit, the door was forced open, smashing back against the wall. He strode into the living room and faced his wife.*

*In reality, Maggie quickly closed her mouth to stop the scream that still wanted to escape. It wasn't Jack, wasn't even a man. The slim-hipped teenager locked her car and walked over to one of the other flats.*

*Quickly, Maggie closed the gap she'd created in the curtains, and collapsed onto the floor, her chest tight, sobbing into her hands. She remained that way for over ten minutes, slowly rocking herself back and forth, stopping suddenly when she heard the knock on the front door, her head whipping around.*

*It was him, there was absolutely no doubt in her mind this time. She knew that when she looked out of the window this time she'd see Jack standing there, maybe looking straight at her. On her knees, using all of the strength that remained in her body, she moved to look, pushing the curtain back a little, creating a space for her to look through.*

*Relief swamped her, making her unable to move for a few moments, when she saw Rob standing on the doorstep with a carrier bag in hand. With one last sob escaping her throat, she scrambled to her feet and rushed to the front door.*

*She flung it open, and Rob's face was consumed with concern. He stepped inside the door, quickly closing it behind him. "Maggie? Christ, Maggie, what's happened?"*

*She couldn't speak at first, just stepped closer to him, resting her head against his chest. As his arms circled her, one hand gently rubbing the base of her back, she felt completely and totally safe.*

*"It's okay, Maggie. Everything's okay." As he had absolutely no idea of what was wrong, he didn't know if everything was okay or not. But it was something to say, and it made* him *feel a little less anxious.*

*Still sobbing, Maggie was able to speak. "He's gonna kill me," she managed to blurt out.*

*"Maggie?" He pulled back, making sure that he could see her tear-stained face. "Who's going to kill you?"*

*"Jack!" She looked at him, as if it should have been obvious, wondering why he didn't know.*

*"What do you mean, he's going to kill you? Maggie, what could have put that in your head?"*

*"I don't know." She looked at him, a resigned look in her eyes.*

*Even though the look in her eyes had done its part to almost convince him, Rob shook his head and pulled her close again. "He doesn't know where you are, Maggie. And even if he did, he wouldn't hurt you."*

*"You haven't told your dad, have you, Sarah? That your mum's here?" It was a quarter past ten, and Maggie had been asleep for almost half an hour.*

*"I said I wouldn't, and, no, I haven't. I'm not going to be the one that kills my father." Sensing that there was something else that he needed to say, she did what she could to neutralise her tone. "Why'd you ask?"*

*Rob sighed. "It's your mum. She's got it into her head that…" he drifted off, trying to figure out how to tell her that her mother was obsessed with the idea that Sarah's father was going to kill her. He came to the conclusion that there was no way he could. "She's having a rough time of it, Sarah. Is there any way you could pop over to see her, or at least ring her, tomorrow?"*

*Now concerned, guilty about her tone at the beginning of their conversation, she asked. "Is she all right, Rob?"*

*"She will be, I think. Can you call round? I think it'd help."*

*"I'll come around. Will you be there?"*

*"I'll go out. Give you two some time to talk." He heard Maggie stirring in the bedroom. "Look, I'd better go. And thanks, Sarah."*

*She started to reply, and found herself listening to the hum of a dead line.*

*He was becoming more and more engrossed in her diary. There were no more murders so far, no more visions, but Jack couldn't tear himself away. It was now a week-to-week diary of her pregnancy, and it was taking him into a part of her mind that he'd never suspected existed. She was so happy and, apart from the side effects that all pregnant women go through – sickness, stretch marks, swollen ankles – things seemed to be all right.*

*Around sixteen weeks or pregnancy, she'd noticed her breasts getting larger and had felt a fluttering movement in her stomach, which she described as butterflies. At twenty-two weeks, October twelfth, she'd had to start undoing her larger sized jeans and skirts so that she could sit down comfortably. After that, she bought herself some maternity clothes.*

*Jack felt a hand clench around his heart as she specifically mentioned the white dress. As they had only found the one white dress in her belongings, he knew that it had to be the one she would kill herself in.*

*Week thirty-one, having realised how soon her life would be changing, with nine weeks to go, Sarah's willpower had snapped, and she bought herself three small bottles of vodka. They'd only lasted five hours, but she had suffered for them.*

Her dream had started off, as the other had, with her walking through the forest and reaching the clearing. Her first sign that something was wrong was when she saw the two figures in the shade. Jack had turned his back on her, and that had distressed her more than anything else that was to follow.

Instead of walking into the sunlight as she had before, the girl remained where she was. On some instinct, Sarah walked around to the pool. Although the water was as dark as before, it was now no longer clean. The smell wafted up to her, a smell of marshland, and she gagged.

"See what you have done." It was a girl's voice, both young yet old.

Obeying, Sarah gazed at the area, seeing that the clean place was no longer untainted. Not only was the pool infected, the grass under her feet was brown and dead. The trees around the clearing were also dead, the leaves and branches skeletal. When she became aware of the changes, the clear blue sky began to darken.

She looked at the girl as the sun was deleted from the sky, and as it went completely dark she could hear footsteps moving towards her, and she compensated by moving backwards.

Two steps and she tripped over rocks, feeling herself falling. The rank water flowed over her face, spilling into her mouth. In the darkness, she began to gag.

She woke herself up by being sick. She rolled off the sofa and landed on her hands and knees as the alcohol was forcibly ejected from her stomach. The pain hit her abdomen and she felt sure that she was going to miscarry.

Tuesday, February the fifteenth came around, and Sarah was anxious. The baby was due and she was suddenly terrified. Because of her actions, the baby was going to have to be born with no help from anyone – how did she know that she'd be able to cope? Part of her told her that her body would know what to do even if she didn't. But another part, a bigger part, told her that she was delusional, that there was no way that she was capable of doing this alone.

She had a small bag packed just in case something *did* go wrong, and it sat next to the sofa. She'd read her book dozens of times, studying it like a manual, hoping that she'd remember everything.

She'd woken up with butterflies in her stomach, and a sense of expectancy. But as the day grew older that feeling lessened and was replaced by impatience.

For nine months she'd carried her baby, had felt it move and kick, had suffered from the bad back, the sickness, and the stretch marks. Now all she wanted was to hold her child.

The heating was on, already switched to the recommended temperature, but she still felt cold. At four in the afternoon, darkness swallowing the sky outside the window, Sarah closed all of the curtains, keeping the night outside.

In her book it said that warm baths could sometimes bring on labour, so as soon as she headed straight to the bathroom and ran a warm bath with plenty of bubbles. She expected her contractions to start the second that she put a foot into the water and was disappointed when it didn't happen. Instead of concentrating on it, she carefully climbed in and lowered herself. Once she managed to lie back against the back of the bath, she was able to relax. All she could see above the bubbles was her stomach, with its new design of stretch marks, and her toes. Looking at them, she realised how swollen they had become.

She'd put on weight. Not a lot but enough for her to notice, but she didn't feel unhealthy. In fact, since cutting out the cigarettes and alcohol, she had never felt better.

Her fingers caressed her stomach, tracing the lines that had appeared, and she failed to realise, even now, that it had been awhile since she'd last felt any movement. Even in the warm water when the baby usually started to move like crazy, she didn't feel anything.

It was well over an hour before she got out of the bath, sitting up and turning herself sideways so that her back was against the side. Using her legs to raise herself, she was able to get out.

She dried herself off and went back into the living room, a dressing gown wrapped around her. With a cup of tea, she settled herself on the sofa and watched the television until she fell asleep.

In total, Sarah was thirteen days past her due date before she went into labour.

She woke up at two that Monday morning, and had been unable to get back to sleep, so simply lay in bed, her back slightly raised on pillows, and watched the patterns thrown up by the moonlight reflecting off the river, watching it dance on the ceiling.

Her hand moved gently over her stomach, and slowed to a complete stop as she realised what she hadn't on the fifteenth – that it had been a long time since she had felt any movements from her child. She stayed where she was for a further two hours, stubbornly hoping that her baby would kick so that she wouldn't have to worry any more.

After those two hours, still with no movement, Sarah made herself get out of bed. It was too much of a risk, she knew that she'd probably get caught, but it was time to put the baby first. Reluctantly, she dressed, struggling to reach past her bump to put on her socks. It was dark outside and she knew that it would be cold, so she dressed in as many layers as she could bear before taking hold of the prepared bag. She struggled down the stairs and out of the main doors, shivering as the cold still managed to penetrate through all of the clothes.

Stretching her hand out towards the car, keys in hand to unlock the door, she felt liquid trickle out from between her legs. Her waters broke and she was debating whether to continue to the hospital or not when her first contraction attacked her stomach. Panic and relief rushed through her and she carefully retraced her steps back upstairs.

She was in labour for over fourteen hours, but most of them were lost in a haze of pain. She didn't know what was happening, but her body took over and there were no real problems with the birth. She pushed when she needed to push, went against the urge when she felt she had to. Sarah delivered the baby's head slowly, her hands between her legs, just as the book had said to, bringing the baby to her chest as soon as it had freed itself from her body.

Shaking and exhausted, it took a few moments to realise that the baby hadn't cried. Looking down, she noticed the colour of the baby girl's skin. It was blue. And she wasn't breathing.

# Chapter Twenty-Eight

She disposed of the placenta, and the sheets that she'd give birth on were bundled up and put in the bathroom. She was exhausted, but she ran herself a clear bath and slowly got in. She expected pain to hit her as soon as the water washed over her, but instead felt herself relax into it. She didn't cry as she thought of her daughter, didn't wail and scream, but she felt the loss just as deeply. Not only did she feel empty in her abdomen where her baby had been, she felt empty in her entire body.

Once she was clean, once all of the sweat of her effort was wiped away from her body, she got out of the water and gently dried herself. She walked to her bedroom, pretending not to notice the smell of the birth in the air, and got a clean nightshirt from the drawers, which she slipped on over her head.

In the kitchen she saw the tin on the window sill, and with no need for her to worry any longer, she took the stale cigarettes out. She sat slowly on the sofa, tucking her legs underneath her so that the sensitive part of her didn't have too much pressure on it.

It was eight in the evening when she put the first cigarette in her mouth and lit it after nearly twenty weeks of not smoking. The staleness burnt her throat, bringing up a taste of blood, but she carried on smoking. Her lungs forced the smoke back out, but as soon as the coughing had stopped she continued. She felt faint and sick, but she forced her body to re-introduce itself to the cigarettes.

She switched the television on and stared at the screen, staring at it but seeing nothing.

When she saw her surroundings, she felt a deep sense of relief. In her dream, she didn't feel empty; her grief was able to rise to the surface. Because of where she was, she was sure that she would at least get the chance to say goodbye.

Not strolling as she had the two previous times, too anxious to see her child, Sarah walked quickly, the hemline of the white dress whirling around her ankles, towards the clearing in the woods. The sun was shining from high in the sky, but Sarah was still aware of the chill that hung in the air, trying to bite through the thin material of her dress.

Her mind was occupied on other matters, and the negative atmosphere didn't register. Wandering under the trees, she didn't notice the fact that the path she'd walked before was more overgrown and that she had to avoid bushes and branches that reached out towards her. Getting closer, the sun was concealed by the dark grey clouds, and she started to jog as she finally noticed where she was.

The area that she ended in could no longer strictly be called a clearing. Weeds and plants that she didn't recognise grew up to her mid-calf and scratched against the skin, not quite hard enough to draw blood. Nearing the pool where she felt she needed to be, her feet fell on sharp stones that were hidden beneath the weeds, and it slowed her down, but it didn't stop her. She was determined.

The rancid smell that she'd noticed in her last dream reached her again, this time worse than ever, and that managed to stop her. Hand covering her nose, she crept towards the pool and looked into its depths. It was more potent than before, the water was brown, and Sarah was sure that if she were to touch it, it would feel slimy. Not that she had any intention of putting her hands in there.

A voice she knew well spoke from directly behind her. She didn't turn around, she simply looked at the water.

"Some things are meant to be, and some things aren't, Sarah. You've got to know the difference."

It began to darken again, and Sarah felt the first tear fall down her cheek as she stopped dreaming.

*Jack wiped at his face, not surprised when his fingertips came away damp.*

*For a short time, he'd tried reading the journal in his living room, in the comfort of his armchair, but it hadn't worked out. He'd become too distracted by the photos of his wife and daughter, and hadn't been able to concentrate. It hadn't felt right, reading it in the same place that he enjoyed reading his novels. That's what the journal began to seem like – a fictional novel that had no bearing on real life. And if he read it like that he could miss something vital.*

*He wondered how he would have managed to cope had their places been reversed, but he couldn't quite get there. He was a man, after all, and childbirth was something he would never be able to go through, could never really understand, no matter how hard he tried.*

*He had absolutely no doubt in his heart that it had something to do with her drinking, and was sure that had probably gone through Sarah's mind as well, not that it would have helped any.*

*In fact, he blamed everything that had happened afterwards – especially Michael Steven's death – on the fact that she blamed herself for her daughter's death. Call it intuition or whatever, ultimately it was all a part of that connection.*

She was on her way back to the car when she saw the pram.

It was a week since the birth of her daughter, March seventh, and the first time that she'd been outside since that day, and her first job had been to get rid of all the things she had bought for the baby. Her first idea had been to burn it, in a kind of private ceremony, but her common sense prevailed, and there was no way she was going to simply throw it in the bin – it would feel like sacrilege.

So she packed her car up and drove to the charity shops. It was a Monday so things were pretty quiet on the streets and she'd been able to park right outside.

As soon as the job was done, she'd gone to the supermarket. After getting a few things (she'd thought about asking them to deliver but then wondered why she'd need; it wasn't as if she was pregnant any more), she took the bags out to the car and was taking the trolley back.

Outside the main doors of the shop, with no one else around, was a travel system with a car seat on top. And inside, wrapped up in an aqua shawl was a beautiful young baby, Sarah guessed no older than a few weeks.

There was no one around, absolutely no one, and Sarah felt two things: absolute sickness that anyone could leave an unprotected baby completely alone, and need.

Her breasts throbbed as they had all week, and she knew that she would be leaking milk into her breast pads, but that was irrelevant. What was relevant was that desperate need. She needed to hold the baby, to cradle it, to love it as it was obviously not loved. She'd be able to give it everything it didn't have, especially care.

Her hands were actually stretched out towards the handle of the pushchair, almost touching it, when she pulled her hands back, crossing her wrists against her chest.

Scared, especially in case someone had noticed her, suddenly remembering that she was wanted by the police for multiple murders, Sarah turned her back on the baby in the pram, and walked as quickly as she could back to her car.

*It was something that pissed Jack off as well. He hated seeing babies left like old bags, and he hated those mothers who obviously had no intention of looking after them, who had them only because they were too stupid and too selfish to do what was right for the child.*

*He'd also nearly done what Sarah had almost done, but for slightly different reasons. While she'd been close to taking the baby for personal reasons, Jack had almost done it for two: for the child's own protection, and to teach the stupid woman who had left it alone a powerful lesson.*

*The only thing that had ever been able to stop him was the thought of his own child – how would he have reacted if someone had taken his baby? It was a thought that had chilled him no matter where he was.*

*In her state of mind, Jack comprehended how much of an effort it had taken for her to walk away, and once again found himself admiring her.*

Michael left the bar with a mixture of humour and despair following him. It was a little strange to think that at twenty-seven years old he was considered by the younger blokes as 'past it'.

Merlin's – the only gay pub in Moss – was on the bank of the river, the opposite side to Moss' residential area, and was a good half hour from where he lived, but it was good to know that there were people like him there. He wasn't looking for a soulmate (or so he told himself), and neither did he want a one-night stand. It was something he'd had to insist to everyone since he'd come out – that all he wanted was a normal relationship.

He went home only to wash and change before going back to the pub. He had hopes of someone his own age being there later.

When he was ready Michael Stevens went back to the pub for the last time.

Three days after almost snatching the baby, Sarah left her flat for the second time in ten days, and the last time in her life.

For March, it wasn't too cold, but she still wrapped herself up warm, putting on her thickest coat. Her head had been aching all day and she thought she might be coming down with a cold.

She had explored her side of the river, but had never looked at what was on the other side of the bridge, so she headed over.

She walked along the riverbank, seeing her flat from the other side. With the sun reflecting off the water, it was a little harder to see, and Sarah had forgotten her sunglasses, causing her head to pound harder. About a quarter of a mile away from the bridge, Sarah's left foot tangled in something and she fell, landing roughly on her knees. If she'd fallen the other way, she would have rolled down the bank and into the river. Moving so that she was sitting on her backside, Sarah managed to untangle her foot from what was wrapped around it.

When she held it in her hands, looking at it carefully, she saw piece of thin wire about thirteen inches long, with pencils attached to both ends. She stood up, still holding it, wincing as black spots began to dance in front of her and dizziness swept over her.

She walked, staggering, to the nearest building she came to, not noticing the name of the pub or the fact that the majority of couples were same-sex.

She got to the bar and ordered an orange-and-lemonade with plenty of ice. The barman started to ask if she was okay – her eyes had a hollow look to them, her hair looked lifeless, and her skin looked sallow – then thought better of it. This woman looked like she had too many problems.

Sarah drank her drink quickly, munching on the pieces of ice, but they did nothing to cool her down. She could still feel the heat in her face and the sweat on her forehead. From a woman sat next to her, she got directions to the toilets and moved as quickly as she dared. Once inside, she rested over the sinks and splashed freezing cold water onto her face. It cooled her down amazingly and she felt not only refreshed but more aware.

She opened the door back to the bar and stopped, the good feeling she'd just acquired being taken from her. She saw gay and lesbian couples, holding hands, kissing, talking intimately.

Sarah rushed back into the toilets, sure that she was about to bring back up her drink. She splashed water on her face again, not able to comprehend how, out of all the places she could have found her way into, she'd ended up in a *gay* bar. It was sick!

Still leaning over the sink, she looked into the mirror in front of her as the door opened briefly to admit a man, a little older than herself, muttering to himself about the queues in the gents' toilets. Sarah looked away from the mirror before his reflection started to change – as she was *sure* it would, after all, he was *gay* – and didn't watch as he walked into one of the stalls.

The piece of wire had somehow jumped into her hands, and she held it by the two pencils, stretching it out to its full length. As the man washed his hands, Sarah calmly walked up behind him and swung the wire over his head, yanking it tight by crossing the wire and pulling it in opposite directions.

He tried to turn around, hands flying to his throat and trying to grab the wire from his neck. It had sunken into the flesh, and he was trying to dig it out with his fingertips.

Sarah was intrigued by the whole situation, especially the way that the wire seemed to have completely disappeared, leaving only a red line in its place. Their eyes locked in the mirror, and her hands relaxed slightly as she saw the frightened look in his.

Before his fingers could find their way under the wire, she tightened it once more.

Within a minute it was over, and so was Sarah Fletcher's belief that homosexuals were evil. For all the time their eyes had remained locked in the mirror nothing had happened, not a single shimmer, not a single change in how he had looked. His mirror image had remained unaltered.

His body fell, and she let it go, her whole mind in an uproar. At the sound of his body hitting the floor she met her own eyes in the glass. It started to shimmer straight away, and Sarah had no option but to watch as her own reflection began to change.

Her face began to elongate, to stretch downwards, until it was almost three feet long. Her face aged, her hair turned white and wiry, the whites of her eyes turned yellow and then green. Finally, tall grey-black horns sprouted above her ears.

In disgust and despair she punched the mirror, glass shattering and shards piercing her skin. One finger was cut badly and she used it to write across the cracked mirror. Then she turned and fled, leaving the wire wrapped around the innocent man's throat.

She went home as quickly as she could, locking the door behind her, and running into the bathroom. She ran the bath and while it filled, she got her white dress from the cupboard and hung it on the back of the door. Then she took the bundle from the bottom drawer of her wardrobe and laid it gently on the bed.

In the shower she quickly and roughly washed her body and hair before getting out and getting dry. The she put on her dress and quickly stopped off in the kitchen and grabbed the two bottles of vodka and her pack of cigarettes, before going back into her bedroom.

There were boxes of ibuprofen capsules in her desk drawer, and she picked them up while also picking up her journal and pen, which were on top of the desk.

She placed the vodka and tablets to one side and lit a cigarette, her hands not shaking now that she knew how things were going to end. It was actually something of a relief to know that there would be no more visions of people's souls, that the responsibility would no longer be hers.

Once the cigarette was finished she wrote a letter, only a few sentences long, and sealed it inside an envelope, then made a quick entry into her journal. She opened the bottles of vodka and the boxes of tablets, and began to force them out one by one, popping them into her mouth and washing them down with the vodka. She lost count of how many she had taken, but the boxes were gradually emptied.

Once it was done, she held the bundle wrapped in sheets to her chest. She couldn't see her daughter, the baby was wrapped tightly, its death-shroud only a bed sheet. She knew that her daughter was dead, but hadn't been able to give her away. With her spare hand, she continued to write in the journal.

She felt tired and it hurt to keep her eyes open so she gave into it, closing her eyelids, waiting for the final sleep to come and claim her, the sleep that she had, in truth, been waiting for. Hearing heavy footsteps moving across the floor towards her, she forced her eyes open one last time.

For the first time in her visions, she could see him clearly, could see the features that had always been hidden to her. He looked slightly drawn but mostly he just looked unhappy.

She tried to tell him that it was all right, but her mouth wouldn't open and no words would emerge, but it wasn't necessary – he was nodding slowly. He understood everything; he always had.

While her mind tried to fall, Sarah finished making her last entry into her journal, fighting against the darkness, needing just a little longer.

She looked up once she'd finished to find that Jack had sat on the edge of the bed next to her. For the last time she closed her book and left it beside her.

With Jack to watch over her, Sarah allowed her eyes to close again, holding her daughter close to her. It was all right now, everything was as it should be, and she could go. As she slipped away, she felt his lips on her forehead, and carried his kiss with her.

Jack carried the journal and letter over to the desk and, after one last sad look at Sarah, walked down the hall towards the front door. He didn't make it though – half way along the hall, he simply faded from existence.

*It was three days after Michael Steven's death, John remembered that clearly. As soon as he'd had the phone call, he'd phoned Jack, and told him to get there as soon as possible.*

*John sat in his living room while the nurse checked over his wife. He had no idea why he'd started thinking about the Fletcher case, but it had just popped into his head all of a sudden. He wouldn't have been surprised if he'd found out that Jack had at that moment finished the journal – in his own way, John had his own connection with them.*

*A woman in the flat below Sarah's had phoned them, stating that she was* sure *that that terrible woman that she'd seen on the news was living* right above her*! They had to come and get her now!*

*When he had phoned Jack, he'd expected him to be really excited, and hadn't been disappointed. By the sound, Jack had already left in spirit and was just waiting for his body to catch up.*

*They'd waited the hour it had taken Jack to get to them and then had moved en masse to the flat. John had been disturbed to find that Jack grew more and more silent, and seemingly more depressed, the nearer they got.*

*It had been Jack they had all followed up the stairs, Jack that had walked into the flat first when they'd received no answer, and Jack that had stood over the body, looking down as if he was looking down at the body of a dead friend.*

*Through it all, John had known that it had always been Jack. He'd felt the closure of a circle without knowing that he'd felt it.*

*He looked up as the nurse entered the living room, her face grave, and all thoughts of Sarah Fletcher and Jack Daniels were catapulted from his mind.*

*He'd looked at her last note, reading the last four words aloud. "Jack it's almost over."*

*Then he looked at the newspaper clippings that were taped to the back of the journal. They were all the clippings about the people she had killed. The first one he came to was about Lenny Peterson, and the last at the back of the book was about Tony Aldridge. Both her lovers, both killed by her hands, only separated by years.*

*He closed the journal, but couldn't shake the feeling that it wasn't supposed to end this way. When he'd seen Sarah's body he'd known that it was right, no matter how sad it made him feel. But there was something wrong about this ending so…so quietly.*

*"Are you ready to see what I have to show you, Jack?"*

*Her voice brought him back, and he looked around, starting to feel that sense of rightness again, to see Sarah standing beside him, looking beautiful in her white dress, her hand held out to him.*

*It felt right when he took her hand and let her lead him to his destiny.*

# Epilogue

*She was on her own again, Rob had gone to work, and the flat seemed too big when she was alone, empty and always too cold, like a crypt. Totally different when Rob was there, always warm.*

*The postman had knocked on the door earlier that morning, and it had taken her a minute to get the courage to open it, and she'd only been able to manage to do that by checking through the window first. She'd scolded herself for being so stupid, for acting like such a stupid little girl, afraid of shadows that were only shadows and held no monsters.*

*So when a knock came at the door that afternoon and she had started to walk to the window first to have a quick peek, she became angry at herself. Stopping before she got there, and telling herself once more to grow up, Maggie changed course and walked to the front door.*

*There was no glass panel in the door, so she couldn't see the shape of the person who was waiting. Although she was terrified, Maggie forced a smile and opened the door. It fell from her face as she saw her husband standing there.*

*He had a smile on his own face, and Maggie thought that he actually looked good-humoured, but she was still scared, and prayed that she was only dreaming again.*

*"Hello, Maggie." He started to walk forwards, forcing himself into the doorway, Maggie backing away from him.*

*"How'd you know I was here?" Her voice trembled and she was too scared to even attempt to try to steady it, and she continued to step away from him.*

*"Sarah told me."*

But she said she wouldn't, *Maggie nearly said, but seeing the look on his face, that distant only-half-there look that she knew so well, she knew that he wasn't talking about their daughter.*

*"She came back, Maggie. Just to tell me about you."*

*Maggie's back hit the wall, and she stopped with nowhere else to go, she stood there, trying to convince herself that it wasn't really happening. Jack could never really hurt her. Not Jack. It had to be a dream.*

*Even when his hands were wrapped around her throat, squeezing against her windpipe, making black snow fall before her eyes, she was still trying to deny it. As she died, she was still thinking that she would wake up from the nightmare.*

*Jack let go of her, watching as her body slipped down against the wall. He walked into Rob's bathroom and saw one of Maggie's lipsticks. As he glanced into the mirror on the cabinet, he wasn't surprised to see Sarah standing behind him.*

*"We've nearly come full circle now, Jack."*

*He nodded and walked back to Maggie's body. His hand moved over her forehead, writing a single word on her skin.*

*Done, he walked back to the front door, marked it with the lipstick, and drove home, leaving the door to tell the world. CHEATER.*

*At home, he went straight to his office and opened his notebook. He made one last entry before closing it and took the photo of Sarah Fletcher from the file. He phoned his station and told them rationally what he had done before carrying the photograph up to the bathroom.*

*The razor was laid out on the sink ready for him. It was a straight razor, given to him years ago, a present that had never been used. He picked it up – its mock-ivory handle concealing the blade – feeling its weight in his palm, then turned the hot water tap on, allowing the steam to build up in the room.*

*He carefully placed the photo behind the cold-water tap so it was leaning against the wall. For some reason, it was important for him to see it when he died. He looked up at the mirror and he was just able to make out Sarah's reflection in the glass as it steamed up.*

*"Almost over, Jack."*

*He shook his head lightly. "It'll never be over, Sarah. Our connection will always hold. It's too strong to simply die."*

*Just before the mirror steamed up completely, Jack saw her nod her head.*

*Without hesitating further, Jack opened the blade from its handle. His veins had become raised due to the heat from the water, and he drew the sharp blade down his arm, from wrist to elbow.*

*He was amazed to find that it didn't hurt as much as he'd believed it would, and he quickly did the other arm, before sitting on the floor.*

*He died with Sarah watching him, her gaze steady on his shrunken form. Once his heart had stopped, she bent over him and kissed his forehead, lips brushing against his cooling flesh.*

*Rob had been upstairs, had seen Jack's crumpled body, blood all over the bathroom floor. Jack had told them when he'd phoned that all anyone needed to know was in his notebook. Knowing the house better than anyone else, Rob went straight to Jack's office and looked at the notebook next to Sarah's journal.*

*His hands were already gloved, so it wasn't a problem for him to pick it up. But still he hesitated. He had a feeling that reading this book would not be the best of ideas, that there were things that he was probably better off not knowing. But he forced himself. And turned to the first page.*

COSMIC EGG BOOKS

If you prefer to spend your nights with Vampires and Werewolves rather than the mundane then we publish the books for you. If your preference is for Dragons and Faeries or Angels and Demons – we should be your first stop. Perhaps your perfect partner has artificial skin or comes from another planet – step right this way. Our curiosity shop contains treasures you will enjoy unearthing. If your passion is Fantasy (including magical realism and spiritual fantasy), Horror or Science Fiction (including Steampunk), Cosmic Egg books will feed your hunger.